I0681331

BLACK CREEK BURNING

The Black Creek Series
Book One

R.T. Wolfe

Photography: S.L. Jones Photography

Cover and Book design by eBook Prep www.ebookprep.com

First Edition, April 2013
ISBN: 978-1-61417-404-2
ePublishing Works!
www.epublishingworks.com

DEDICATION

To my sister, Dian...
because you truly are Liz.

.

CHAPTER 1

The yellow cab turned onto the short cul-de-sac. Brie leaned back, slightly buzzed, and thought of how the dark street looked much the same as it did when she was a little girl.

Deep horseshoe drives, towering trees and well-kept yards framed the pavement. Like her parents' home, many were classic Victorians with small, square porches setting between towering white pillars. An occasional Colonial or English Tudor was thrown in the mix, yet the familiarity of the ancient road gave her a sense of serenity. She smiled even as the smell of stale cigarettes and dirty carpet mats filled her nose.

She and Liz had spent the evening at their favorite hole-in-the-wall pub. Her faded blue jeans and NYU collared shirt fit the nonexistent dress code nicely. Together, she and her sister celebrated the keynote speaker address Brie had landed for their district conference.

Stopping at the curb, she noticed her parents' Lincoln Town Car. They weren't due home until the next day, and she had parked in their spot. She felt a twinge of guilt, realizing they couldn't fit in their own garage. After paying the driver, she stepped out into the balmy, upstate New York night.

The house was, indeed, a classic with decorative latticework framing the awning of the square front porch and windows. It was clear that night, and the air hung stagnant. Brilliant moonlight shone on the bold color of the low-lying dianthus blooming red along the walk that led to the square porch. Her mother preferred bushes, mostly dark green and thick to adorn the length of their home, but always maintained a row of color.

As she meandered up the path to their house, she felt queasy, like she'd done this before. Nervously, she glanced over her shoulder through her mass of wavy brown hair as she kept moving toward the front door. Two people were walking along the street. She stopped and wondered what reason anyone would have to take a walk at this time of night in such an early bird neighborhood.

It was then she heard the shrill of the smoke detectors. Chest tightening, she bolted for the door.

For too long, she fumbled with the keys in one trembling hand before trying the knob with the other. Damn it, it was already unlocked. "Mom! Dad!" she screamed and tumbled inside, spotting them almost immediately as they ran down the long upstairs hallway.

Not again. Please not again, she begged, as she fought her frozen legs to make them move up the stairs. The smoke detectors shrieked in her ears. Or was that the shrieking coming from her lungs?

Her parents yelled her name as they reached for the bedroom door. She couldn't stop gasping for air long enough to tell them to stop. She wasn't in there. Didn't they know? If she hadn't taken her damned sweet time getting in, she could keep her parents from opening the door. They needed to get out of the house. Couldn't they smell the smoke?

Just like each time, her viewpoint from the middle of the stairs showed her the yellowish air sucking under the door to her bedroom. Although trying to use the railing to give her momentum, every part of her felt like it was in molasses. She cocked her head to the side, drawing her eyebrows together. Her gaze locked on the eerie breeze.

Almost simultaneously, her mother rotated the knob as her eyes turned and met hers. For that fraction of a second, her mother understood the fear on Brie's face, but it was too late. It was always too late. As she opened the door, Brie had just enough time to witness her parents engulfed in flames before the explosion blew her back and everything went dark.

* * *

"Brie, wake up. Wake up, Brie. You're dreaming."

She opened her eyes to Brian as he shook her gently.

Sitting up with a start, she took three, quick gasps of air, her tank damp with sweat.

"It's all right now," he said, pulling her toward him.

She swung her legs over the side of the bed. "I just need a minute." Rubbing her hands over her face, she headed down the hall to the bathroom and shut the door behind her. Her knuckles turned white as she gripped the side of the vanity. She looked in the mirror at the dark rings under her eyes and thought of how her mother should be the one standing there.

Although the night of the fire was long ago, the dream's vividness had yet to fade. The taste of the smoke. The crackle of the fire. The rush of the water hoses. The piercing sirens. She splashed water on her face, rolled her head from shoulder to shoulder and put on her running gear. She shook her head twice and headed back to the master bedroom of the home she grew up in.

With her hair tied up and her dog's leash in hand, she found Brian waiting in her bed, slouched with his back against her headboard. He ran a hand over his short crop of hair; the man who had been a good friend to her, the man who helped put out the fire.

His eyes turned to her as she noticed the single, deep rise and heavy fall of his chest.

"Got a minute?" he asked.

"Sure. Will you need a ride to work? I should get Macey out for a run first."

"One day on and two days off, Brie, same as always. You picked me up from the station yesterday. Sit down, will you?"

She sat on the crumpled sheets, faced him and crisscrossed her legs. "I guess you'll need to take me to work then." Forcing the corners of her mouth up, she folded her hands in her lap. "Today's going to be a busy work day."

Brian sat up and faced her. "You were dreaming about the fire." It wasn't a question.

Shrugging, she looked away.

"You were amazing, you know."

She jerked back to face him and felt her face scowl.

"With the back of your head bleeding, you came to, still strapped to the gurney, and started shouting orders to the crew. The guys at the station still razz the rookie who forgot to secure your legs and ended up with a face full of your foot. He may have bled more than you did."

He paused long enough to make her uncomfortable.

"You couldn't have saved them."

She stiffened. "I know that."

She concentrated on his eyes. They were acorn brown, framed with a short buzz of blond hair that stood straight up. Why did he look so sad? It wasn't like this was a new dream.

His shoulders fell forward as he reached for her hands. "You won't let me in."

She paused, keeping her focus on his expression. "I can't give you more, you know that." Although she knew he wouldn't be surprised, the quick wince of his face caused her to drop her gaze to her folded hands.

Brian took a breath, cupped a hand under her chin and slowly lifted. "I know and I'm sorry, but I can't keep chipping away at this ice. I need to be done."

Looking back up, she turned her head away slightly. "Ice? Are you serious?" Instinctively, she pushed at his hand.

"Sorry...sorry. I didn't mean *you're* ice, just that...come on, Brie, we've been friends for too long. I don't want this to end badly."

"It won't. I'm okay." Picking up the leash, she walked toward the hallway.

"Brie, we swore if this didn't work, it wouldn't end the friendship."

She stopped when she reached the doorway, placing one hand on the jamb. She didn't face him. "It's really okay. I'll bring some food by the station the next time the Giants play." She let out two short whistles, and a golden retriever followed her down the stairs and out the front door.

Ice. Great.

"You fucking idiot," Rob repeated to Brian as they pulled up to the fire station.

"How many more times you gonna need to say that?" he grunted.

Rob slowly shook his balding head. "I'm not sure. You idiot."

"Should I have stayed with her after six years of being friends and months of dating that weren't any more than us being friends?"

"Were you having sex?"

"You picked me up from her house this morning, asshole. You know we were sleeping together."

"Sex with a low-maintenance brunette who has a great rack. Sounds like more than friends to me. You idiot."

"Yeah. You're probably right." He stepped out of the car.

"I guess that just clears the way for me to move in."

"You even think about it and I'll kick your ass. Friends don't move in on friend's ex's." He dug uncomfortably for his keys out of the pockets of yesterday's wrinkled work pants.

"I laid off for how many years while you figured out how to get her to go out with you? Now, I still have to lay off? Well, fuck me. Who made up these rules anyway? Just kidding, man. Come on, cheer up. I'm only going to give you shit about this...well, always."

He opened the door to his car as Rob walked up to the station. "I'm just going to go in and tell the B-shift what a fucking idiot you are before I head on home and go back to bed."

She sat in the drive in her seasoned truck, enjoying the look of how everything lay covered with a fresh blanket of snow. Brie wondered why she wasn't pouting in her bedroom, but she simply didn't feel sad. Worried, definitely, at the fact that she couldn't even make it work with nice-guy Brian McKinney, but not sad or really even disappointed. Maybe she was ice, she conceded.

She looked up at the west side of the home she had rebuilt. The two stories included rows of windows on each level. The pillars had been salvageable after the fire. They were painted with a fresh coat of white each year just like when she was a child. White shutters framed each of the windows as well as miniature balconies for the ones on the second story.

Only the landscaping had been altered. Inkberry holly and spring-blooming viburnum stood leafless in the fresh snow. The upright junipers that grew at the corners of the house were the only winter green. She carefully chose an array of plants that

9

alternately bloomed throughout the spring, summer and fall, yet presented an organized, sophisticated look that blended with the appearance of the house.

Putting the car in gear, she tried to prioritize the list of things she had to do before the end of the work day. She still had enough time to arrive a full two hours before her first meeting. Between that and the appointment with the assistant superintendent after school, she needed to find time to finish the comments on her report cards by the four o'clock deadline.

She took in one fast, deep breath, let it out slowly and pulled out, noticing she made only the second set of tire tracks in the morning snow. The sun was just coming up, the evergreens and naked oaks casting long shadows over the white. The wind was calm, but the air bitter cold. She didn't mind the cold. However, the drive did little to settle her.

Ice. Get over it, she convinced herself. So, she wasn't interested in love and marriage. She had always been honest about that.

Thinking of the upcoming winter break, she considered how nice it would be for her students to have some time to spend with their families before the demands of second semester began. She, too, could use the break, take some time for herself and get ahead on work. Her sister, best friend and fellow teacher in the same building, called it detox time, and they christened each with a night at Mikey's Pub and Grill. She probably should have called Liz before work to tell her about Brian, but she wasn't ready to go through that story with her just yet.

After eight years of working at Bloom Elementary, Brie moved toward more district projects rather than keeping her focus solely on her classroom. The staff seemed to trust her ideas, for the most part, and her research. However, not everyone admired her knack for teaching adults as well as children. She'd been asked to give a handful of presentations on the research regarding society's preconceived opinions of students' academic abilities based on social and economic backgrounds. It was no secret she turned down offers to move into administration. She simply wanted to work with children.

She was one of the first to arrive, so the hallways were quiet and some still dark. As she walked past Susie Phillip's second-grade classroom, she noticed the light on and popped her head in the doorway. "What are you doing here so early?"

Susie turned and leaned back in her chair. "Report cards. How about you? I figured you'd be done days ago."

"Every time I'm done, I think of more comments to add. Will you come for New Year's Eve?"

"Of course. Wouldn't miss it. You know we used to have staff Christmas parties around here until you came along with your New Year's Eve deal. I heard our favorite boss is going to make an appearance."

"Ouch," Brie grimaced. "At least she never stays too long. No television cameras or news crews."

Susie shook her head and turned to her computer. "I'd better get back. Deadline is looming."

She continued down the empty hallway. Her sensible, low-heeled pumps echoed as she turned the last corner. Purposely, she always dressed for work conservatively in slacks and basic-colored blouses with an occasional blazer. The feeling of cool air blowing from her classroom caused her to wish she'd chosen the blazer that morning. The noises from portable radios and the voices of men caused her to hesitate. They were speaking to her principal, Sandy Finley. She considered stopping to listen but understood her shoes had likely given away her presence in the hall. Instead, she walked in. Her eyes went first to the shattered wall of windows, then moved to the same two officers that had come the last time this happened.

CHAPTER 2

Taking a deep breath, Brie lifted her chin and addressed the trio. "Good morning, officers, Sandy. Do we know what happened?"

"It looks like rifle practice, along with a few large rocks this time. Seems your windows must be an easy target, being in the back of the building and all," the first officer answered, chewing on a plastic coffee stirrer. "Do you have any reason to think this would be more than a coincidence now that it's happened twice this year, Miss Chapman?"

She felt cool droplets of sweat form along the back of her hairline. She thought of the other incidents but decided they had nothing to do with this. "No," she answered, pulling on her ear. "Nothing, officers. Is there anything I need to adjust for my class today? Sandy, do you want me to relocate?"

The second officer interrupted, "Plywood should do for now. The glass repair crew can come tomorrow. Mrs. Finley assured us the shards on your floor will be cleaned up before the students arrive." He jotted something down in a small ringed notebook.

"Very well. If you don't mind, I have some things to finish in the workroom. Please let me know if there is anything else you need. Thank you for your time, officers, Sandy." She walked out calmly and with purpose down the hall, stopped, leaned against the wall and closed her eyes.

* * *

The class was wired for Christmas. How could her lesson plans compete with the excitement of Santa? Brie decided to give in and just go with it. Writing was to be about what they wanted for Christmas. Math included the use of geometrical shapes to create Christmas trees.

She grinned as Sean raised his hand to read his story made up of a full page of misspelled words. She remembered the first few weeks of school. The boy had been insecure and barely able to write his name. He had been afraid to try, afraid to speak. Now, he was confident and writing extensive, coherent stories. She laughed out loud as he explained that he drew a new snowmobile, since that was what he asked Santa to give him for Christmas. She wondered if his mother knew. She decided if this boy got a snowmobile before she did, there was something very wrong with the world.

Suddenly, she felt better and remembered why she loved this job.

The intense morning meeting with the Department of Children and Family Services had left her tapped before her class even arrived. Brie started putting up chairs for the custodian and shook her head in disgust as she thought about young Aaron Babb. His explosive father would have a lot to answer for. He would be furious, but she didn't care. She did her part to end the cycle of bruises Aaron had likely put up with since birth.

The rest of the day flew by teaching twenty-five first-grade students, then a meeting with the assistant superintendent. She was spent and ready for a breather. After putting the final touches on her report cards, she loaded her bag down before heading to turn out the fluorescent lights. As she walked to the door, she glanced back at the plywood covering her windows. Her shoulders jerked as she felt a chill.

She flicked the lights, just when her sister stormed around the corner. "All right, spill." Liz was as direct as she was selfless. "Why do I work in the same building as my baby sister and am only now hearing your windows were shot out again?" Liz set her hands on her hips as she blocked her way while peering over Brie's shoulder at the plywood.

She could make excuses by taking Liz step-by-step through

her hell of a day, but instead she let out a sigh and simply answered. "Sorry, I was just coming to find you, and they were not *shot out*. It was mostly rocks," she lied. "After several questions from the kids, they moved on to obsess about Christmas. Are we still on for tonight?" She changed the subject, walked around her sister and headed toward the school office for her last stop on her way out.

Liz adjusted her heavy bag and took up stride with Brie's longer legs. "Of course we're on. It's tradition. I heard it was another rifle. And my students are too old to admit they're obsessed with Christmas."

"I need to take a shower, then meet with Mrs. Melbourne before we go. Is eight too late? Will you owe Tim for having to put the kids to bed?"

"Tim knows the drill. Detox time at Mikey's the last day of school before any break." Liz draped her free arm around Brie's shoulder. "And he knows his payment will be well worth it," she said with a sexy grin. "Are you sure you're okay?"

"I am, thanks. I'll meet you there. I think I'll get a cab tonight."

"I'll pick up you at eight and have Tim drop us off; we'll share a cab home," Liz said.

Brie pulled open the door to the front office to let the secretary know she was leaving. Mrs. Seward was as big around as she was tall, and as scary as they came. She was also conscientious and made sure to keep everyone on their toes. Her walls were wallpapered with neatly displayed schedules and calendars.

"Theme tests are due before you leave, Miss Chapman, Mrs. Brownley."

Brie pulled out a small tin of cookies with a bow. "Merry Christmas, Mrs. Seward."

"Thank you, Miss Chapman. Theme tests are still due before you leave," she said as she stapled a phone message to a note card.

She smiled at her favorite secretary. "You're welcome, and I turned them in yesterday."

Liz flipped through the papers she had pulled from her office mail slot as she followed. She grinned and glanced up. "Don't look at me. I turned mine in last week."

"You're getting a new student when we return from break,

Miss Chapman, and Dr. Tyman wants you to call her. Something she forgot to mention in your meeting this afternoon." Mrs. Seward turned to peck furiously at her document.

Liz's eyebrows went up at the mention of the assistant super.

Blowing the hair from her face, Brie stopped and turned back to Mrs. Seward. "What is the spelling of their first name? Do they ride a bus or a car, and did you tell Dr. Tyman I would call her back today?"

"Sylvester, spelled the regular way. Bus fifty-one, and I told her you were already gone for break." Winking, Mrs. Seward dipped the few files left on her desk neatly into drawers. "Enjoy your break, Brianna."

Four wide eyes looked out of a shiny black truck as they turned onto the gravel drive of their new home. The snow had to be a plus, Nathan decided. His nephews had played in snow when they visited their grandparents up here, but they'd never had it in their own backyard. He could tell Duncan, the older of the two, was wondering if people could actually live in the place. He'd tried telling them it would be an adventure. He said the three of them would be like pioneers.

Snow crunched under his tires as the truck pulled to a stop. He looked over at the boys' cautious expressions. "Come on, men. We'll get her put together in no time. We're bachelors now." He laid a reassuring hand on Duncan's shoulder.

"Do you think Goldie will like it here?" Duncan asked.

He figured his nephew wasn't really asking about the bouncing yellow Lab in the backseat, although taking care of Goldie and his little brother were first priorities for Duncan, even if he was only eight. He thought about how much Duncan looked like his dad with his deep brown, wavy hair and serious sable brown eyes. Duncan's soft nose and chin were the only features he had inherited from his mother.

"I think he already does. What do you think, Andy?" He glanced over at his younger nephew.

Goldie, not quite two yet, yelped and jumped in the backseat. With his tongue hanging to one side, he pressed his wet nose against the window.

"'Course he'll like it. Look at the creek and the lake," Andy defended. "He can fish and chase birds."

15

Andy not only inherited his mother's looks, but her personality. Optimist. Adventurist. Like his brother, he had his father's wavy brown hair. But his eyes were light brown, soft and full of wonder.

The extended cab, eight-foot-bed pickup was packed full. Bungee cords tied down mattresses, sleeping bags, suitcases, a card table with chairs and a cooler of food along with a handful of puzzles, Legos and Duncan's drawing supplies. It was enough to get them through until the first moving van came with more. The rest would be retrieved from storage as the house became ready.

The boys climbed out and stretched from the last hours of driving like they'd just woken from a long nap. Nathan grabbed Andy, tossing him effortlessly onto his shoulders. With Andy's hands wrapped under his chin and his feet tucked around the sides of his back, he couldn't resist pulling out the new notebook he had ready in his back pocket and the pencil from behind his ear.

He opened it to the first page and jotted down notes about the shutters. They would need to be discarded and completely rebuilt. The porch was littered with rotting boards that needed to be replaced. Some were still in good condition and just needed to be planed, stained and sealed. The railings, however, were going to be all new and all his, part of a giant wrap-around porch he envisioned. The wood siding needed to be scraped and painted. Some boards needed replacing there, too. He jotted down notes about finding a good painter and roofer. He wouldn't have time for that if he was going to finish the beauty by summer's end. The outside of the house would have to wait for better weather, he decided.

"Dad, Goldie wants out. Let him out and let me down." Andy squirmed as he fumbled the notebook back into his pocket. "Can we go around back?"

"I'll come with. Stay where I can see you." He let Andy down and took Duncan's hand. He noticed that Duncan held on a little tighter than usual.

He opened the door of the packed truck for the jumping, barking dog. Taking a giant leap, the dog tried to run before his legs hit the ground. Stumbling and rolling twice before regaining his footing, he took off around the side of the house. They followed through the deep snow as they zipped coats and pulled on gloves that were too thin for staying out very long. Snow already began dipping into their shoes, but they didn't seem to care.

A floodplain encompassed the creek, twenty-five yards on each side and seemed to flow downward toward the house, away from its adjoining lake. Between the small lake and creek was a spillway built with a concrete wall and watermelon-sized rocks. Hundreds of rocks that looked like they were keeping the lake water from running like a river. Houses lined around, and the floodplains boasted fields on both sides, butting up to generous backyards. Several of the yards around the lake ended abruptly with snow-covered docks over the frozen water.

Patches of tall grasses and frosty cattails lined the creek. He learned it was named Black Creek due to the dark mud lining the bottom. The lake looked frozen, but near the spillway crystal water slipped stealthily under the ice, trickled down the rocks and flowed through the dark creek bed. The frigid water ran around snow-piled patches of grasses and rocks, making them look like huge marshmallows floating in black coffee.

As they made it to the back yard, one corner of his mouth curved up as Duncan finally dropped his hand. The boys ran, squealing as they slid down the slope that led to the field. Goldie ran circles around them and rolled in the white. He noted the weeds poking out through the yard and added a landscaper to his list of people to hire. This was a far cry from the tight rows of yards in the South Carolina neighborhood they'd moved from. He would need more than a little flower box this time around.

While he watched the boys, movement from across the creek caught his eye. A woman with a light blue coat and brown hair pouring out from under a matching hat was running full speed around the side of a traditional Victorian home. He tilted his head as he watched the cape of hair that flew behind her and stopped at the middle of her back. It wasn't until he noticed the charging, growling dog at her heels that he found himself running.

CHAPTER 3

The dog leapt at the woman, trying to get at her back. Nathan was nearly to the edge of the floodplain when the sound of laughter made him skid to a stop.

The woman rolled in the snow with the dog in apparent delight. He watched as she grabbed it by its cheeks, nuzzling their foreheads together. Jumping to their feet, they both stood with wide stances. The woman leaned over with her hands on her thighs. The dog seemed to mimic the position with its front legs flat on the ground and head down.

He couldn't help but stare at the playful standoff. At seemingly the same time, they broke their freeze, took off around the side of the house and disappeared as quickly as they'd appeared.

"Is it okay to go in, Nathan?" Duncan tucked his arms inside his coat. "I think Andy's cold."

"Am-m-m n-not!"

"Of course. The bank promised they would have at least arranged for running water and all the parts of the bathrooms in working order if we just agreed to take it off their hands. Pioneers, remember?"

Andy rolled his eyes and followed him with Duncan around to the front of the house.

He worked on scrubbing the floor of the enormous master

bedroom. Nathan decided after he finished with the master bath, he was definitely hiring someone to clean the rest of the house. They would camp in here for now. He had plans for a small walk-out balcony in the back with French doors, where he could sit and watch the boys play.

Quarter-sawn oak would be a perfect match to the furniture that waited patiently in storage. In his mind, he could see the three-panel doors, the base and window trim. He planned on small, protruding corbels to mark the corners of the doors and windows. Beams would intersect each other along the ceiling, and a few shelves inlaid into the walls would showcase antique pottery. He took down the dimensions for each and moved to the master bath, where he measured for tile and decided on a separate shower and tub.

"Anyone home?"

At the sound of the visitor, Goldie howled and rolled over in his scramble for the door. Downstairs working on puzzles, Duncan and Andy howled, too. Two boys and a dog ran to her, all three of them nearly knocking her over.

"Be careful with her, boys. She's not nineteen anymore." He felt a sense of calm blanket him as he yelled down the stairs and headed for his mother.

Mackenzie Reed wrapped a tiny, but strong arm around each boy. She was barely more than five feet tall, with brown hair the color of her grandchildren's, showing streaks of gray. Her eyes, however, were a sky blue color that matched Nathan's. She was in her early fifties and looked more like her early forties.

"I'll have you know your father and I just returned from a long weekend in a tree house hotel. You are as old as you think you are, and I think I'll be nineteen for today." She gave each boy a noisy kiss on the top of their heads. "How are my favorite grandkids?"

"We're your only grandkids, Grandma." Duncan smiled, keeping his eyes closed with both arms wrapped around her narrow waist.

As Nathan reached her, he kissed her cheek. "Oregon was it?" he asked as he absently turned to lead Goldie out the front door and hooked him to the leash on the porch.

His mother walked with the boys to the grubby dining room. "Yes, Oregon. When are you going to let us take these boys out for a trip? Just a short one. Maybe Niagara Falls."

She pulled out a washcloth from a plastic baggie and started wiping down the card table and chairs the two boys and he were using as their kitchen table.

Nathan rummaged through the picnic basket his mother had set on the floor. "We just got here, Ma." He turned and wrapped his arms around her waist, and rested his cheek on the top of her head. "It's good to be back. We need you. I need you."

In the mudroom off the garage, she knocked snow from her boots, then hung up her coat. Shaking the snow from her hair, Brie thought of the family that, from the look of the overflowing truck bed, must be moving into the old farmhouse. She wondered why anyone would buy that place, let alone a family, dog and all. Was the dad really planning to fly through the icy creek to save her from her ferocious dog? She laughed as she looked at Macey. The adolescent retriever was curled up on her oval braided rug, biting tiny snowballs from between her toes. She rubbed her dog's ears and mussed her light-brown head.

"Come on, girl. Let's get us something to eat."

She stopped in the doorway of the mudroom and looked out to the open layout of the home she'd grown up in. Large archways separated most of the rooms with the exception of the library and formal sitting room. The hardwood and ceramic floors had the same flat finish they always had. The only change she'd made was carpet in the family room.

The quiet was deafening.

For her, this home still meant two noisy older brothers, a squealing sister and parents that were either scolding them or laughing with them—sometimes both within the same breath. Being already married with their own homes, her siblings inherited trust funds and bonds. She inherited the house.

Her salary was small, even with the growing landscaping business she maintained on the side. She probably should have saved some of the insurance money from the fire to help her with the upkeep of such a large home and help pay the taxes. But she had a need to restore the house to its original state, right down to the oval braided rug Macey lazily stood up from.

Rolling her shoulders, she grabbed an apple and headed for the bag of dog food, and then a shower.

* * *

Her hair was still damp when Brie signaled for Macey to stay on the concrete porch as she knocked on her next-door neighbor's door.

Mrs. Melbourne peeked through the beveled glass. "Who is it?" Her quick, gruff voice was a stark contrast to her elegant appearance. She was a slender woman with silver hair curling just above her shoulders.

Without giving Brie time to answer, she opened the door. The house was femininely decorated with floral printed wallpaper and large rugs covering hardwood floors. It smelled of lavender potpourri. "Well come in if you have to, Brianna. I was just about to see Ethel out. Go on to the kitchen. I've been baking." She handed a check to her housekeeper. "Did you dust the baseboards, Ethel? I can't stand dust on the baseboards."

Ethel was in her late forties with deep lines around her eyes. She had salt and pepper hair that didn't move an inch from its bun as she shook her head. "I do the baseboards on Tuesdays, Lucy. You're just mad because I won in Canasta." Her voice was easy and southern-touched. "This here is Friday. Do I need to get out the contract again?"

Ethel let out a huff as her plump behind followed her to the door. "If you want to add a third day, you just let me know. I left fresh coffee in the pot and your favorite cups and saucers on the counter. Good night, Lucy, and good luck, Brie. She's in an especially grand mood today."

"A third day? Do I look like a rich old widow? I can hardly afford two days for what she charges."

The kitchen was scattered with vases of artificial flowers, decorative canisters and crystal bowls. Without waiting for her consent, Lucy poured two cups of coffee. She'd known Lucy all her life.

"Oh, Mother. You could afford to have Ethel here every day of the week," Lucy's daughter walked in the front door as Ethel left. "In fact, you could afford to hire Ethel to live here if you weren't so stingy." Walking into the kitchen on four-inch designer heels, the tall, thin blonde made her way directly to her. "I'm thankful you put up with her, Brie," she said and kissed Brie on each cheek.

"Ethel made coffee, MollyAnne. I'll pour since my help left at such an inconvenient time. I know you like yours black, Brianna." Lucy handed Brie a cup and saucer.

"I brought cookies." Brie pulled up a stool next to her.

"Are they the kind with those Christmas sprinkles you always bring over when you're trying to soften me up before telling me you're going to have that loud party until all hours of the night again?" Her eyebrows lifted high as she peered inside the cookie tin and took out one on top.

Molly let out an overtly loud sigh and turned to her mother. "With as soundly as you sleep, you wouldn't even know there was a get-together if she didn't come over here to tell you beforehand. Don't pay attention to her, Brie. She has no appreciation for tradition. I think it's wonderful you continue to invite your parents' friends and the neighborhood over for a very tasteful celebration of the coming New Year. I know I wouldn't miss it. I'm bringing a date." Molly winked as her mother straightened up.

"Of course, I'm the last one to know. Ungrateful child." Lucy slowly lifted her chin. "Is it the Logan I so detest?"

"No, Mother. This one's name is Roger. Roger Swindley. I met him on my last buying trip."

"I don't know how you call shopping a job, and for fancy clothes even." Lucy closed her eyes a little longer than a blink as she took a bite of the cookie. "In my day, shopping was something you did to take care of your home and your children. It looks like I'm not getting any grandchildren out of you anytime soon. Brianna, when are you going to marry that firefighter and pass on those genius genes of yours to some babies of your own?"

She shifted in her chair. "They're not exactly *genius* genes. I'm just good at taking tests and—"

"I wouldn't call testing out of high school in two years," Molly interrupted, "and a full-ride to med school just any tests, Brie dear. No one thinks badly of you for turning down your career in medicine." Molly smiled at her as she added another scoop of sugar to her cup.

"Regardless of my genius or not-so-genius genes, Brian broke it off." There. She said it.

"Hmm." Molly ran her forefinger across her chin. "Such a waste of a great ass." Molly grinned at her as they both suppressed a laugh. Lucy looked like she was going to blow a gasket. "Speaking of tradition, your sister should be here soon. It's the last day of school before break, and by the looks of that other tin of cookies, it seems like you still need to get across the street and bribe Mr. Piper into using his home for the party babysitters."

Mikey's was a favorite spot for a good burger and kicking back. The seats were nicked and set too closely together. The air held scents of grilled meat and grease. There were plaques and photos of years of local softball tournaments mingled with yellowing newspaper articles about the pub that were laminated and pinned to dark-paneled walls. Large posters with the Giants' and the Jets' game schedules covered the wall closest to the flip-up counter that gave an entrance to behind the bar.

"I say to you for the second time today, Brie, spill. Why is Dr. Tyman meeting with you and leaving you messages?" Their waiter brought them a first round of beer and buffalo wings. The two were the kind of friends only sisters could be—unconditional. Liz supported her when she'd changed college majors after two years, putting her on a six-year graduation plan. She put up with her neurotic need to have everything replaced in their parents' house just as it was before the fire, right down to the single bathroom upstairs for all five bedrooms to share.

Brie plopped her chin in one hand on the table. "She wants me to team up with her to vertically align the district math curriculum with a focus on common vocabulary."

"Ugh. Sorry I asked. So, she wants you to *team up* to work at no extra pay on a project that will make her look good. What else is new?" Liz folded her hands neatly on the table.

"Not every administrator is out for number one, Liz-the-union-rep." She grinned. "Besides, I offered. Really, Liz, I don't mind. I have time after school until spring hits. Brian broke up with me this morning," she added, trying a subject change.

Liz stared into her eyes clearly analyzing. With a touch of humor, Liz asked, "This morning? Don't tell me you were in bed when he broke it off."

"Pretty much, but I guess that part isn't such a big deal since he called me 'ice.' Although the comment didn't have anything to do with the bed." She stopped and placed her other hand under her chin with the first one. "At least I don't think it did. Oh, hell." She took a sip of her beer and grabbed another wing.

"Bastard. He spent how many years of his life trying to get you to date him, and he doesn't even make it six months. Did he really say 'ice'? Bastard." Liz sat back in the hard wooden bench. "Are you still inviting him to the house for New Year's Eve? It would be a waste for us not to be able to at least look at that great ass."

They both laughed until their sides hurt.

"I sort of already did. You know, before. And if I'd known everyone thought his ass was so great, I may not have let him go."

"Yes, you would have."

Brie froze just before her next bite of buffalo wing touched her lips. Her eyes drew up to her sister's.

"I'm sorry," Liz said. "I didn't mean it. Well, I did mean it, but who cares? I just don't like seeing you alone so much. Brian's a great guy. In fact, you always date great guys. Oh, wait, except Doug. He really was a bastard. What were you thinking?" Liz curled up the corners of her mouth.

Shaking her head, Brie thought about Doug. "Yeah. I guess Molly didn't have much better luck at that. At least I didn't marry him." She let out a sigh, thinking of her childhood friend. "And divorce him."

"She bounced back pretty fast. Molly's never alone. There's always someone chasing after those long legs." Liz finished her first beer and picked up the nearly full one in front of Brie. "Why do we always get a cab? You never have more than one, maybe two beers. Light beers."

"I like to have options."

A dumpster sat in front of the house. Tire tracks and footprints flattened the snow around it and down the tree-lined drive. The crew Nathan had hired to finish scrubbing the rest of the house had just arrived to finish the job.

"Not that we mind, but why are you having us clean everything if you're just going to rip it all out?" asked the woman in charge.

"The kids should have a clean place to live while I rip it all out. Stay as long as you need. Find me when you're done. I'll likely be in the garage and will get you your check." He headed off to the foyer to help Duncan and Andy.

He expected another crew soon to work on installing a spray room in a corner of the enormous garage, but he couldn't put the boys off any longer. They were too excited about his promise to let them play in the snow before their grandparents arrived. While the boys wrestled with their winter gear, Goldie ran circles around the three of them. The slope at the end of the backyard was perfect for an eight- and a six-year-old boy to use for sledding. They each owned a shiny new red sled.

"Dad, why couldn't we get those wooden sleds with the metal thingies on the bottom?" Andy zipped his coat, tucked his hat on tighter and held out his hands with fingers spread for Nathan to put on his gloves.

"The plastic ones go faster." He wiggled his eyebrows as he pulled on Andy's new snow gloves, carefully tucking them into the sleeves of his coat. "All set."

It took them several small steps to turn and face the front door. They made their way around to the back.

"Look," he said to the boys. "Our footprints are still here."

The boys carefully put their feet in each leftover print until they realized there was no need with their snow pants and boots. They, then, barreled through the snow and around back with Goldie racing, falling, rolling and running again.

At the top of the hill, he started to remind them to keep the string from dragging under the bottom of the sled. Instead, he gave them both a running push down the little hill. They would figure out that sort of thing best by trial and error. Goldie ran next to them so fast his feet couldn't keep up with his body. He somehow ended up on his back. Nathan grinned as he watched the dog get stuck, even if for just a second, like a turtle on its back, kicking his legs in the air.

As the boys pulled the sleds back up the hill, he felt better about his choice to uproot them from the South, from the only place they remembered living. Not to start over, but to start fresh.

As Macey waited by the front door, Brie laced her worn running shoes and tied her hair back in a few quick twists. Her dog's tail thumped against the umbrella stand. Clicking on her leash, they started out the door.

There wasn't much traffic to dodge other than an occasional car or snowmobile. She and Macey ran in the street where most of the snow had been cleared. She thought about the neighbors who had lived here longer than her. Lucy Melbourne had lost her husband years before. Clifford Piper, who also lived in their short cul-de-sac. His granddaughter, Amanda, lived with him on and off over the years.

As she rounded the corner with Macey at her side, she looked at the lovely Colonial-style home the Delaneys lived in. They must be at least eighty by now. Still, they got out to pull weeds and sweep the walk when the weather was nice.

She did the major projects for them. She ran in the street over the bridge that crossed Black Creek. Macey didn't hesitate at the swimming huddle of ducks but did manage to give them a yearning gaze. "Good girl." She gave Macey a quick scratch on the top of her head.

Their feet crunched through the snowy street, and the breath that steamed just in front of her led the way. As they rounded the next corner, a familiar, large, yellow Lab came bounding toward them with its tongue hanging to the side.

CHAPTER 4

Macey stopped and dropped her head. Pulling her ears back, she exposed her teeth and let out a deep growl.

"Down girl," Brie commanded.

Macey quieted, although she didn't loosen her stance. Brie recognized the Labrador as it galloped down the weedy drive of the old farmhouse as belonging to the new family. The dog's front legs locked as it halted at the sight of Macey's teeth. Then, it rolled on its back, legs in the air. Brie couldn't help but smile.

The dog must have decided it was safe and flopped around like a fish before making it back to its feet. It circled Macey, sniffing her. When it passed her back side, Macey looked up at her, desperately seeking permission to take a bite out of him. Brie grinned, but when the dog started to climb on Macey's back, she took it by its collar.

"Whoa there, stud. That's where I draw the line." Simultaneously, she tugged on his collar and down on his back, easing him into a sitting position. Opening her hand, she placed her palm in front of the dog's face, far enough away in case he decided to take a bite of her. "Sit," she said in a commanding tone. Keeping her fingers outstretched, she scratched his head with her other hand.

Out of the corner of her eye, she saw the man walking with a slight swagger toward them. His work boots were soaking wet and mostly covered by faded blue jeans. A layer of stubble men often thought of as sexy covered his face, not that she didn't. It was just annoying. A mass of jet-black hair curled just around his ears and down to the collar of his coat. As he neared, she realized she had to look up to keep eye contact. Not many men were much taller than her five feet, nine inches.

He had nearly run again—saving her this time from his obnoxious dog. But Nathan understood for the second time that this woman didn't need his help. She wore a pastel yellow fleece jacket and was taller than she seemed from her backyard. Her glossy brown hair was tied in a tail that threaded through the back of a Giants' ball cap. She wore loose, black running pants.

The woman was different today than when she rolled in the snow, laughing with her dog. Her chin was up, her shoulders stiff. Nonetheless, he felt a tug in his gut. "How did you get him to do that?" he asked as he tilted his head toward his still-sitting Lab.

"Easy. Is he fixed?" The woman turned her head slightly to the side, keeping her eyes on his.

"If you mean neutered, no. I keep meaning to, but I just don't know if I can do that to a fellow member of the male species. I'm Nathan. The boys making their way down the drive are Duncan and Andy, Duncan being the taller of the two. And the overly anxious dog is Goldie. Come meet our first neighbor, boys," he called out over his shoulder.

Now that she was closer, he saw her eyes were an intense, moss green. Her lips were full, her skin golden. She wasn't pretty in the standards of society, but she carried herself with an attractive self-awareness. The tug turned into a pang. He'd been celibate for so long, he'd forgotten what that felt like.

"Goldie?" Her eyebrows lifted to him before she squatted down and rubbed around the dog's ears.

He bent down next to her and placed his hand on his dog's head. He noted that she moved back as he moved down. "It's the name the pound gave him. I couldn't get the boys to change it. Andy got the notion I just may change his name, too."

"Dad, I did *not*." Andy stomped his foot and buried his head in his side.

"Duncan, Andy, this is..."

"Brie, sorry. I live—"

"I know where you live." He stood up slowly and hooked his

thumbs in his front pockets.

He lifted one side of his mouth.

"Right," she answered. "This is Macey." Brie took a step back, placed her hands on the backs of her hips with her thumbs facing forward.

He looked down at the dog that hadn't moved through the introductions. "It's nice to meet both of you. If I scratch her head will she chase me around my house, lunging and trying to bite me?"

Brie grinned.

Not much to say, but a very nice smile. A warm and sexy smile. Down boy, he told himself. Gloves hid whether or not she wore a ring.

"No. You're safe. I, um, heard you say I'm the first neighbor you've met. There'll be a gathering for New Year's Eve at my home. Most of the neighbors stop by." She paused. "You could come."

"No sitter, but thanks." He looked over and noticed the boys moving snow to form what looked like a wall for a fort or maybe a foxhole.

"We'll have good babysitters at Mr. Piper's. He lives across the cul-de-sac from me. If you're comfortable, they're welcome there."

He narrowed his eyes as he noticed hers were focused behind him.

"You're about to get pelted. I'm going to finish my run. Nice to meet you. It starts at eight."

He watched as she ran. He held onto Goldie's collar to keep him from chasing after her. A snowball hit the side of his head, then one on his leg. He let out his own growl and started balling up snow before the boys ducked down safely below their makeshift wall.

He worked the house from top to bottom and front to back. Systematically ripping down window and door trim, Nathan kept what he liked, if it could be salvaged, and labeled each piece carefully as to which room and wall or window it belonged. He made notes as he measured each room, calculating how much material he'd need to purchase to replace rotted boards and add what he wanted.

The formal dining room would showcase cross beams along the ceiling, much like the master bedroom. He planned for tight-grained, rift-sawn oak for most of the first floor. On the pages of his notebook reserved for the dining room, he drew a quick sketch of an arched entrance along the eighteen-foot-wide opening. A shipment of hardwoods would arrive soon, and he could start on it all. He pondered using the attic space above the garage to store it.

He heard tires coming up the gravel drive and realized he'd gotten carried away with his piles of trim. He was ready for a disruption. When he heard the air release of the braking system, he figured it was the moving truck and headed out to help the driver unload.

Pulling out his notebook from his back pocket, he wrote as he walked, jotting down that each garage door needed replacing. The garage was one of the reasons he had picked the house. Double-deep, it could easily fit six cars, but that wasn't what he wanted it for. It was added on years ago and nicely done. The roof dipped from the line of the house just enough to give character and yet balance to the home as a whole. The end of the garage bumped out slightly and gave the back of the house added personality. It was large enough to hold all of his tools, his work space and his truck, along with his Saab that waited in storage with the furniture. A guy's gotta have his toys. Only the basics would be on this truck. Still, he rubbed his hands together in anticipation.

He helped the movers unload and carry the kitchen appliances to the mudroom for now. It was his tools he was anxious to retrieve. Other than his truck, the garage was empty, clean and ready for his planer, table saw, and all of the hand tools and boxes of drill and router bits he needed to make this ancient home live again.

As he and the movers placed each tool and work table precisely where he'd planned, a squad car pulled up behind the moving truck. He set down a box of routers and hand sanders, and let out a long whistle as a police officer walked through the entrance to the front of the garage.

"Aren't you looking important? You're gonna make the neighbors think I brought trouble." He gave his childhood friend a quick embrace of two, quick thumps on the back.

"Nathan, what are you thinking? This place is a dump." the

cop said.

"Don't hold back, Davey, tell me what you really think."

"Son-of-a-bitch, Nathan, don't call me Davey. We're not in high school anymore. I have a rep."

Dave towered over the movers. Nathan remembered him to be right at six feet, four inches. Brief introductions were made with Dave's partner as they looked around at the tools.

"Where're the boys?" Dave asked as he walked around the spotless garage, hovering over boxes.

"My folks are taking them for a few hours during the day until school starts so I can get going on the place."

"I thought maybe they already carted them off on a trip. You were hardly in town growing up."

"We just got here, but I'm keeping an eye on that. I want them to get a feel for the place, start feeling like home, and besides, it's good for them to chip in and learn something."

"I expect they have a *feel* for this place." The radio at his hip beeped.

"Time to go. Good luck with the house. We'll have a beer soon," Dave said, walking to his squad car. "Welcome back. Tell the boys I said, 'hey,' and that I've got a present for them."

The movers unloaded the boys' bedroom furniture. Their rooms would be the first Nathan would finish. He walked over and ran his hand across the top of Duncan's dresser. He noted the dent in the side from when Duncan fell into it with his baseball gear. Duncan felt so badly at the time. He was much like his dad; he had to be in control and be the responsible one. Nathan had assured him it was only wood and could be repaired. Now, he couldn't bring himself to fix it. Memories, he figured.

He stood back, remembering each tool he'd used to make the distressed marks on their oak furniture. Chains, hammer and chisel. The stain pooled perfectly into the marks, giving the wood a mood of comfort and age.

By nightfall Nathan's hands were filled with nicks. He was sore and tired, and he wouldn't have traded it for anything. Duncan and Andy talked him into making a fort using extra blankets over the mattresses they slept on. With Goldie already belly up at their feet, he zipped the boys in their sleeping bags as he looked out the back window.

He noticed a fire pit blazing on the patio in Brie's backyard. What the hell? In December? He couldn't help himself. He dug out some binoculars from his still unpacked suitcase. This wasn't like being a peeping Tom, he assured himself. He would have to be looking in her bedroom windows to be a peeping Tom. This was neighborly curiosity.

She'd scooped out snow all around her. Her dog sat at her side, looking comfortable in the frigid night. She read a book using a book light that hooked to the top of a page. Very interesting, he thought. Very damn interesting.

The Novicks would be home from their cruise on Christmas Eve. They expected her to have their outside lights up on their return. Brie couldn't put it off any longer. Her side jobs brought in good money. She'd almost saved enough to buy the living room furniture Liz was always hounding her about, but she really had her eyes set on a shiny new Jeep Wrangler. Regardless, it was the only house left on her list to decorate, and the forecast was for snow that night. The Novicks would come home to a beautifully lit home with a fresh coat of snow covering her tracks and the lights.

Taking off her fleece jacket from her morning run, she walked to the kitchen to brew some coffee before heading out. Her feet stopped before the rest of her. She stuck her arms out to catch her balance and then rocked back on her heels. Her hands went instinctively to her hips as she looked through the glass of the back door at the bloody, mutilated animal strung on her deck rail.

CHAPTER 5

"Oh, hell. Not this again," Brie said out loud. Who had nothing better to do than leave ripped up animals around people's homes?

She grabbed two plastic grocery sacks, doubled them as one and snatched up a hand shovel. Without bothering to put on a coat, she walked out to the deck and tried to scoop the thing into the bags. Rabbit. The slash from mouth to tail caused its insides to protrude from its belly. She fumbled it and watched as it tipped over the side of the rail on the five-foot-high deck onto the snowy yard. Storming down the stairs, she marched around to the carcass. Finally maneuvering it in the bag, she tied it and stomped with an outstretched arm to the garage.

A figure stood anxiously between houses, waiting in the cold to watch Brie's reaction. To see fear from the arrogant bitch. To see her distress, maybe some sobbing or running to big sister for help.

Instead, there was a bit of frustration and a quick, efficient clean up. Clenched fists caused white knuckles. Cutting up the rabbit had been exciting. The thought of Brie finding it was arousing. Now, there was only disappointment.

"Low-class slut. I will find what makes you snap. I have all the time in the world."

* * *

Carrying a load of rotted boards to the dumpster, Nathan slowed down as he noticed someone arranging outdoor Christmas lights across the street. As he tossed the boards into the huge metal box, he recognized the light blue coat, the matching hat and the brown hair falling out the back. She hadn't tied it in a tail today. He wanted to walk up behind her and pull off her hat to see what all that wavy hair looked like falling around her shoulders. Instead he made it to nearly the foot of her ladder without her noticing.

"Is this a prank?"

She jerked and nearly fell off the ladder. "Didn't your mother ever tell you it's not nice to sneak up on people like that?"

"No. My mother was mostly the one doing the sneaking. What are you doing?"

She kept working. "Putting up Christmas lights."

"I can see that. Why isn't whomever you live with putting them up for you?"

"I'm going to ignore the chauvinist comment. If you know what I'm doing, why did you ask? And I live alone."

So, this wasn't going to be simple. Hmm. Walk away? He considered. Or stay and poke. Poking was much more fun. "Because I find it strange to put up decorations two days before a holiday when the rest of the world generally does it weeks before. Oh yes, and there is the whole *This isn't your house* question."

She took an exaggerated deep breath and turned. "This is what I do. The home belongs to the Novicks. Nice neighbors. You'll like them. Recently retired. Travel a lot, but friendly people. They, as have several people of the good town of Northridge, hired me to put these up. Since they don't return from their cruise until tomorrow, I saw no reason to do this any sooner."

She does cranky well, he thought.

"And I'm sorry for being rude. I've had a bad morning."

Interesting again. Cranky, but interesting. "No problem. Want some bad morning coffee? I've got some fresh in my kitchen. Well, actually in my mudroom that is my kitchen right now, but the coffee's good."

She turned away from him and continued working. "I've been curious why a man would move his family into that old place.

Picturing your kitchen stuffed into a mudroom makes me curious enough to ask."

When she reached the end of a light strand, he absently handed her another. "Several reasons. Mostly to be closer to my folks."

"Aren't there nicer homes closer to your folks?" She winced. "Sorry. That, too, was rude. You don't have to answer that. I really should just finish up here."

"There are nicer homes, but I would just tear them up anyway. I like a house done my way. And I work a lot in the garage. Can't beat the garage on that old house. Come by some time for that coffee. I'll show you around."

She turned to say something not quite so curt, but he was already walking that swagger of his back up his drive.

It was cold enough overnight to make the snowfall light and dry. Brie had been right; it coated everything with a fresh blanket of white, including her tracks in the Novicks' yard. Waking, she gave a long sigh at the thought that it was Christmas Eve. She stuck another pillow under her head, propping herself up enough to pretend like she was at least starting to become vertical.

She looked around the enormous room and remembered when it belonged to her parents—passed down to them from their parents. It had been filled with antique furniture that was covered with knick knacks and different sized photos in frames that didn't match. The walls had striped wallpaper along the bottom, a wooden chair rail and a floral pattern covering the upper section.

She thought of when she would bounce into the room and nose herself between the two of them early on Christmas Eve, trying to convince them to allow the opening of presents a day early. Her father worked as a home builder and rarely had days off. Yet, he would patiently explain she would find only coal in any opened-early gifts.

She sat up and crisscrossed her legs. That room was gone. The furnishings and keepsakes had all been scorched as well as most everything throughout this side of the house. Pulling herself up, she went to look out her back window.

The spectacular blanket of snow shone in the moonlight in the still dark, morning air. She decided to use her snowshoes and take Macey for a walk. Afterward, she would take a hot bath and read a book. The dog slept curled in a ball in the corner of the room. She gave her a little nudge.

"Come on, girl."

Macey recognized what the tone meant. She stood, stretching her legs and arching her back.

She was five minutes from making it out the back door when the phone rang. She piled on thermal wear and extra socks as she answered it, then rolled her eyes.

She knew Liz hated that she insisted on being alone on Christmas Eve.

"I knew you'd be up. One o 'clock tomorrow, and bring Macey. My kids won't forgive me if I didn't remind you to bring her."

"I'll remember, and stop worrying about me. Macey and I have plans."

"You should be with family on Christmas Eve."

"Sounds like a greeting card." She held the phone between her head and shoulder while lacing her boots.

"Okay, but you know our door is open."

"I know and I love you. See you tomorrow." She zipped her coat and lifted her snowshoes from the hook in the mudroom. Macey would do without a leash this morning.

Nathan stood at his bedroom window sipping coffee. The boys were still sleeping as was their dog that lay at the foot of Duncan's mattress, belly up, legs in the air. As usual, Andy had moved to Duncan's mattress sometime in the night. And as usual, Duncan moved over for him.

The sun was just beginning to expose the homes, the trees and the lake that was covered in a blanket of white. Nathan noticed something moving in the light of dawn. He recognized the dog. The coat. The hat. He wondered what she was doing out at this hour. Were those snowshoes? He shook his head as he thought she looked like a postcard walking in the endless snow along the creek that sprouted tall pieces of white-topped brown from the plants that lay dormant. Her dog buried its nose in the snow, looking for something that must be waking from the night—or possibly just nestling in. He grinned and turned to make his way down for breakfast. He and his nephews would spend the day at his folks as they did every year. Only this time, they'd arrive by car instead of plane.

The world seemed to finally slow to a peaceful pace when the Christmas rush ended. Brie still had a few days before the first of the year when she would need to start taking down all the lights she had put up. She scooped up the paper off her front porch and toed off her shoes from her morning run. Walking into her kitchen, she headed for the coffee grinder before noticing the new neighbor's dog wandering in her backyard.

Macey snarled and pressed her nose against the glass of the doors that led to the deck. Her fur stood straight on the back of her neck. Goldie jerked his head when he heard her and began wagging his tail furiously, tumbling up the snowy steps of the deck. Macey's snarl turned into frustrated barking. This time the yellow Lab seemed clueless to Macey's warning and started whimpering like he'd found a long lost friend. She couldn't help but laugh. She gave Macey the command to stand down and opened the door.

She hadn't considered how Goldie might have gotten over to her place until the dog bounded into her kitchen with sloppy, muddy feet that must have trudged through Black Creek. Macey, the traitor, started whining with Goldie and nuzzled noses. As they circled each other the Lab spread black prints over her ceramic floor.

She pressed her hands on top of her head and tried, "No. Down. Lay. Stop!" Both dogs ignored her and continued their circling and sniffing around the kitchen island. She stomped to the mudroom to pull down Macey's leash and slipped on her boots. Grabbing her light blue coat, she headed back to the kitchen. The dogs had moved their reunion to the family room, trailing footprints of mud all over her carpet.

"Stupid, stupid dogs. Idiot man."

The dogs sensed the fun was over as the leash clicked on Goldie's collar. She faced Macey, held her arm out, elbow locked and pointed toward the mudroom. The dog's tail went between her legs and her ears lay back as she slumped obediently to her rug. Goldie tried to follow, but Brie maintained a good hold on him.

She went out the door the mongrel had entered; the door she had so generously opened for him. Together, they stomped through the shin-deep snow of her backyard and along the creek's floodplain. When Goldie tried to bolt for the water, she gave the leash short, quick jerks to bring him back to her side. By the time they reached the road and started over the bridge, she couldn't help but be impressed with how quickly he was learning to heel. She scratched his head as they walked. It wasn't the dog's fault his owner couldn't keep an eye on him. As they rounded the corner, she had to work a little to get her mad back up again.

She walked up the drive, noticing a dumpster that overflowed with old carpet and rotted boards. The snow on the drive was packed, the garage door open. She saw Nathan bundled up, wearing headphones and using thick chains to beat on some very long boards that were draped across large rectangular tables. This was the strangest man. She had to tap him on the shoulder to get his attention.

Normal people would jump if they were alone, listening to music and someone tapped them on the shoulder. Nathan Reed simply stopped beating the wood, turned his head and lifted an eyebrow. His eyes met hers, dropped to her leash, then down to his dog. Soon after she saw the realization in his eyes, he turned his head and shoulders to look at the door leading from his mudroom to the garage that hung wide open. He shut his eyes tight and turned his head back to her as he slid off his headphones.

Oh, yeah, her mad was back. She pulled on Goldie's collar as she eased his rump down. Placing her open hand in front of his face, she gave him the command to sit. "Do you know what your dog has done? Did you know we have a leash law in upstate New York? He came running through the creek and trailed a muddy mess through my house. And why the hell are you beating on that wood?"

Add temper to cranky, Nathan decided. Yes, very interesting. He'd have to remember to keep an eye on the temper. Watching the rant, he thought she had the prettiest mouth he'd ever seen. He hooked his thumbs in his front pockets.

"You just told me what my dog has done. I know the laws in upstate New York as I'm originally from here. And how did he get inside your house?"

Brie let out a quick, "Huh?" and put her hands on the back of her hips. "I...let him in." She sighed as her shoulders dropped. "I didn't notice the muddy paws, and you still haven't answered my question about why a grown man is taking out his frustrations on perfectly good boards. They look new."

He considered letting his dog run loose more often if it got her to talk this much. "I'll apologize for the dog. I didn't realize I'd left the door open. Looks like I've been heating the neighborhood." He kept talking as he meandered over to shut it. "I'm not beating on the boards. I'm distressing them. Come, I'll show you."

He reached to take the leash from her. No gloves today and no ring. Add intriguing to interesting. As he reached, she pulled back. He decided he would have to work on the personal-space issue slowly.

"I thought I'd tie him up for a while. Seems he'd rather be outside. I've got a nice long rope around front." He took the leash from her.

As he walked out and around to the front porch, Brie waited in the garage.

"Nice one, mutt," he muttered to his dog and couldn't decide if he meant it sarcastically or appreciatively. Not sure if Brie had stepped out to watch, he turned his back toward the garage to conceal that he scratched his dog's ears before leashing Goldie to the porch. But she wasn't there when he turned.

He found her still in his garage, bent over, face close to one of the boy's bedroom dressers. Two of them stood side by side next to the two full-sized beds, matching dressers and nightstands. Once again, he found himself merely watching her. She rotated her head to the boards he'd been working on to match the furniture, then back to the dresser. As if it might bite her, she slowly reached out and ran her hands over the finish, stopping at the indented distressed marks.

The generous reaction from the public toward his work was always flattering, but this was more. The awe in her eyes and her cautious touch was...humbling. It reminded him of when he'd learned the magic of creating the comfortable look in the wood.

"As I said, it's called distressing, but it works on frustrations, too."

Her hand jerked back. "Sorry. It's beautiful." She didn't turn to him. "Where is your family?"

"You need to stop apologizing. The furniture's been in the rooms of young boys. It's been through worse than a woman's touch. They're with my folks." He placed his hand on top of hers, ready for the escape attempt and placed it back on the dresser.

She ran her hands along the top, along the smooth marks. "The ones you moved to be closer to."

"Yes." He handed her leash back to her. Those eyes. So much going on behind those large, green eyes.

She shook her head slightly twice and stood. "I can't have your unneutered dog around mine."

Startled at the turn of the conversation, he paused to gather his thoughts. "It's a little hypocritical to give me grief about my dog not being fixed. I'm assuming you don't want him around because yours isn't fixed, either." The corners of his mouth lifted.

Brie gave another, quick shake of her head. "I'm waiting for another golden retriever to come of age to breed her. She's about three, and I'd like her to have a litter of pups before I have her spayed."

His mouth opened, then shut again. He pulled his head back. "*Bred?* She doesn't have a say in it? That's rough."

Brie shook her head more dramatically, this time, and smiled just a bit. "Just keep him out of my yard," she said as she headed down the drive.

CHAPTER 6

Brie's brothers and sister would arrive at seven thirty; guests would begin showing up shortly after that. She stood in baggy, gray sweat pants and an oversized flannel shirt. The clothes were a stark contrast to her finished makeup and hair piled high on her head. Standing with arms crossed and legs locked, she stared at the folding chairs that still stood stacked against her foyer wall as she mentally went over the list of things yet to be done. Why, she wondered, hadn't she listened to her sister and bought that family room furniture she needed—or dining, or sitting room furniture either?

Oh, well, she thought, pulling nervously on an ear, and turned to head for the kitchen. People liked to stand and talk at these things.

There would be a band and spirits downstairs. The main floor would be more for talk and food. She needed her brothers to help her move the large oak table from the kitchen nook to the dining room for the food that waited, neatly arranged on platters, in the fridge and on counters. Candles were scattered and ready to be lit. Coolers of soda and beer needed to be hauled from the deck, where they stayed cold, to the buckets that were scattered around the house.

Rubbing her hand along the back of her neck, she realized it didn't matter. It would never be the same. Never like it was when her parents were the host and hostess. Yet, the same people would come. She took a slow, deep breath and straightened her shoulders, listening as the sound of her house shoes changed slightly when she moved from the foyer's hardwood to the kitchen's ceramic tile. It would be nice to catch up with old acquaintances and visit with good friends, she convinced herself.

When the doorbell rang, she looked at the clock and glared. Six o'clock. Who would dare? Liz didn't even have the nerve to come this early. She opened the door and stood with brows tucked tightly together. Nathan Reed stood on her porch in black jeans that matched the color of his slightly damp hair. Okay, so the unshaven look must have been out of comfort rather than for appearance, as he was clean shaven tonight, but what the hell was he doing here two full hours early?

The boys stood frozen, each holding a container covered in foil as Nathan walked past her without so much as a polite *hello*, let alone waiting for an appropriate invitation. "Thought we would make up for the muddy carpet and come by to help. Boys, you remember Miss Brie."

She found herself a little speechless as she moved out of his way. The boys followed at his heels. "I'm sorry, Nathan, wait— stop! I said eight. You're...early."

He walked through to the kitchen. "I said we're here to help, not socialize. I have great southern hospitality. I imagine anyone who waits until the day before Christmas Eve to put up lights might also wait until the last minute to get ready for guests. You have a nice home," he added, moving his eyes in a first-time-around glance. He paused at the traditional lattice detail garnishing the corners of the entrance to the dining room. "What did you do with all your furniture?"

The crooked smile softened her...a little. "There was a fire. Can I speak with you privately?" She forced a grin as she tilted her head at the boys, still frozen, each with their dish of food and bulging brown eyes. She squatted down in front of them. "Duncan, Andy, I have new boxes of toys the clerk at the store said were the latest thing. They're some kind of monster-type people with cars that match. I don't know that much about them. Do you think I could take that food from you and maybe you could get them out of the boxes and try them out for me? The children will have plenty to play with tonight at Mr. Piper's, and I don't want to send over new toys if they aren't any good.

That could be very embarrassing."

"Yes, ma'am," Duncan said.

Nathan took their coats and hung them over the newel post of the staircase. He ran his hand up the rail. "Walnut. It's what I'm planning to use on mine."

The boys wore nice jeans and shirts. Their hair was cut short and neat around their ears and necks. They sat down on the carpet in the family room next to the boxes and began tearing them open as she made her way to the kitchen.

She noted Nathan's sweater matched the blue of his eyes, making them all the more striking. His hair waved slightly at the ends. "Listen, we could discuss the walnut stairs at eight; I don't have time right now to entertain—"

Nathan opened the back doors. "We'll save that for later, then. It looks like you have plenty on the deck that needs to be moved. Where to?" He walked back in carrying the cooler that was filled with hard lemonade.

Brie tried to think of something catchy to say but simply pointed to the opening leading downstairs.

When the drinks were settling on ice in wicker-covered metal buckets around the house, they moved to transfer the kitchen table to the dining room. Talk centered mostly on the boys and where they had lived. Every few minutes they would hear a loud, 'That's not fair!' or noises that sounded surprisingly similar to loaded sports cars.

"When is the rest of your family coming?" she asked before she realized how that sounded.

"Rest of my family?" Nathan tilted his head toward the boys who were gleefully battling scar-faced monsters driving Corvettes and Camaros.

"You made reference to your wife." Her eyes moved around thoughtfully. He said that, hadn't he?

"I would not have made the reference, since there isn't one. I'm divorced."

"Yes, you did. You said your family was at your parents' home when I came to bring your dog back to you."

The two of them centered the table under her traditional, crystal chandelier.

"The boys *were* at my folks and they *are* my family. You know, you wouldn't have to move your kitchen table if you had one for your dining room."

"I told you, it was burned," she said quickly.

"I guess I thought you were being sarcastic. How did it happen?"

"That's a subject I don't have time for." She turned and started upstairs. "I need to change."

She felt his fingers, rough and possessive, wrap around her arm. Gently, he turned her around. He held on carefully when she tried to pull away.

As she looked into the blue, he whispered, "I'm sorry. I know what it's like to suddenly lose someone you love."

Shaken, she felt exposed as she responded, "I never said I lost anyone."

Nathan released her arm and lifted his hand near her face. He paused as she watched him before running the backs of his fingers down her cheek.

"True. I'm going to work on setting around your stack of folding chairs."

As she moved up the stairs, she laid the palm of her hand where his fingers had touched her and swore she felt heat.

From her bedroom, Brie heard the front door shut and Liz's voice playfully threatening her kids with bodily harm if they tracked their snowy feet through the house. She touched up her makeup, tucked a few loose strands of hair back into place and decided on her silver jumpsuit. She heard her sister's footsteps on the stairs and grinned at the thought of the look on Liz's face when she'd walked into the house to find a strange man and his two children setting up chairs and playing with action figures.

"Come in and tie up my back," she said to the tap on the door.

"I don't generally tie women up on the first date. Where would you like coats? The closet in your foyer's not big enough." Nathan smiled as he watched Brie catch herself on the open drawer of her dresser.

She placed a hand over the neck of the jumpsuit. "Do you *generally* barge into the bedrooms of people you hardly know? And this is *not* a date."

"I didn't barge in. I knocked. You invited. And why do you always back away from me?" He lifted a corner of his mouth.

She wore silky silver that went from high on her neck to her feet that stood in strappy, black heels. Trying not to be obvious, he couldn't help but notice how the material clung to her slightly more than should be legal. Finally, he got a glimpse of the form that was under the sweatpants and fleece jackets. And it turned intrigue into a moment of straight lust. She wasn't the skin and bones so many women think men wanted. She was merely built and all female.

Brie placed one foot down, then the other, like she was stopping a cowardly retreat. "I don't know what you're talking about. What do you think you're doing?" she said, putting her free hand out, palm forward as he walked toward her.

"You asked me to tie up your back."

He gently took the wrist of her outstretched hand, felt her pulse quicken under his touch and turned her around. It was his turn to be flustered. The upper half of the back of her top was missing, replaced with zigzagging strips of silver strings. Not skin and bones, no. Her back was smooth and golden lined with a hint of muscle he fought not to touch. He tied the strings at the top and stepped back.

Standing next to the open drawer she'd knocked into, he turned and looked in. "Is this what you wear while you're running around in snowshoes and putting up other people's Christmas lights? There's nothing but lace in here." He grinned as he picked up something pink and stringy.

Brie stepped forward and, hands shaking, yanked the panties out of his hand. Throwing them back in the drawer, she slammed it shut. "It's no one's business what I have on underneath when I have on my snowshoes or anything else. Come on, pushy new neighbor. I hear a car door. I need to get the sitters set up across the street." She stepped around him and made her way for the door.

Brie stopped in the family room and plopped down on the floor in her silky jumpsuit and heels. Andy lay on his stomach with his tongue sticking out of the corner of his mouth as he carefully lined up his monsters with plans to defeat Duncan's.

"I heard Mr. Piper has set up a table full of Play-Doh and those machines that let you push it through to make strings that look like spaghetti." Andy turned his head to her in interest.

She turned to Duncan. Good luck with that one, Nathan thought. "And there's always a game of Twister going." Duncan politely nodded his head. Tilting her head dramatically, Brie tried again. "The babysitters are arriving. If it's okay with your dad, after tonight I really don't have a place to keep the monsters and their cars. Would you mind taking them home with you?"

At that, Andy ran over to Nathan as he leaned against the entrance, thumbs stuck in his front pockets. Andy locked his arms around one of his legs. He squeezed his eyes shut and whispered, "Pleeease, Daddy?"

Duncan followed. "Can we, Nathan? It would keep the kid happy."

"The kid?" He grinned at Duncan's obvious attempt to impress Brie. "Well, I suppose we could find a place for them for *the kid,* although I notice you have them lined up pretty carefully for war." Duncan's face flushed, but not enough to keep him from jerking a bent elbow back and letting out a fisted "Yesss," before heading to pack them up.

As the boys gathered the toys, the doorbell rang. Without waiting for an answer, a tall man walked in carrying large speakers. The band, he figured. He felt a twinge in the back of his neck when Brie walked right up to him and kissed the guy on the cheek. No worry about personal space there, he noticed. Shit, shit, shit. He knew she lived alone but never really pushed to find out if she was seeing anyone. She turned back to him for introductions. He let out a small sigh of relief as he noticed the similarities. Same color hair. Same eyes.

"Nathan this is my brother, Chase."

The man pulled his arm from around Brie and held it out to shake Nathan's hand.

"He bought the old farmhouse across the creek."

Chase raised an eyebrow. "Really?" He walked to open the door to two teenagers carrying pieces of a drum set. "It's got a great build to it, loads of structural personality, but it needs work. You hiring her out?"

"Chase is an architect," Brie interjected. Female bickering came from the kitchen. "And I had, uh, better see to that."

"Only some," Nathan responded, all but ignoring Brie. "I won't do the painting, or the roof or much carpentry. I've got a small crew coming next week to help knock down a wall and enlarge the kitchen. The home was built in the late 1800s, but you probably know that," he added awkwardly.

"Yes, I know," Chase said before turning to the teens. "You can take those down to the basement. Your cousins are already down there. They can show you where they go."

"Drummer?" Nathan asked, thinking Chase carried himself as more of a cello player.

"No. That would be my brother. I live in the city and keep a set there for him since he flies in from Pittsburg. I'll be taking care of the keyboard for the night. Mostly, we use a DJ system, but guests seem to move easier to live music." He shrugged. "Nice to meet you, Nathan..."

"Reed. Nathan Reed," he said as he turned to make his way cautiously to the kitchen.

"Nathan Reed," he heard Chase mutter. "Rings a bell."

Nathan walked in to find four women leaning against the counters in close conversation. He could tell right away which woman was Brie's sister. Her hair was shorter and she stood several inches under Brie, but other than that they could nearly pass as twins. The other two he figured were Brie's sisters-in-law. One was tall, thin and dressed in a sleek, black dress. The other was more conservative, yet still wore a pantsuit he recognized as upper-middle class. Other than their clothes, all four women carried themselves as casual and warm—until Brie's sister spoke up.

"Why does he get to come early and help?" Liz poked a finger toward Nathan. "You've never let any of us come early to help. Hello." She turned. "I'm Liz." She didn't offer a hand but instead laced her fingers in front of her and turned back to Brie.

He watched as Brie's chin dropped slightly. Amused and interested at being the subject of the conversation and at this new timid side of Brie, he joined the other two women leaning against the counter and watched.

"I didn't let him in. He just barged in and started setting things up," Brie huffed. "And believe me, it won't happen again."

Hmmm, he decided, a challenge. Temper and cranky at the same time. So sexy.

"I'll just remember that for next time." Liz poked the finger toward her sister and turned back to him. "I'm terribly sorry for the scene. Are those adorable boys out there your sons and why does the older one call you by your first name?"

He grinned at Brie's outspoken sister. "Yes, they're my

sons...now. Their parents, my brother and his wife, died in a plane crash when the boys were two and four."

CHAPTER 7

Nathan answered Liz's question matter-of-factly, then without bothering to quiet his voice added, "Duncan still feels a duty to his father. He may decide to always call me by my first name. It's up to him." He casually reached to snack on the neat rows of bruschetta.

Suddenly lose someone you love. Brie recognized Nathan's efforts to keep the subject relaxed and admired his openness. She also felt a jolt of pain in her stomach. She'd judged him. Judged him the way she told others not to in her stuffy presentations. She'd seen a lazy man who would subject his young children to filth so he could pawn them off on his parents and have time to play in his garage. She respected his need to distance himself from pity with his casual response to Liz and felt exactly that, pity. Pity, with a feeling that Brian was right. She was ice.

Closing her eyes, she also thought of how she and his nephews had more in common than either of them had known. She knew exactly what it was like to lose your parents. The difference was she took part in a lifetime with hers before losing them. Taking Nathan's lead in keeping the conversation light, she smacked the back of his hand away from the thin pieces of toast and salsa.

"Those are for later. You'd better get their coats. It's time for them to head across the

* * *

Nathan spent much of the evening analyzing how this odd mixture of people ended up at the same place to celebrate the holiday. Brie had been right; he was able to meet many of his new neighbors. Most were either empty-nesters or retired. From the easily overheard conversations, he learned there were several firemen and a large group he was sure were either social workers or teachers.

Brie spoke to everyone while paying attention to the drinks and food. She nursed the same glass of champagne for hours, and as composed as she carried herself, often rubbed the back of her neck or pulled nervously on her ear.

There always seemed to be one bombshell at these sorts of things. This one must be a close friend of Brie's as she was often hanging near her. She had pencil-thin legs and long, straight blonde hair with a date that followed her around like a lost puppy. A balding man that he concluded was in the firefighter group kept an eye on her ass whenever she shook it through the room in her skin-tight, strapless red dress. A blond, buzz cut man with baldy gave Brie looks that gave Nathan an urge to pound on something.

Brie headed upstairs from the basement, juggling an armful of dirty dishes. He followed to help, but the firefighting duo fell in stride behind her first. He noted they *didn't* attempt to help. Instead, baldy backed off and split away as buzz cut walked to her with a long neck in his hand. A woman stepped in to make small talk with Nathan. It suited him as he could see Brie and GI Joe from where he stood, and hear them.

"You haven't been by the station," the man said as Brie set the dishes in the sink and began to rinse. "You said you would come by."

"I've been busy. End of grading period, you know?" She loaded the dishes into the dishwasher.

He watched GI Joe and baldy as the woman spoke of drinking too much and coming here each year for this. He was only half listening. His interest remained with Brie and how she moved uncomfortably around the live action figure.

The man stepped closer and said something he couldn't hear. Then, the dude circled his hand around Brie's upper arm and pinned her between the counter and open dishwasher.

"Excuse me," Nathan said quietly as he stepped around the woman mid-sentence and headed for them.

"You've had too much to drink, Brian. I want you to back off." Brie pushed him with her forearm and spun around, almost running into Nathan. She caught her step and looked up at him.

"You okay?" he whispered with his lips close to her ear while looking Brian in the eye.

Brie nodded before picking up her step again toward the dining room.

Brian started to head past him to catch up with her.

Nathan stepped to the side, blocking his path.

Stuttering to a stop, Brian gave him a once over. "What the hell?"

Nathan saw red and fought to keep his voice down. "She obviously doesn't want to talk to you," he growled.

"Who the fuck are you?" Brian slurred as they squared off.

Hands pumping into fists, Nathan inched closer until they were nose to nose. "I'm the one you have to get through before you lay a hand on her again."

Baldy conveniently stepped between them. "Whoa. It's a party, remember? Time to move along." He took Brian by the arm and pulled him back toward the basement.

Brie seemed to handle GI Joe better than he had although she didn't come out completely unscathed. He decided on providing her with a distraction. He walked up behind her, whispering in her ear once more. "How is it that your guests sit in folding chairs while you have the biggest television I've ever seen in your basement?"

"It's none of your business how I spend my money." Hearing the snap in her voice, Brie closed her eyes, paused and turned around.

"Football," she corrected with a smile that didn't reach her eyes.

"Football?"

"Yes. I have my priorities. The Giants deserve a big screen. You mentioned that you moved from the South? Which state?" She placed her hands on the back of her hips.

"South Carolina. We lived in a small town near an old growth forest."

"Ah. The Panthers then, is it?" she said, making sure to keep her eyes focused on his. It occurred to her it wasn't hard. The blue was such a contrast to his jet-black hair. His eyes were intense and analytical and...observant. She couldn't help but smirk at that damned sexy, crooked smile. Shaking her head, she wondered how he could seem so comfortable around all of these people he'd never met, carrying on conversations with complete strangers and seeming to pick out the ones that would now be considered both of their neighbors.

"Jets." His hand lifted toward her face, then down again.

"Huh?"

"The Jets. I'm a Jets fan. You forgot, I'm originally from here. This town even."

"I did forget, and I forgive you."

"For you forgetting I'm from New York?"

"No, for being a Jets fan."

The doorbell rang. She tried for her warmest smile and gave Nathan's hand a friendly squeeze before leaving to answer the door.

"Hello?"

She groaned as she recognized the voice already walking through her foyer. Her boss was clearly lifting her nose to her as she looked her up and down.

"I'm glad you could make it, Sandy." Not. "Did the windows turn out okay?"

"I wouldn't miss it. Yes, they're good as new." Sandy handed her coat to Brie dismissively.

"Cassandra, Susie, Randy, and some others are still here. A few have left already. You're later than usual this year. You'll stay for the countdown, I hope."

She handed her boss a flute and reached for a bottle of champagne to fill it.

"Yes, I partook in other engagements earlier this evening. Of course I'll stay."

When the time arrived, guests slowly meandered to the basement where the TV was tuned to the big, red apple ready to begin its drop a minute before midnight. She spoke with Susie Phillips while checking the clock on the wall often.

Noting the time, she excused herself and dutifully began topping off champagne glasses. The band stopped playing and everyone shouted a loud countdown as the apple started its sixty-second drop.

Nathan held out his flute and she obliged. When she lifted the bottle, he took it from her and set it aside. Her insides began to bubble as his eyes locked on hers. He slid his hand around her waist, stopping on the small of her back. She felt the warm, firm skin from his hand between the silver strings of her jumpsuit. His face dropped closer to hers, stopping just before their lips touched.

She could smell him, a mixture of wood and man. Flustered licks of heat erupted at the unexpected closeness. She wasn't ready for this. The muscles in her stomach lurched, and the air left her lungs as her eyes dropped to his mouth.

"I'm going to kiss you," he said as a statement and curled his other hand around the nape of her neck. Her skin flamed beneath his fingers as they ran under the pieces of hair that escaped her pins. He drifted his thumb along her jawline, painfully slowly, before resting it under her chin.

"I can see that."

"You're trembling," he said as he used the thumb under her chin to lift her face closer to his. Her warm breath flooded his mind.

"It's th-the champagne."

"You've hardly drank a glass all night."

Gently, he closed the distance between them. His lips brushed over her yielding mouth. He stopped and savored the taste of her before diving in. Gliding his hand possessively up her back, he pulled her body into him. There he found flesh. Stunning, sexy, smooth flesh.

He parted her lips with his tongue and was lost. The taste of her sent him drifting. Her arms wound one around his back and the other over his shoulder. He heard a soft purr from deep in her throat as she fisted the back of his shirt. Their bodies fit together and their mouths moved in slow, cool sync.

Just as quickly as he took her, he pulled away. The countdown was over. He kissed her quickly once more and placed his hands on her shoulders. As he looked at her, he slid them down her arms to her hands. Twining their fingers, they turned to send out greetings of the New Year to friends and family.

More than one set of eyes watched the embrace. A fiery sensation burned between temples as one guest lifted a shaking glass of whiskey to dry lips.

"I'm in no hurry. I will break you.

"Fucking bitch."

CHAPTER 8

hands around the warmth of her coffee mug, Brie stood at her back door watching the sunrise. Long, wispy clouds swept orange and yellow along the horizon. It felt good to have family in the house again, even if it was just for a few days. She felt strangely refreshed after such a late night and already had much of the mess picked up.

On the kitchen table, breakfast warmed under serving plate lids. She understood her nieces and nephews weren't tots anymore and would likely sleep late. So would the adults, she conceded.

She looked at Macey. "Come on, girl. Let's take a walk."

The geese on the lake were crammed into the area near the spillway that seemed never to freeze. Several flapped their gray wings as they woke like they were checking to make sure everything still worked after the long, cold night. Her dog ran without a leash around the field and near the water, scattering the flocks before they were ready.

It wasn't long before Nathan's dog discovered them and darted down for a greeting. She thought of the toe-curling kiss with his owner as she used a fallen log to quickly cross the creek. She intended to head off the Lab before he could reach the water. Macey followed easily behind. The greeting between the two dogs seemed like more of a long-waited-for reunion, but she was able to steer Goldie's attention away from her dog with a whiff of the bacon she carried in her pocket.

"Get a new dog?" Chase called to her as he walked down the frozen slope of the floodplain.

"No," Brie said loudly while slightly turning her head. "This one belongs to a neighbor. What are you doing up so early?"

"I could ask you the same. Is this the same neighbor you were lip-locked with last night?" He brought the mug to his mouth in a miserable attempt to hide his smile.

"I was not locked and yes, this is his dog. Anyone else up yet?"

"No. My family will sleep until the afternoon if I let them. Something going on between you two?"

"No, I hardly know him." She sighed, then added, "He moved in not too long ago, and I'm a grown woman, Chase. I can kiss a man."

"Just asking. What are you doing to him?" Chase tilted his head as she pulled Goldie with one hand over the creek and onto the fallen log. In her other hand, she dangled the bacon in front of his nose.

"I'm not doing anything to him. I said it was just a kiss."

"I meant the dog," he said as the two of them landed safely on the ground.

"Oh." She pulled on her ear. "He gets out and comes to the house. He's already tracked creek mud through the kitchen and family room. I'm going to teach him to stay clean."

"Probably just jump in after he walks across on the log. Remember catching crawfish in this creek? You had a knack for finding them." He stood with his free hand in the pocket of his coat.

She moved back over the log nimbly, although the dog looked just as clumsy. "Just have to turn over a few rocks. Look for bubbles."

Chase followed along without spilling a drop of his coffee. "Since I'm already halfway there, I'm going to go on and give Nathan Reed a house call."

"What? Why?"

"He invited me. Well, not necessarily for this morning, but his dog needs to be returned."

Both dogs ran ahead and she and Chase followed. She softened at the sight of the worn path obviously made from the boys' sleds. There was another that looked like a footpath leading around the side of the house to the front.

The backyard was a mess. Weeds as tall as her knees poked brown through the snow. The deck looked hazardous. She figured it was why they came from the front.

She and Chase entered through the tidy garage. The doors were already up.

"Whoa. Great space in here," Chase ogled. "Son of a bitch, look at his tools."

"I won't mention to our brother you said that." She grinned at him.

"Smart ass," Chase muttered as they peeked through the door leading to the mudroom/temporary kitchen that stood wide open—again. Brie gave her dog the command to wait outside, led the reluctant Goldie in and shut the door, still following her brother. Letting out a *hello*, a response came from the front of the house. They found Nathan sitting on the floor, leaning back against his front door. With legs straight out and crossed at the ankles, he stared up at his stairs. A notebook sat in one hand and a pencil in the other.

"I noticed your family walks right on in to your house. I didn't realize it was a neighborhood thing," Nathan said while his eyes moved from the stairs to his notebook. He wore blue jeans worn at the knees and brown, lace-up work boots. His untucked Henley draped over the sides of his loose jeans.

"You left your door open again. We brought your dog back." She hadn't been inside the house since they moved in. The rooms had been completely stripped except for the floors, which were rows of battered wood.

They craned their heads to see what Nathan was looking at. At that same time, they heard the mudroom door release and both dogs run through the open space like roller derby competitors.

"Stupid dog," Nathan said as he tossed his notebook on the floor and stood up to grab hold of his overly excited Lab.

"Not stupid. Not stupid at all. Very clever." She slowly shook her head in amazement while she watched the two bump shoulders. "He's opening your door to get out, or in this case, to let my dog in."

Nathan stood very still for a minute. "Even though you seem to have a psychic connection with canines, I have to disagree. The dog has no thumbs and no general intelligence. That dog cannot open a closed door." He smiled at her with one side of his mouth.

She took Nathan's hand and led him to the back of the house. Standing, she let out two short whistles. Macey trotted over and Goldie followed. "Watch." She pushed her dog back out to the garage and pulled his in the house, shutting the door once again. The three of them watched as Goldie didn't hesitate to use his mouth to turn the knob and open the door to the garage. This time the dogs escaped out to the back.

"Well, I'll be damned."

"Save yourself on your heating bill, Reed. Get yourself a child cover for the doorknob," she said.

He shook his head and headed back to the foyer. Picking up his dropped notebook, he turned to her. "Are you here just to return my dog?"

"No," Chase interrupted. "I came to take you up on your offer to show me what you've got planned for the place." Chase glanced at her. "I couldn't keep my sister from tagging along."

Giving her brother a healthy smack on the arm, she motioned to Nathan's notebook. "Do you draw?"

"No. No, not really, just sketching. Planning mostly." He started to stick the notebook in his back pocket.

"Can I see?" she asked.

Nathan shrugged and handed her the notebook while turning to Chase. "I was just figuring what to do with the stairs. I think I'm going to start from scratch."

"This is what you call *not really*?" She turned the sketch to face Nathan and Chase.

"Mmm. Give it back if you're going to embarrass—"

"Nathan frigging Reed." Chase hit his forehead with the palm of his hand. "I knew I recognized the name. You're Nathan Reed. You own Woodridge Studio, don't you?"

"Did. I sold the place."

Brie looked from Chase to Nathan and back again.

"What the hell are you doing here? Why did you sell? Sorry, none of my business. Are you still making pieces? I've got two end tables from your place...your old place. They're Greene and Greene. Mahogany with little square, ebony inlays and box joints." Chase wrung his hands and rocked up on his toes.

"I know what tables you're talking about." Nathan stuck the

notebook back in his pocket, slipped his pencil behind his ear and tucked his thumbs in his front pockets. "Made a few sets of them."

"You still taking orders? I'd really like a coffee table to go with the end tables."

She was confused as she watched the two of them. She'd never heard of the studio or Chase's obsession with upscale furniture. Her brother looked like when he was a kid working their mother to buy him a new instrument.

She followed as they talked.

"No. No orders. I'm on leave."

"Not even for an across-the-creek neighbor's brother? After all, you did kiss my sister," Chase added with a toothy smile.

"My priority is this place. I plan to have her done by summer's end. I also plan to kiss your sister again," Nathan said as he led them up the creaky stairs.

"Standing right here," Brie murmured to herself.

"I'll tell you what, if you still want it come fall, you'll be my first post-home-remodel order." They walked up the curving, creaky slats, then along the stripped hallway to the bedrooms.

As Nathan opened the door to the first room, she drew in one deep breath. She stuck her chin out, walked in slowly and looked around. It was simply the most stunning room she'd ever seen. In it was the wood he had been beating on...distressing he'd called it. It was stained with a comfortable light color now, yet maintained the smooth look that made her want to touch it. It was all around the windows and doors and even crowned around the ceiling. The tops of the windows and doors held taller layers of wood.

Arranged in the room over rows of thin strips of tight hardwood and a large rug was the furniture he'd brought with him from the South. The walls were painted a homey sage green with curtains and a messy bed comforter that matched. On the walls were two framed pictures, one of a house in a compact neighborhood with towering trees in the background, the other of a rocky beach along an ocean. She walked closer to look at the pictures and noticed the frames had pieces of something that looked like they were stuck in the wood. She ran her fingers over the silver pieces, then turned to look at Nathan with an expression he read.

"Silver inlays."

"How do you get them in there?"

He lifted a corner of his mouth. "Carefully."

Her eyes drew back to the picture. They were both signed *Duncan Reed.* "Duncan drew these?"

"Yes. You can see why I don't claim to draw with him in the house."

"Where are they?"

"Still asleep in the next room. This is Andy's room. He generally makes his way into Duncan's sometime during the night. You usually do the floors all at once in a whole-house remodel like this one, but I decided to go ahead and get their rooms done."

She felt a tug on her heart as she watched him speak of his nephews with all the adoration any father would show for his sons.

Chase made his way to look out the back window. Curious, she followed. They looked toward the house that had been in their family for three generations. The double-leveled deck she had hired out blended well with the Victorian theme from up here. She couldn't see the basket weave pattern of the bricks on the patio she dug and laid herself from so far away, but the shape was nicely symmetrical.

She noticed Chase staring down toward Nathan's huge backyard filled with weeds.

"I know a good landscaper," he spoke up.

Brie gave him a discreet elbow to his kidney.

"You do? I've got that on my list, but seeing that summer is so far off—"

"Spring or fall is when you do the work, and it's not far off," she couldn't help but interject.

"Give me the name. I'll call," Nathan said.

Chase answered, "It's Brie. I thought I was being sarcastic. She didn't tell you?"

"Hmm," was all Nathan said in response.

She enjoyed watching her brother's childlike enthusiasm oddly mixed with Nathan's slow swagger as he animatedly described his plans for moving walls, adding bathrooms, and enlarging the kitchen. He spoke excitedly about the projects that the boys would help with.

Absentmindedly, Nathan placed his hand on the small of her back as they headed for the front door.

It wasn't an absentminded gesture for her. The earlier tug on her heart changed to a solid punch. In her head she carried a short debate with herself about the foolishness of her reaction to such a mundane gesture. "I'm impressed. It seems...overwhelming. You can get this done by summer?"

The dogs were crashed on the holey porch, sitting in the snow the same as they might by a cozy fire.

"*End* of summer," Nathan corrected. "And remember, this is my job for now. The furniture's mostly built and waiting in storage."

Nathan grabbed his dog as she split two, short whistles.

"Thanks for the tour." Chase shook Nathan's free hand. "Let me know if there's anything I can do to help. Or have Brie do to help so you can start on my table sooner." He smiled and headed around toward the back.

Pleasantly worn from taking down lights from fourteen homes in forty-eight hours, Brie lay in bed thinking back on the past few days. She and her siblings had told stories about their childhoods—embarrassing stories, heartwarming stories. Nodding, she thought of the feeling of contentment from that part of her life.

Her brothers had joined their sons in tussles over football. Her nieces had debated the true New Year's Eve Twister champion. Enough food had been made to feed a small country. She sent her brothers off with to-go bags of food. Kisses were passed and promises made to spend time with each other the coming summer.

And the house had become silent again.

Chase had tried to fill his role of eldest brother after their parents died, but Brie shut that off. His children were just reaching adolescence. It made more sense for Brie to handle the affairs since she lived locally. She had nothing and no one, then or now. It suited her. She preferred it that way, as Brian so aptly pointed out for her.

She grinned as her mind flipped to the small tantrum her brother had pitched when Chase told him the Nathan Reed that bought the old farmhouse was Nathan Reed, founder of

Woodridge Studio, and had agreed to make a coffee table for Chase's front parlor. His reaction confirmed that her new neighbor must have built up quite a business. She wondered what made him leave that kind of success. So his nephews could be closer to their grandparents?

She thought of the conversations with her brothers and sister, reminiscing about their parents, this house and the neighbors who made this their own little retirement community. Gossip was that Clifford Piper had been spending an awful lot of time over at Lucy Melbourne's. Mr. Piper's house was near the entrance of the short cul-de-sac, just a few houses from hers. Brie could see it from the window as she rode in the back of a yellow car. A cab. This was familiar.

Fear seeped into her spine. She couldn't quite think of why she would be afraid. Someone was walking. She remembered someone was walking. A couple. Don't take time to stare at them, she told herself. Don't take time to look at the red flowers her mother had planted as she walked in the moonlight. She felt an urgency to get in the house and then realized it was too late. It would always be too late. Failure and guilt took her.

Everything came back. She knew she had to go in and watch her parents die and that she would be useless in saving them. She recalled that her legs weren't going to run. So, she just walked. She stood this time at the bottom of the stairs and let the tears stream down her face, feeling mortified that she was actually eager for the moment that her mother would turn to look at her one last time. When their eyes met, Brie simply cherished their last connection and brought her arms out to her sides waiting for the explosion. Her eyes opened and she was lying in her bed. She rolled over and buried her trembling body in her pillow until sleep took her.

Brie woke to a dreamless morning. It was a good sign for a new day, a fresh start to a new semester. She felt worn from poor sleep, but relieved she'd woken with a blank mind. She called out to her dog even before lacing her running shoes. She tied her hair back in two quick twists as she walked from the bathroom and down the stairs to grab her yellow fleece jacket. Snatching her dog's leash from its hook, she went into the garage and pushed the button to open the door.

"Damn," she said out loud. "Damn, damn, damn it."

Punching the garage door button with more force this time,

she went back in to schedule a cab ride to Bloom Elementary. If someone was trying to scare her, all they were really doing was pissing her off.

As she ran, she considered who might have a grudge against her. A parent of one of her students? The Gradys never missed a chance to tell her she had ruined their son's academic career for having him repeat first grade. Poor kid. He had moved from school to school and could hardly write his name when he had started in her class two years before in the middle of the term.

Hmm. Confidentiality would keep Mr. Babb from knowing who reported his abuse to the authorities.

She rounded the corner as Nathan's dog came running down the drive. This time, Macey completely ignored Brie's command to heel and yanked the leash out of her hand, dragging it through Nathan's yard.

Nathan meandered down his drive to greet her.

"I'm sorry, Nathan," Brie said impatiently, "but I don't have time to talk. I have a new student coming today, my car broke down and I need to get back to catch a cab to work. Please help me get the dogs."

"I'm afraid I can't have you taking a cab. I'll drive you. You have a new student? To train for landscaping? In January?"

"No, in my classroom. Macey, come!"

"Classroom? You teach landscaping?"

"No," she said, picking up Macey's leash and wrapping it around the palm of her hand. "I teach over at Bloom on Millcreek and Prairie. Landscaping and holiday decorating are a side job. I have a cab coming. Thank you. I need to get going." She turned to take a step.

"Wait." Nathan grabbed her arm. "Duncan and Andy are starting today at Bloom. First and third grades."

CHAPTER 9

Without fully turning, Brie stopped. Her mind did a fast-motioned circle through several possibilities.

There was a mistake.

She knew Andy was six.

There was no Andy starting in first grade at Bloom. She would know that kind of thing.

She assumed they were starting at a private school next week with the rest of the private schools. Nothing really to think about there.

Back to there-is-a-mistake.

She turned to face him. "Have you registered them yet?"

"Yes. They have Mrs. Whittier and Miss Chap...oh." he said as his eyes wandered up and to the side.

"I'm Miss Chapman." Brie dropped the leash, not noticing her dog running off again. "There is only a Sylvester registered to start in my class today."

"Well." A large smile filled Nathan's face now. "Sylvester Andrew Reed. It's my father's name. You can see why my brother chose to go with the middle name."

Brie felt sick and started pacing back and forth in a short path. "Oh," she said with legs shaking. "No, no, no, no. This cannot happen." Her mind did another circle.

She'd kissed him.

Kissed a parent of one of her students.

In front of her colleagues.

She'd kissed him in front of her boss.

This was beyond wrong. She pressed her fingers against her temples while continuing to carve a path in the snow.

"I can fix this," she said aloud as she stopped and put her hands out, palms down. "I'll go right to my boss and expl—"

"You mean that judgmental fish you said was your boss is the principal of my boys' school? Huh. So...just asking, don't you check last names and addresses of your new students?" he asked still smiling from ear to ear.

"No." She went back to pacing. "Research shows if teachers know the social and economic backgrounds of their students, they may make preconceived judgments of the student's...oh, never mind. This is unprofessional. Backward. I don't kiss parents of my students." She started pacing again. "And, ohhh, Sandy saw me kiss you. Sneered at me. Even made the jab that you're 'not quite the firefighter.' I can fix this. I can get him moved to another class."

Nathan stepped in her path trying to slow her down. He framed her panicked face with his hands. "Slow down. Where is the wrong here? Andy likes you already. He'll be happy. I'm happy." His eyebrows dropped when Brie didn't soften her expression. "We didn't do anything worthy of a scandal." Not that he wasn't thinking about it. "No wrong. I'll take you to work. I'll bring the boys when it's time. They'll have a great first day at school. Andy is very well behaved, so his other teachers told me." He didn't let go of her face but pulled his head back some. "Firefighter? So, GI Joe *is* an old boyfriend."

Brie sighed deeply. "Nathan. I can't do this. I can't have you drive me to work like we just had some steamy night of sex before dropping off your nephew in my classroom. It's too late to have him switch rooms. I have to figure out how to patch this over with my boss. With the teachers that saw...us. And I have to change all of the places in my room that say 'Sylvester' to read 'Andy.'"

He had a hard time listening after the comment about the steamy night of sex, but he tried to smooth over the situation. "Okay. You take a cab. Leave your back door unlocked. I'll catch up with your dog and get her back home for you."

Brie took off the way she'd come. He rocked back on his heels and shook his head. He hadn't even made the connection with her last name, he berated himself. Southern hospitality my ass. Dumb ass was more like it.

His image of Brie had been pretty well set. Small business woman. Works with her hands. Seems to enjoy living alone. Outdoorsy. Not the overly flirty Barbie-type. He stood in the doorway of her classroom studying her. She was dressed in low-heeled pumps, gray slacks and a white blouse with her hair bundled up on her head. He thought she was just as pretty as she'd been in her silver jumpsuit.

This was a side of Brie he enjoyed watching. She didn't speak down to the kids like many adults did. She was warm and approachable, and...attentive. Cleverly, she kept a close proximity to Andy, letting him feel safe but not obviously so. He seemed comfortable, for the first day, and remembered to call her "Miss Chapman" like he'd been told a hundred times on the drive to the school. It occurred to him that this was the first time he had seen her really smile. Nathan didn't stay long, and he respected Duncan's wishes to steer clear of his class. He drove home and thought of the parts of him that were awakening, parts that had been asleep for a very long time.

Nathan stopped at the end of his long drive and pulled yesterday's mail from his rusty box. Walking back to his pickup, he flipped through the few envelopes. Damn it, he thought. They've found me already. He tossed the mail on the passenger seat and drove the rest of the way to his house.

When he opened his garage door, the dogs jumped out. He'd have to get that child cover for the mudroom doorknob after all. Grabbing hold of Brie's dog, he snapped on a leash. There was no sense trying to keep Houdini back, so he put one on Goldie, too.

Steering clear of the creek, he led the two of them on a walk in the snowy street around to Brie's house. He realized he'd never seen the front of it in the daylight. The drive was cleanly shoveled and the yard had neatly scattered, snow-topped bushes of brown and dark green. As he walked around to the back, he noticed clusters of different kinds of dormant plants and bushes sticking up from the snow around the perimeter of her home.

Every inch of her yard was littered with footprints, animal and human alike. Her brick patio was a perfect, large circle and had been shoveled and swept clean. Three-quarter height windows lined the basement and under her deck. He walked on the brick to reach the deck stairs.

She had remembered to leave the door unlocked. The house was spotless. It was hard for him not to snoop, but he'd come with a purpose and not just to return her dog. Walking to the garage, he wondered if she spent any time in the house at all.

He froze when he opened the door. "What the fucking fuck?"

He looked at her old-model pickup, just starting to show spots of rust. It sat in the middle of her garage with all four tires flat from gaping slashes. He reached for the phone. If this was what she called a broken-down car, she would just have to deal with him prying into what the hell was going on.

Dave was working and answered on the second ring. "Officer Nolan."

"It's Nathan." He went through the story of the psycho-slashed tires and mentioned the fact that Brie lived in a peaceful, tucked-away cul-de-sac with mostly retired neighbors. After giving her name and address, he hung up and waited. Paced. Opened the garage door and paced some more.

Dave wasn't long. He came in, ducking as he walked under the door. He walked around looking at the car, around the garage, at all the doors. "Nothing's been tampered with inside?"

"I don't know. Not that I can tell, not like that."

"It looks like whomever did this either has a key to the door leading out back or is a professional. There's no evidence of a picked lock as far as I can see. I ran Brie's name through the system on the way over."

"You son-of-a-bitch. I asked for your help. That's bullshit."

"Touchy. I'd say we're looking at more than just a spunky neighbor. She's had her windows shot out at work twice since September. There's more. Not saying it's connected. Any of it. Just saying what I found."

"Go on."

"There's an open case involving her. An arson six years back. She made it out. Her parents didn't. You sure you want to be involved with this woman? Seems like a lot of baggage if you ask me."

"Just do some more digging, would you? Let me know. I need to think."

"Can't call this in unless it's her that does the calling. No crime in having a car with flat tires in your own garage."

They stopped talking at the sound of footsteps crunching the snow in the street. Up the drive walked a short redhead with chipmunk cheeks. She walked with quick steps but kept her distance.

"Is there a problem officer? My name's Amanda Piper. I live across the street."

"No, ma'am. Just helping out an old friend," Dave answered.

"Can I ask what you're doing in this garage in front of the owner's car with...flat tires?" She craned her head, leaving room between her and them.

"I'm Nathan Reed. I moved in on the other side of the creek. Came by to help. Brie's at work. You're Clifford Piper's granddaughter? My kids stayed at his place New Year's Eve."

"Oh." Her posture softened. "I didn't make it back in time for that. Yes, I'm his granddaughter. I guess I'll head back then. Uh...thanks for helping." She turned and left with the same, quick steps as when she'd come.

Nathan was right, Brie thought, Andy was delightful. She decided to sit him next to Aaron Babb. They'd both moved into new situations recently; Andy into a new state and Aaron into his new foster home. Maybe they could find a common thread. She was able to test him on his reading and math skills. They were a concern, other than his spatial sense—which topped the scales.

This might not be so bad, she thought. She could keep her distance from Nathan. She understood that when you lived in the school district you taught in, you might have a neighbor in your class.

Then, she found the message in her office box. "Miss Chapman: See me before you leave." Great. Her boss never called her "Miss Chapman" unless it was bad.

She picked up her room and quickly laid out her things for the next day. Liz was giving her a ride home and needed to get to her sitter's to pick up the kids on time. Sandy's door was open, but Brie knocked anyway.

"Come in and shut the door, Brianna." Sandy leaned back,

placed her elbows on the arms of her tall-backed chair and folded her hands in her front of her. She wore her usual tailored, pinstriped suit, complete with designer pumps Brie couldn't see but knew were tucked under the desk. This had to be either Sandy's way of intimidating those who entered her office or making herself feel more important. History would prove it was probably both.

"You have a new student."

Here we go. "Yes. He'll need help with numerical sense and reading fluency, but excels in geometrical concepts." She knew Sandy didn't care about any of that.

"This is the son of the man you were with at the staff gathering in your home. I saw him here this morning dropping off his two boys."

"I'm not sure what you mean by *with*. Do I need union representation?"

"That's your right. What you do in your personal time is also your right. I called you in here to let you know I don't appreciate you meeting with the assistant superintendent without my notification, and that I consider it unprofessional to socialize intimately with parents of your students." She steepled her fingers together.

Brie reminded herself she knew this was coming. Well, part of it, anyway. As far as informing her boss about her plans with Dr. Tyman, she wasn't prepared for that part of the conversation. She decided less was more and that she wouldn't play into the "intimate" comment.

"I'll keep that in mind. Is there anything else?"

Sandy stood, opened the door and smirked. "Yes. I want you to consider why someone would want to vandalize your windows...twice."

Brie tried to explain the Nathan Reed situation to Liz on the way home, but her sister laughed so hard tears dripped from the corners of her eyes. The only way she could stop laughing was to tell her what their boss had said about it.

Liz quieted. "That sounds like 'better watch your back.'"

"I thought so, too. I can handle her."

"Pretend to listen to me, Brie, just this once. You've been working at Bloom for six years. Moved up the ladder fast, kept your nose clean. You're keynote speaker at conferences, some of which other teachers from our building attend. A few are teachers you had when we went here. You're rubbing noses with the assistant super. It doesn't sit as easy with people like Sandy Finley, who need to look the best and get the most attention.

"I'm not telling you to stop what you're doing to appease insecure colleagues or Sandy, just be careful. Principals can make your life...difficult."

Liz pulled into the drive, pressing on the brakes without putting her car into park. "Good luck with the car. Are you sure you don't want me to have Tim take a look at it?" she asked, shifting the gear into reverse.

And see the tires? I don't think so. "No, I've got it." She shut the door behind her and said her thanks loud enough for Liz to hear through the window.

As she made her way to her front door, she lifted one hand to wave goodbye to her sister and juggled her keys to find the right one with the other. Checking the knob, she realized the door wasn't locked. She stopped and saw something move across the frosty side lites of the door. A figure. A person. She turned to gesture at her sister, but Liz was already down the drive.

CHAPTER 10

When Brie heard the happy noise her dog made on the other side of the door, she relaxed. Still a little breathless, she opened it to Macey dancing around with her regular end-of-the-day greeting and Nathan Reed standing in her foyer with his thumbs in his pockets. It wasn't hard to see he was angry.

She took a deep breath, lifting her chin as she hung up her coat and dropped her bag. "Thank you for getting my dog back, but what are you still doing here? Where are the boys?" she asked while trying to think of what needed to be said here.

"My mom's with them. Why didn't you tell me your tires were slashed? In your garage? With the door closed and locked?"

"Listen, I appreciate you getting my dog back and your worry, but I can take care of myself and...I hardly know you. You hardly know me." The bottoms of her low-heeled pumps clicked as she made her way across the hardwood and onto the ceramic of the kitchen floor.

"We need to take a step back here, Nathan. Not only do I not kiss the parents of my students, I don't entertain them in my house. We're going to need to set some boundaries if I am going to continue to be Andy's teacher."

Red filled his face. He jammed his hands firmly in his pockets. "I'm not talking about you and me, although I have my own ideas about that. I'm talking about some nut-case putting at least a half-dozen slashes in each of your tires in your locked garage.

And I don't care for you threatening me with Andy."

"I'm not above doing that. You should know that. I can take care of my own car." She turned as she thought of just how she was going to do that, and reached up to pull out a single tea bag and mug. "And there is no you and me. It was just a kiss. Now, we have to move backward for Andy's sake." And mine, she thought.

He made his way to her in three long strides, picked her up by the shoulders and plopped her on the kitchen counter, smashing his mouth to hers. Framing the side of her face with one hand, Nathan laced his fingers in her pinned up hair with the other.

She couldn't think and for the first time in her life let go. Slipping away from her blessed control, she blocked out the possible consequences and surrendered to the now. Her skin nearly ignited from the feel of his body as she pulled him in closer. She held onto his lanky back, his strong arms, feeling his rough hands on her face, in her hair. His mouth and his tongue emptied her mind. She clamped her eyes shut and wanted to stay right there.

As he'd done at the midnight hour in her basement, he pulled away as quickly as he took her.

Nathan whispered close to her face, "Just a kiss my ass."

When she tried to speak, he put his fingers to her lips.

"You're right. I don't know you...well...but I plan to. The parts I've picked up so far tell me you work with animals using unnatural patience. You took a lot of extra trouble to get this house rebuilt as it would have looked when your parents lived in it.

"Yet, you don't want to spend time here. You spend more time outside in the cold than most people do in the summer. You've not made it your home. You invite a hundred people here but only pretend to enjoy it. You love your family completely, and your job is the only thing that makes you truly smile."

Her eyes remained on his, and she didn't speak when he moved his fingers from her lips.

"But I want to know you. Tell me about the tires."

She looked at him in silence for a long time. He pegged her in ways that should have made her uncomfortable and normally would have made her push away. Instead, she just laid her forehead on his shoulder and answered, "I don't know."

He slid an arm around her waist while picking up the phone and dialing his mother. "It's me. I'll be longer than I thought. Yes, I'll be back in time to go through all that. I owe you—again."

"Come." He eased her down from the counter. "Let's get something to eat. You have nothing. I checked."

"I can't be seen with you, Nathan. You shouldn't even be here. My boss got after me today. Unprofessional this and that. *She'll be watching* written all over her face. We don't get along."

"Okay. Pizza delivery." He picked up the phone again.

Brie let out a heavy sigh. "I'll go change."

She came down wearing faded jeans and a sweatshirt. Her feet were bare, Nathan noted, but she left her hair up.

"Tea?" she asked as she walked through the kitchen.

"That'll work." He sat at her kitchen table with Macey at his feet. Scratching the dog's head, he began with a question. "You have no idea who would have done this?"

"No, not *no* idea." She pulled down a pot for water and an extra mug. "There may be some disgruntled parents. I'm not sure."

"Would some kid's dad get so mad he would break into your house and go crazy on your truck?"

He walked to her and reached for the teapot. "I'll get it."

"Already done," she said as she filled it with water. "Parents can go off the deep end. There's one that makes sure to give me an earful about retaining his gifted child. There's another that lost custody due to abuse I reported. Who reported him should be confidential, but it's not unheard of for that information to be leaked. I'm not so sure it isn't just ornery kids and I'm not just letting my mind wander." She handed him a full mug and tea bag.

"You've put thought into this." He sat back down and leaned back in the chair.

Taking a sip, he watched her face.

She nodded.

"This isn't the first time," he said as a statement.

"No. It's not. I mean it is for the tires, but there are other things. They're probably—"

"What other things?" he interrupted as he pushed the mug aside and put his hands on his legs under the table, gripping his thighs.

"Animals. Broken windows." She didn't move her head, but turned her eyes to his.

It took some effort to keep his temper from showing on his face. "I'm listening."

"My windows at work have been shot out with a rifle. Well, the first time a rifle and the second a rifle and rocks." She paused. "Some animals have been...I don't know...killed. And left strung from my deck. On my porch. Over my deck rail. I realize this sounds crazy, and I'm not saying it's all connected. Most of it's probably kids and-"

Nathan pushed away from the table and walked to her family room, running his fingers through his hair. She's lived here alone, he thought. Dealing with this alone.

"Listen, I'm all right. It mostly just makes me annoyed and angry."

"Whoever did that number on your tires isn't trying to annoy you. They're trying to scare you."

"I'm not scared."

"I called a friend. He's a cop."

"You're a pushy man, Reed. I don't need your help."

"I don't need your permission to ask around. You should know I'm not above doing that. I know a guy who can get you new tires—"

"I'm going to let you talk to your cop friend, because I can't stop you. I guess I'd really like to know if he thinks any of this is connected, but you're not fixing my car. I can take care of it myself. I can take care of me. I won't like it if you crowd me."

Nathan sat with Dave at his card table in folding chairs drinking dark beer from glass bottles. Goldie snored at his feet.

"I requested the case to my captain if Brie ever decides to move forward with any kind of investigation. I'm not up for detective for a few months yet, but my captain thinks this would be a way to get my feet wet. I've pored over the files."

"Anything linking then to now?"

"What makes you think this could possibly be linked to an arson that happened six years ago?"

"You think she just happened to be victim of an arson that ended in the death of both of her parents and then just happens to have another nutcase leaving her mutilated animals, shot out windows and slashed tires?"

"Okay, okay. But what doesn't make sense is why someone would wait six years in between." Dave sat back, took a drink of his beer and flipped through his notes. "Confirmed arson. One witness. Called in by the next-door neighbor at eleven forty-two. A Lucy Melbourne. Says she made the call because of the noise from the explosion, before looking out her window. Some kind of backdraft was set in what was, at that time, Brie's bedroom. The file suggests that whoever set it knew what they were doing."

"Backdraft?"

"Set especially so it can't spread at first. Uses all the oxygen from the room. When the fire gets a new dose of air, such as opening a door...boom. The parents were the ones that opened the door. Died instantly. Brie was blown back from the kick. Hit her head. Knocked her out. Treated for head injury and smoke inhalation.

"It said in her formal statement she saw two people walking as she pulled up in a cab but couldn't remember anything about clothing or faces. Not even gender. Both her sister's and her alibis for the evening were confirmed."

Nathan leaned forward. "You suggesting they might have blown up their own parents?"

"Just saying what I read. They were seen that night by several bar patrons. Bartender remembered them, too. A neighbor also said she remembered seeing someone out walking. Not so strange to take a late night walk if you ask me, but both Brie and the neighbor said it was odd for the neighborhood." Dave tossed his empty bottle in the paper grocery sack next to the dog and opened the cooler for another. "Have you talked to her since the tires?"

"Just stuff about Andy. She's touchy about the whole getting-involved-with-parents-of-students thing."

"That is weird. If I had a kid, I wouldn't want his teacher running around with some classmate's dad. Shit, it's still weird to think of you as a dad."

"She supposed to be the Pope? And being a dad's still weird

for me, too. I don't know what the hell I'm doing."

"Is that why you came back?"

"Pretty much, yeah. My ex wanted the divorce. Andy's teachers basically told me I was doing a rotten job. The shop was taking all my time." He looked into the paper sack at the growing stack of empty bottles. "They're piling up in there."

"Yeah. I think I'm sleeping on your fucking filthy floor tonight."

"It's not a fucking filthy floor. It's just a fucking unfinished floor and don't talk about fucking. It's been too long for me." He stood up slowly. "You're welcome to my extra mattress, and I have a Spiderman sleeping bag that might fit your right leg."

CHAPTER 11

Nathan had Duncan pulling orange and white stickers from the new windows and working on installing the screens.

"The windows are all different sizes. There are too many screens. I'm only eight." Ironically, Duncan tried to reason like an adult about his young age, but Nathan wasn't budging.

"Mmm hmm. You *are* only eight. That's why I'm only giving you this one project for your Saturday." He continued spreading stain on one of the twenty-seven interior doors. "And remember to only put in the screens on the first floor and basement daylights. Just lean the screens next to the windows upstairs."

He stacked doors on drying racks throughout the garage. They, too, were different sizes but all matched in design, each with three flat panels boasting the straight lines that fit a Mission-style home. The wood, however, differed depending on which room it belonged. The master bedroom, bath and closet doors were made of quarter-sawn oak, the boys' rooms in distressed oak and the rest in riff-sawn.

Andy's chores stayed in the garage where Nathan could keep an eye on him. The younger boy's job was to replace router and drill bits to their proper spots. Since it was much like completing a puzzle, it was just the right task for him.

He knew the house didn't look like much had been done, but he'd checked off plenty from his list over the weeks. Besides the new windows, the electrician had finished. The plumbing was ready for sinks and fixtures. He'd changed his mind and decided on a shower that had both high and low spigots for all three upstairs bathrooms. The plumber wasn't too happy about the change and took his time making the extra return trip. Nathan didn't mind. He wouldn't have the new sinks picked out for some time anyway.

He'd given Brie time to think and the space she'd asked for. He'd never had time for clingy women. Following her suggestions, he worked with Andy each night, reading the books she sent home, doing the worksheets, flashing the flashcards and all that. As he and Andy worked on his assignments, Duncan worked with pencil and water colors on the view of the lake and Black Creek. The scene was becoming a nightly routine, and it felt right.

For the first time, he was beginning to feel like a real parent. The studio wasn't calling. He wasn't working late. The letters requesting work piled up, but he could ignore those easily enough.

His folks helped and had already convinced him into a few day trips with the boys, one hiking around the Finger Lakes and another ice skating in downtown Northridge. The boys seemed to get into the cold as much as his hard-shelled neighbor. He saw her almost daily and let his dog out to play with hers when the two of them came around to her backyard.

He stopped what he was doing to watch out one of the windows in the back of his garage. There she was, working with Goldie. His dog trotted across the log without her coaxing him now. She plopped his butt down and put a hand in front of him like a stop sign, then walked away. The mutt sat watching her. Brie patted her leg and he ran to her, looking like he was going to knock her over. Instead he slammed on the brakes, then sat his butt down again. Go figure.

Brie always had some kind of treat in her pocket for a reward. He thought that was cheating. He tried to get Goldie to sit and stay for him once, but the dog played dumb. If he didn't hear from her soon, she would have to deal with him breaking the don't-come-to-my-house request.

Andy learned quickly. Brie was determined to catch him up. Not because of anything that included Nathan, but because it was her job. She learned that he loved to build. There wasn't a lot of that in the first grade, but she made some adjustments to allow for it. The other kids were drawn to him. He was fun and had a likable personality. It was often too cold to go outside for recess. On those days, the students played in the classroom after lunch. The other children liked to give Andy something to build with, sort of a challenge. Cards, blocks, books.

She decided to ask about Duncan and stopped in to see his teacher on her way home. She knocked on the open door. "Elizabeth? Did I catch you at a bad time?" Mrs. Whittier was in her early sixties. Her hair was stark white and her skin well cared for. Not too many lines for a woman her age. She generally wore dresses with large floral prints and laced shoes with large heels.

"No, no, Brie. Come in. I expected you long before this."

Honestly confused, she asked, "Did I forget something we were to do?"

"No. I expected you to check on the Reed boy before now. Aren't you still seeing his uncle?"

The *Reed* boy? Brie thought that was cold. "I was never seeing his uncle." She reviewed the night of the New Year's Eve party in her head, trying to remember if Elizabeth had been there. "Who told you that?"

Elizabeth's brows lifted. "I'm not sure really, everyone I suppose. The boy is doing well. He's smart enough, although the children are giving him a go. Sorry about the assumption, by the way."

"Apology accepted as long as you mention that it's not true the next time you hear it. What do you mean 'giving him a go'?"

The third-grade teacher stuffed papers into a bag covered with pictures of cats. "They call him a girl. He does like to doodle on a lot of his notebooks and papers. Mostly trees and people. The teasing doesn't seem to bother him. He's content."

"I see you're on your way out. I'll let you get going. Have a nice night, and thank you."

Brie kept running back the phrase "but he does like to doodle" through her mind, like it was enough of a reason to call him a girl. As if it was his fault the other children were calling him names. Like *any* child was content with being teased. That woman needed to retire.

As she drove home for the long weekend she thought of stopping by to see Nathan. Not to mention what Mrs. Whittier had said. She had her own ideas about how to handle that. She hadn't seen Nathan since she'd went over to give him the rundown on Andy's test scores and her plans for catching him up. That was a regular home visit, she convinced herself. She made plenty of home visits over the years.

Nathan respected her request not to crowd her. Points for him. She saw plenty of his dog, however. Goldie made almost daily trips over to wrestle with Macey. So much for the child lock on the door. She had to admit she enjoyed working with him. He thrived on learning and not only could successfully maneuver the log whenever he came over but had all but mastered most of the routine commands. She decided on calling instead of stopping by. Safer.

"You're calling me," Nathan said.

Smiling at his reaction, Brie held the phone between her ear and shoulder. "Yes. Don't you get phone calls, Reed?"

"You're calling me from your house?" he asked as a question this time.

She walked to her freezer and pulled out a bag of coffee beans. "I want to see if your cop friend found out anything."

"You can run miles every morning, make my dog go crazy at the crack of dawn when you go by, but you can't walk over two fields and a creek to ask me?"

"I didn't realize we were making your dog go crazy. I can run a different route. And I didn't know if you'd be home."

"My dog's in your yard right now. I can see him. Don't run a different route."

Still holding the coffee beans, she went to look out her back window. She could see Goldie tugging at a stick with Macey like they were joined at the head. And she could barely make out a figure in the glass doors leading to Nathan's kitchen. She smiled and bit her bottom lip.

"You haven't put the child lock on your door yet." She paused a moment. "Are you staying away from me to respect my wishes or to make me want to see you again?"

"Which answer gets you to go out with me tonight? I'll see if the cop can come along. We'll make it business."

"Either answer works, but I can't tonight. I'm watching my sister's kids."

"Tomorrow then."

She thought a minute. What the hell was she doing? "Okay. I'll bring a friend, too. You know a pub called Mikey's?"

"I know the place. I'll pick you up at eight."

She thought again. "No. I'll meet you there."

"We're both going to drive when you live close enough for me to see you standing in your kitchen?"

"Absolutely."

"Eight o'clock, then."

"Why don't you have a hill on your side of the creek?" Liz's daughter asked Brie. She sat back on her little heels on the floor in front of Brie's back window watching Duncan and Andy sled down their hill. Elbows resting on the chilly windowsill, her niece propped her chin in her hands.

Brie walked over to her and sat down, looking out the window with her. They watched Nathan pulled Andy up onto his shoulders, carrying him back up their short hill that was worn from use. Duncan got a running start, then dove head first onto a red sled.

"I guess my ground decided to be flat. Too many trees over here anyway." She mussed her niece's hair and stood up to answer the knock at the door.

Without waiting for an answer, Clifford Piper's granddaughter walked in, closing the door behind her.

"Amanda. I was just getting ready to call you." She hugged her longtime friend. Smiling, she shook her head as she thought of what Nathan had said about people walking into each other's homes in this neighborhood. "Hey, Rose." She squatted down to Amanda's five-year-old daughter and her shocking head of strawberry blonde hair.

"Hi, Bwie." Rose waved her hand once like a windshield wiper.

She looked at Rose face to face. "Where've you and your mom been this time?"

Rose tugged on her mom's shirt sleeve, pulling her head down so that her little mouth could reach her mother's ear.

Amanda answered for her. "The Dominican Republic. That one's a mouthful for her. We helped clean up after Hurricane Emily." She turned to her daughter. "I think I hear Liz's kids in

81

the family room."

Before Amanda had finished, Rose took off through the open space of the foyer back to the family room.

"How long are you in town?"

Amanda tossed her coat over the newel post. "Hopefully 'til at least summer. I'm enrolling Rose in school. They say they want her in the bilingual class at Marsh."

"No kidding? I thought you were doing home schooling and tutors while you're abroad. Marsh is a great school," she added as she picked Rose and Amanda's coats off the post and grabbed hers from the closet.

"That turned out to be harder than I thought. It seems she needs to settle somewhere, for a while anyway. We'll see how it goes. It's really great to see you."

"You, too. We miss you around here. Too many old people."

Amanda walked into the kitchen, opened the cupboard and pulled out a glass. "Who are you kidding? You love old people."

"Sure, but the ones I know are not the kind you can go out with for a drink and some laughs. Speaking of going out for a drink, I need a favor."

"Son of a bitch, girl, I just walked in the door." Amanda poured herself a glass of water and headed for the family room.

"I know, and it's really big." Brie followed. As they watched the kids, she went through the abbreviated version of the tires.

"You mean the cute new neighbor is who we're meeting? I came over when they were playing Starsky and Hutch in your garage. And he's bringing the sexy cop? I'm in, though I think the chaperone thing is stupid."

The kids had dressed Macey in a shirt and hat. "Who's ready to crash a party?" Brie asked, saving her dog from further humiliation. "Get your stuff. We're going sledding."

Nathan recognized Liz's kids walking across the fallen log. He thought the tiny woman helping the little girl across was the Amanda he'd met the day of the flat tires. A thrill struck him when he saw Brie take up the rear with a paper grocery sack in one arm and sleds balancing on her other shoulder. Her mass of wavy hair was pulled through her cap. He jogged down to help. "Here, let me help you," he said as he reached for her sleds.

"No. I've got it." She smiled. "Are you up for a few extras? I brought hot chocolate."

Amanda approached him before he could say hello. "Remember me? Flat tires? Checking up on Brie's house?"

Rose ran off toward the little hill without stopping for introductions.

"Yes. Good to see you again. Is she yours?" he asked, gesturing to the screaming girl pulling the old pink, circle sled that Brie brought with her.

"Yeah. That's Rose. What'd you find out about the tires? Brie tells me there's been trouble."

"I didn't say *trouble*," Brie interrupted. "I said to look out for odd pranks or strangers walking around."

"I agreed to come and supervise the discussion of the dire situation," Amanda said sarcastically. She walked away and gave the kids a running push down the hill.

They stopped for breaks to sip the hot chocolate Brie brought in two large thermoses. It was dark, but the white snow lit in the moonlight. After some time, they decided on pizza for dinner and dragged their frozen bodies around the front and into the warmth.

"You finished the stairs," Brie said.

He felt humbled that it was the first thing she noticed. The rooms on the first floor were still just as bare, but his stairs had the rows of straight spindles topped with his smoothed railings. They didn't have the delicate look of the stairs Brie had replaced in her house. He'd used more lines than curves, and he'd made the newel post with enormous tops and layer upon layer of thick wood.

She leaned over for a better look at the panels in the posts when she said, "These patterns in the grain look like swirling cumulus clouds."

"Burled walnut veneer," he answered. "I probably should be finishing the upstairs, but I couldn't get the picture of the stairs out of my mind."

"Hey, babysitter, you gonna help these kids? Or let me do it all?" Amanda methodically pulled off wet gear from the kids and tossed it randomly on the floor.

They ordered pizza. After eating their fill, Andy and Rose went to the part of the bare room with Andy's Duplos. The older kids headed upstairs to play in Duncan's room. Nathan and

Brie each sat in a folding chair and sipped on a glass of chardonnay while Amanda sat on the floor, legs folded.

"That's not what you do with those," Andy told Rose.

She stuck the Duplos together in a single, tall row. "There's no wules," Rose said with her head tilted down and eyebrows stuck together.

"You're supposed to make something," he said reaching for her toys.

Nathan started to move toward them. "They seem tired. I'll just—"

"Let them figure it out," Amanda interrupted and held up a hand.

Squinting at Andy, Rose responded, "I am making some-fin."

As soon as Andy's hand touched her Duplos, Rose fisted him in the face.

Blood started dripping.

Andy screamed.

Rose crossed her arms, chin tucked.

Nathan let out an, "Oh shit," as he grabbed up Andy and stuffed some paper napkins under his nose.

The adult chuckling just made Andy cry harder.

"Well, I guess that's our cue to head out. Sorry about the nose, kid," Amanda said as she rubbed Andy's hair and headed for the front door. "We'll let you care for the injured while we take the long way around back home. Thanks for the pizza and the hill."

"She hit me!" Andy said with a little shake of his head as Nathan carried him off to bed with short legs wrapped around his waist.

"That's true." Nathan checked his nose as he carried him up the stairs. "Looks like you'll survive."

"She didn't even say sorry!"

Setting him on the end of his bed, he responded, "That's true, too."

"She's supposed to say sorry!"

Nathan pulled the covers down. "You might not want to mention that to her next time you see her." Pulling the sheets up to Andy's neck, he kissed his forehead. "It seems telling her what she's supposed to do is how you ended up with a bloody nose in the first place."

Brie was in Duncan's room. She made sure her niece and

nephew had picked up before they went downstairs and got ready to head back to her house. Framed sketches of a woman and a man she assumed were Duncan's mother and father hung next to each other on his wall. The drawings were excellent. The man had Duncan's eyes, a darker brown than the woman's, and the same color hair. The woman looked more like Andy, she thought. While Liz's kids trotted down the stairs, Brie stayed. "Is this a drawing of your parents?"

"Yeah," Duncan said as he closed the sketchpad he'd been working on.

"I lost my parents in an accident, too." She was careful not to look at him and kept her eyes on the pictures.

"I heard Nathan talking to Officer Dave. He says it wasn't an accident."

So mature for his age. "No. It wasn't an accident. You call Nathan by his first name," she said as a statement.

"I always do."

"But Andy doesn't." She turned her eyes to him now and sat down on his floor, leaning her back against his wall.

"He doesn't remember our mother and father."

"Do you think they would want you to grow up without a dad?"

There was a long silence as Duncan zipped up the case for his chalks and pencils. He placed the case in the cubby where it belonged in the door of his desk. "They divorced because of us. Nathan and his wife did."

She didn't argue the point. "He loves you and Andy. He loves being your dad and would like it if you would let him." She decided to change the subject. "So, Mrs. Whittier says some kids are poking fun at your sketches. Goes to show how much they know."

"She's dumb." His eyes darted to hers. "Sorry."

"Don't be." She kept her expression purposely casual.

"I don't care what they think anyway." He rolled his shoulders as he pulled his sheets back.

She walked to him. "I think you should draw some of those monsters you were playing with at my house. Oh, and their cars. Draw them right on the front of your binders."

When he crawled into bed, she pulled the covers up to his shoulders. And just as Nathan had done with Andy, she kissed him on the forehead. "My class has recess when yours eats. I'll stop in at lunch sometime if that's okay with you."

"Sure, that'd be fine." He rolled over but not so far that she couldn't see him squeeze his eyes tightly.

She flipped the lights off on her way out, leaving the door cracked open. On her way down she ran her hand across the top of the smooth stair railing.

"Thank you for allowing the unexpected visit." Brie picked up her coat.

"It's too cold and too dark to dredge through the snow back to your house. Take my truck."

"No. I can..." Brie turned to see the kids struggle to pull on their wet gloves. "All right. Thank you."

He took her hand and rubbed his rough thumb across her knuckles.

She felt her skin jump several degrees.

"Will you do me a favor?"

"Depends."

"Will you wear your hair down tomorrow?"

She pulled her hand away in a knee-jerk reaction, sighed then responded. "I'll think about it."

CHAPTER 12

When the kids woke up, Brie had chocolate chip pancakes and sausage links ready. She was sipping coffee, listening to her niece and nephew's chatter when her sister walked in.

"I thought I'd get here before you were up," Liz said to her kids as she kissed each child on the top of the head. "I knew I wouldn't beat you awake." Liz turned back to her. "Thanks for keeping them."

"Did you and Tim have a nice time?" She took out a to-go cup for her sister, knowing Liz wouldn't stay long.

"Very." Liz poured herself a mug and then glanced at her kids. "Are you about done? You've both got swim lessons today." Liz touched Brie's shoulder and nodded her head toward the foyer. As the kids ate, Liz guided her by the arm to the front of the house. "So, listen. I know it's your business if you have a man spend the night at your own house, and I know you would be discreet..."

"Liz, no. Nathan's not here. His truck is parked out front because I borrowed it."

"I'm talking about Brian who I just saw pulling out of the cul-de-sac."

She paused to think. "Are you sure it was him?"

"White Mazda? Very sure. He didn't come by?"

"Maybe he did and thought the same thing you did when he

saw Nathan's truck in my drive."

"Aunt Brie held hands with Mr. Nathan." Her niece grinned at being the one to say so.

Liz turned to her daughter. "Really?"

"Tattle." Brie gave her a small push to the side of her head.

"And they're going out together tonight," Liz added, ducking her head close.

"You've all worn out your welcome." Brie handed her sister a cover for her coffee and helped them out to their car. She could hear them talking as they walked through the cold.

"And we went sledding. Mr. Nathan's dog is awesome. It pulled us in the sled around the field; can we get one?" her nephew said all in one breath.

"Talk to your father." Liz lifted a hand. "See you, Brie."

"Thank you," the kids said simultaneously.

Dave and Nathan arrived early and slid into a booth.

"Who was the neighbor that saw the two suspects?" Nathan didn't waste any time.

"You gonna make me say all this again when she gets here?"

"I don't think Brie needs to hear the parts she already knows." He motioned to the waitress. "I haven't mentioned the idea that anything might be tied with the arson. Was it Lucy Melbourne who spotted them?"

"They're not *suspects*. The files don't even read *they*. The neighbor couldn't verify she saw more than one person on the sidewalk. There's no identity and if there was, they're not suspects, more like a person or persons we'd like to bring in for questioning. And it's not Melbourne who saw, it was Amanda Piper, who, if I understand right, is the gal Brie is bringing as her bodyguard against you tonight."

"I'd tell you to piss off if you weren't helping me. I still might."

Dave looked over Nathan's head. "They're walking in. That Amanda's a looker."

Brie's coat was already tossed over her arm. No purse. She wore loose khaki pants and a white sweater that buttoned down the front. He'd expected her to wear her hair up, mostly because he'd asked her not to. A solid punch of lust hit him straight on at the sight of her wavy brown hair draped over her shoulders and around her face. He shouldn't have asked her to wear it like that, he decided. He was having enough trouble with restraint when it was up.

Sliding in next to him, Brie looked over to the bartender and spoke up. "Glass of Merlot tonight."

"Let me get that." Nathan tried nudging her back out.

She wouldn't budge. "No. I'll buy this first round. Thank you, though. What do you want, Amanda?"

"Bottle of light for me. I'll get the next one," she said as she slid in next to Dave. "Wouldn't have recognized you without your uniform."

"Good to see you again." Dave took a long swig from his bottle.

"Is it all right to talk about this in front of Amanda?" Nathan asked.

"Always." Brie smiled toward her friend.

"I need to start by telling you this is unofficial," Dave began. "There cannot be any kind of an official investigation unless you formally report the incidents. What we know is that you've had sporadic vandalism over the past few months. Windows shot out in your classroom." He flipped through a page in his notes. "September 22nd and December 21st."

"You didn't tell me about your windows at work," Amanda interrupted. "Sorry, sorry. Pretend I'm not even here."

"What can you tell me about the animals?" Dave asked Brie.

"Animals? What animals? You said tires." Amanda stopped talking when their heads all turned to her. She made a motion of zipping her lips with her fingers.

Brie shrugged. "It's likely what you just said, 'sporadic vandalism—'"

"If you say *it's just kids* one more time," Nathan interjected, "I'm going to get really pissed off."

Amanda's eyes went from him to Brie and back again several times before pulling her chin back and shooting her brows up.

Brie turned her face matter-of-factly to cover her nerves. She'd never said the whole of it out loud before. "The first was a mouse or a mole or something. There was no head. It was tied to my deck rail by its tail. The next was a snake on my porch. Its head was smashed, but at least still on its body.

"The last was the day before Christmas Eve, the day Nathan found me putting up lights for our neighbors. It was morning. I went to start my coffee and saw it lying across my deck rail. It was a rabbit, cut from head to tail along its belly. It was a mess. I could hardly tell what it was at first. I just bagged them each time and tossed them in my garbage."

Everyone was silent for a few minutes, and she realized why she would have nerves. Dave sat back, clearly waiting to see if she was done. Nathan's face turned all kinds of red. Amanda's, on the other hand, was paler than her usual pasty white.

"I guess you already know about the windows and tires. So, that's about it."

"It would help if you would write it all down." Dave leaned forward. "Think about it for a few days, then read what you wrote and add to it if you can. Try to remember dates, people you saw any time before or after each incident, including the windows. List family members." He put up a hand when she opened her mouth. "Not that your family could be involved, but it could be someone they're friends or acquaintances with or have seen around. If it is just coincidental vandalism..." This time, he held his hand in front of Nathan. "It won't hurt to write it down. If it's not, the details will help give a timeline." Dave tucked his notes back into the inside pocket of his coat, leaned back and took a drink.

"I need a pack of gum. I'm going to run next door." Amanda's voice was shaky. "Be right back."

"I'll go with you." Dave scooted out with her.

"You okay?" Brie looked at Nathan.

"Aren't I supposed to ask you that?"

"I suppose. How was your day?"

He tucked her hair behind her ear and slid his hand around, cupping the back of her neck. "Productive. Tile guy finished in the upstairs bathrooms. Heated discussion with my carpenter about making the master bath bigger for what I have planned for the vanity. You?"

She felt heat where his hand touched the skin on the nape of her neck. She tried to remember her day. What had she done? Oh, yes. "Chocolate chip pancakes for, Liz's kids. Relentless hounding from my dog because I ran her late—due to the chocolate chip pancakes. Landscaping plans for a new construction site the owners think will be ready for me to start in April, but will likely need to wait until fall."

"I need someone for my yard." He slowly ran his hand over her shoulder and down her arm before twining his fingers with hers. Her lids closed as he did.

"I don't work for family or anyone I'm close to."

"I'm not family," he said with a crooked smile. "So, that must mean we're close."

She let out a quick sigh and smiled back at him, her eyes dropping to his mouth. "Close enough not to do your yard, but you need to line someone up soon. Spring's around the corner and the schedules of the nurseries in town fill up fast."

"I'll get to it."

They talked of plans for his house. The Giants chances of making playoffs. The progress she'd made with his dog.

Eventually, they realized it had been a while since Dave and Amanda had left. "I'll go check on them," Nathan offered.

"If it's all right with you, let's just leave them," she answered. "I really don't want you to think Amanda is loose. Well, too loose, but they're not coming back." Brie took the last sip from her wine. "And I really should be getting home. It's late."

"Not coming back? Well I'll be damned. That's not exactly like Dave, either. Lucky shit." His eyes darted to hers just as Duncan's had when he'd realized what he said about Mrs. Whittier. And just as Duncan had, Nathan quickly apologized. "Sorry."

She laughed. "No one's keeping you from going out and...being a lucky shit yourself, Nathan." She put on her coat before he could help.

"I'm okay." He smiled and added, "I know how to be a lucky shit all alone."

Shaking her head, she gave his hand a discreet squeeze and headed for the parking lot. "Thank you for getting involved with my...incidents. I'll try to be more cooperative."

He opened the door and placed his hand on her lower back.

She winced.

"You're not going to let me kiss you, are you?" he asked as they walked.

"No. Not here. Not that I wouldn't like to, but no. I know you don't understand. I went to the school I work at when I was a little girl. It's been hard enough for me to gain the respect of my colleagues. This would be just the kind of thing that could set them off."

"We could go back to your place, and I could kiss you there."

She smiled at him. So cute. "I'll write out that list for Dave. Thanks again for your help."

CHAPTER 13

An early warm spell stayed so long the snow all but disappeared. With the ground saturated, Brie was careful to run Macey in the street through the morning mist. A car approached as she moved toward a stretch of sidewalk. Squinting at the white compact car, she recognized Brian and waved awkwardly.

He wasn't smiling. "Morning, Brie."

She stopped and Macey sat at her left side. "What brings you here at this hour?"

He ran his open hand over the top of his blond buzz. "I just got off, thought I would stop by to see if you were up for coffee before you went to work."

"Did you come by a few weeks ago?"

"Uh, yeah. Looked like you had...company."

"Liz's kids."

"Really?"

Pulling on her ear, she answered, "I actually need to finish up my run and get to work."

"I miss you, Brie."

"We've been over this, and I really should be going. Have a nice couple of days off." Waving, she took off uncomfortably with Macey keeping pace at her side.

On the way back, she noticed Molly's car in her mother's drive and decided to visit the two early birds. Even with the caution of keeping her dog out of the mud, she still needed to clean paws in the mudroom before letting Macey loose in the house. Accustomed to the routine, Macey looked like she would have rolled her eyes if she knew how, lifting each paw one at a time.

Showering washed away any thoughts of the uncomfortable run-in with Brian. She dressed in a pair of dark brown slacks with matching pumps and an ivory blouse.

A fresh-baked-goods smell blew over Brie when Ethel opened the door. "Good day for an inside visit, Brie. Come in, come in. They're back in the kitchen."

"Brie." Molly walked over to greet her with a kiss on the cheek. "We were just talking about you." Molly was dressed in olive, flowing slacks and patent leather black boots with a coordinating linen blazer over a white blouse. Her straight blonde hair bundled high on her head.

"I hope it was good." Brie walked over to kiss Molly's mother who didn't get up.

Lucy placed her cold hand on her cheek. "We were wondering how long your family stayed over the holidays and if you had a nice time. You don't have enough visitors for a young, single woman."

Lucy looked more vibrant than usual and so early in the morning. Her hair was already styled in lose, silver curls around her shoulders, and she wore a coral pant suit. Pouring Brie's coffee in one of her favorite china cups, she set it in a matching saucer before handing it to her.

"They stayed just two days. It was wonderful. I'd just seen them at Thanksgiving, but I think the kids have grown. It was nice to reminisce." She placed two fingers on her chin as she leaned over to decide between a blueberry and a cinnamon scone.

Molly smiled a thoughtful grin. "I had the biggest crush on Chase when we were children. He was six years older and didn't give me a second look, but yet."

"Everyone gave and still gives you second looks. *I* was the geeky chunky girl." Brie laughed. "Still, it was nice to speak of the times when my parents were still proud of me."

Molly shook her head. "Oh, honestly. Your parents didn't care what you chose as your career. Granted, *they* may have preferred you stay in med school on scholarship rather than NYU. It didn't hurt that you landed a job that wasn't a thousand miles away."

Molly put a cinnamon scone on her plate for her. "They would want you happier now. What about the attractive, skinny neighbor? Have you gotten over your silly notion that you shouldn't have a relationship because you have his nephew in your class?" Molly looked toward her mother who pretended not to hear.

"I don't need a man to make me happy, and he's not so skinny anymore. One of the rooms in the second floor has been transformed into a workout area. He mentioned that's one of the reasons he sold his business, to have time to get back in shape." Brie paused to sip her coffee. "Did I tell you he owned a business? Woodridge Studios? It's high-end furniture, so I thought maybe you would know about it. Chase was all Nathan Reed this and Nathan Reed that. He has some of Nathan's work in the parlor at his condo."

"I'm more in the clothing line, but the name sounds familiar."

"Man's been without a job for two months, now? That's no man, Brie. You can find plenty of working men to use those brains on." Lucy stood and wrapped up some of the blueberry scones in clear plastic wrap.

"I need to stop and see Amanda before she has to get Rose to school. Shall I take those over for you?" She smiled innocently at Lucy.

"Take what over where?" Lucy looked to the pastries she was placing in a box. "Oh." She handed the box to Brie. "Suit yourself."

As Brie walked around the end of the cul-de-sac, she gazed at her neighbors' brown yards that had been buried under white for so long. The green would return soon. Her spare time would turn to clearing out her customers' flower beds and on the new construction site design.

Just before she reached the Pipers', a police car pulled in the drive. She almost shouted hello to Dave before she saw Rose come tearing out of the house with her school clothes, coat and backpack already on. A few steps before she reached Dave, she jumped in the air. In what looked like a practiced routine, he caught her and sat her on his hip. Rose dug in his shirt pocket until she found what she was looking for. She unwrapped something small and stuffed it in her mouth, keeping her legs wrapped tightly around his sides. Amanda made her way to him by the time the stunt was finished, and Dave leaned down to kiss her.

Look who's been sneaking around, Brie thought. She wondered if Nathan knew.

"If you're gonna get that comfortable, you're gonna have to help me fill out some of these reports."

Nathan's feet sat annoyingly on the corner of Dave's metal desk. They hit the ground with a thud when Dave pushed them from the corner of it with his left hand as he kept writing with his right. Feeling guilty, he decided on a disclaimer. "I don't have anything new to tell you until she fills out a police report. If you're going to get comfortable, how about you get comfortable with some coffee and get me some while you're at it?"

Damn it, he had work to do and now all could think about was Brie's cold case. His gut told him there was more than one person guilty of the double murder walking around free, and it ate at him.

As he thought, he put his pen between his teeth.

Nathan came back with coffee. "Come on, Dave. Think about it. The cold case file says the backdraft was professionally set."

Caffeinated bribery. "Seemed professionally set."

"Okay, seemed. But then Brie just happens to become buddies with a firefighter? Ends up dating him?" Nathan propped his feet back on the corner of Dave's desk. "That's a really big coincidence, don't you think?"

"Yes. I've thought about it. And I have a lot of work to do. Get her in here to make this official, and I'll enjoy hauling his firefighting ass in for questioning."

She finished her midterm assessments. Brie grinned, pleased with the progress of her students, especially Andy. So, how did he fall behind in the first place? she wondered. She decided to leave work right after her students and stop by to share the news with Nathan before Andy's progress report was mailed.

There were a handful of pickups in his drive and one white box truck. It looked like a bad time for an impromptu conference, but she couldn't help feeling curious about the action. It occurred to her she'd never really stopped by his house during the day in the middle of the week. She walked right in, laughing to herself that she didn't knock.

There was a crew of men working on the walls in both the front sitting room and the enormous foyer. Scaffolding reached the open foyer that went up to the landing of the second story. The men walked around on stilts as easily as they would on flat shoes. It was hard to watch, dizzying.

Endless plastic covered everything. Painters worked in the long hallway at the top of the stairs, along the tall landing and back to the bedrooms. She could hear Nathan's voice from the back of the house, bickering with someone. She walked toward the sounds, noticing the child lock on the mudroom door knob as she searched. She found them off the kitchen, past the large pantry room, and in a tiny bathroom she never knew existed.

"There's no damned room to make this any bigger," said an irritated voice.

"It can go this way," Nathan retorted.

"Not without butting out the damned side, changing headers and studs."

"So?"

"Listen, I pushed this up for you because I owe your pops a favor. This'll take twice the time. It's just a small bathroom."

"The *small* is what I have a problem with."

Brie turned to leave, then stopped to listen.

"I want it bigger without making the pantry smaller."

The two walked out as they debated. The contractor cursed and wrote notes on a small yellow pad.

Nathan stopped when he noticed her and smiled big enough to show the beginnings of lines radiating along his temples, making him look smart and sexy. "You're here."

"I'm sorry to interrupt. I can come back later." She tugged on her ear. "Or just call. It's nothing, really."

"Is this her?" the man asked.

"Yep." Nathan offered introductions before turning back to him. "Call me with the new estimate." He held out a hand to shake.

"Pretty, aren't you?" The man tipped his cap to her as he shook with Nathan. "Tell your dad I've got an order for tops coming up." He walked out jotting notes on his yellow pad as he left.

"Is *what* her?" she asked.

"Doesn't look like much yet. The upstairs bathrooms are done. Painters just finished the bedrooms this morning."

"Can I see?"

"That's the third time you've asked me that question." He tucked a loose strand of hair behind her ear. "That's not why you came."

"No." Her breath caught at the feel of his touch. "But I'd still like to take a look."

They walked around men and plastic Visqueen as they made their way upstairs.

The tile was striking. It covered the large tub and separate shower in the master bathroom. The floors were speckled beige with smaller, matching tiles behind the vanity. The counters looked like slabs of stone with tumbled edges. A huge mirror was framed with tight-grained wood embedded in the tiles, matching the vanity. Instead of blinds, stained glass in a matching frame covered the single window with a hinged side.

"The pattern of the stained glass matches the front of the vanity doors," she said.

"You're observant. I made it that way."

She took a step forward and ran her fingers across the glass, then opened it using the knob in the bottom corner. The window faced the back of the house. She pondered over the generous yard space. She wondered if he knew some of his trees were not dormant, but dead. She imagined a corner plot with a handful of Foerster grasses for a canvas backdrop. Lines of Yellow Yarrow mixed with red Penstemon behind groups of purple Liatris would do nicely in the southern sun along with clumps of Shasta daisies for cutting.

"Who did you end up hiring for your yard?"

The corners of his mouth lifted. "Haven't got around to that yet."

"Technically, you can lay sod anytime, but summer means heat stress and constant watering and late spring means the crabgrass is going to take root...in the next few weeks." She lifted to her toes and looked back out the window. "It's really recommended that you get started before the weeds start to germinate."

Yes, and I can hold out much longer than you can, Nathan thought. "The other bathrooms look much the same, only I chose a faint peach coloring for the tiling."

"You're not calling anyone anytime soon, are you? You are going to have a beautifully finished home with an overgrown yard."

"Noted." Her frustration was sexy and her professionalism impressive. "Why did you come by?" he asked, walking back out and into his freshly painted bedroom.

"Nothing that couldn't have waited. Andy's midterm test scores came back. You'll receive a report soon, but I wanted to share with you that he's doing very well. Almost completely caught up. I can tell you're working with him at home."

"That means a lot. His other teachers told me I was basically doing a bad job. We just do what you send home with him."

"I forget how hard all of this must be for you, and you're not one for excuses so I'll just say that he's doing amazing work and this place is coming along beautifully. I heard the man you were arguing with mention that he works with your dad. I realized I don't know what your parents do."

He slid down to the floor and leaned against a wall. "Mom retired early. She was a nurse. They like to travel and her schedule didn't suit her. Dad has his own business. He works mostly with plastic laminate."

She looked puzzled as she sat down next to him.

"Countertops and cabinets made with a plastic, counter-top material, like for business reception counters. His place is just a few miles from here." He stretched out his legs and crossed them at the ankles. The master bedroom contained hardly more than his messy mattress. "He's scaled back a lot. Wants to spend more time on sporadic trips with Ma."

Brie leaned a shoulder against the wall. "What will you do when you're done here? Do you miss owning your own business? If you don't mind me asking, how can you afford to do all of this with no income?"

"That's a lot of questions. Let's see. I miss building for people, but not the being-in-charge-of-employees part or the bookwork. I have plans to start up again when I'm done here—on a much smaller scale. And I'm rich."

She turned her head to the side but kept the moss green glued to him. "Excuse me?"

"To which part?"

"The rich part, I guess," she said, eyes wandering.

"I have a lot of money. People like to pay for my work." He shrugged a shoulder. "Plus, I sold the studio with the shop attached and most of my larger equipment."

"How much is a lot?"

He grinned at her forwardness and simply answered, "Millions."

Brie choked. "Millions of *dollars*? What are you doing in this neighborhood? Why didn't you buy a place already done or hire people to finish this one before you moved in?" She paused and pulled on her ear before she added, "That came out wrong. I'm sorry."

"Don't be. I like the older homes in this neighborhood. The lake. The creek. I told you before, I'd just rip up a finished place anyway. I like a house built my way. It's good for the boys to learn to use their hands. Not enough people do that anymore."

He saw his opening and went for it. "Why do you blame yourself for the fire?"

Brie started to stand. He'd expected it and gently grabbed her arms, bringing her back to the floor. "You can ask personal questions, but I can't?"

Patiently, he waited through the line of silence.

"Fair enough, but first tell me what makes you think I blame myself?"

"I'm observant...especially when it comes to you." He made sure not to crowd her.

Her shoulders visibly loosened. She rested her head against the wall with her eyes on his. "You're always so composed," she said. "In control, even the times when you're angry." She turned her eyes to the bedroom window and took a slow breath.

"They'd been out of town. They hardly ever got out together, just the two of them, but they had that week. They came back a day early, later in the evening. They thought I was home. My car was in the garage, in their spot. I took a cab because Liz and I were out celebrating a keynote speaking address I'd landed. I knew I would likely have a few extra drinks—which I did. I saw their car, but I stopped in the drive to watch a couple of people who were walking up the street.

"I should have been home. Someone set a fire in my bedroom. A fire that was set to explode when my door was opened.

"I stood there wasting time, thinking how odd it was for someone to be out so late in this neighborhood. Stood there instead of getting inside to keep them from looking for me." She closed her eyes. "I figured out later the people walking must have been the ones that broke in and set the fire. The fire that was meant for me, not them. I started back toward their house and stopped, even again, to admire how the color of Mom's flowers lit in the moonlight."

He remained silent and resisted the urge to wrap his arms around her.

"She never grew flowers anywhere but along that walk. Such an efficient woman. She kept them meticulously weeded and watered. I heard the smoke detectors and stood at the front door, wasting more time fumbling with my keys. I didn't even try the door first. It was unlocked. I saw them running down the hallway, heard them yelling my name as they reached my bedroom.

"They still had on the silly tropical shirts and cargo-type pants they liked to travel in. I froze in the middle of the stairs, staring at this yellowish air that sucked under my bedroom door." She shook her head like she was trying to remain in the present.

"The rest is in the files."

"Counselors have already given me the no-one-could-have-known talk. I hung on to the night to survive. I push relationships away to survive. I'll push you away. I've already pushed, but you seem to maneuver around me. You don't pull at me. I haven't figured you out yet, Nathan. I don't have a good track record with relationships. You shouldn't wait for me like this. My last boyfriend called me ice. He wasn't wrong."

He used his thumb to wipe away the single tear that escaped her expressionless eyes. "You open yourself to your students. You take extra time to help a boy who's struggling with reading. Duncan's a hit at school, because you told him to draw Corvettes on the cover of his binders. You keep the memory of your parents alive because you love them, not because you feel responsible for their deaths. And I'm not a child who needs attention. Don't look so deeply into us, Brie. Let go. It might just feel good."

CHAPTER 14

Nathan watched as Brie pulled in her drive. Macey's head stuck out the truck's back window. He'd waited patiently on her front porch, leaning back against one of the pillars and reading the newspaper. Brie let the dog out, then walked toward him. Macey ran ahead and sat on his feet.

"You didn't come by this morning." He turned a page.

"Come by?"

Folding the paper, he reached down to rub Macey's ears. "Each day for the past three months, you've run by my house with this dog, sending mine into a fit. You didn't come by this morning. I overslept. Everything okay?"

"Well, come in off my porch. We'll have something to drink and I'll explain."

He noticed a grin and the way she practically bounced past him.

She was still in her work clothes. He watched the pieces of her hair that had escaped her pins move around her neck as she walked.

"Macey didn't want to run this morning. I was worried and got her in to see her vet after work." Brie took down two glasses and an unopened bottle of wine.

"Is she okay? Let me open that," he offered.

"Got it."

Of course you do, he thought.

"We'll need to celebrate." She had hardly gotten the cork out before turning. "She's pregnant!" she said and ran to him.

He barely had time to brace a leg behind him before Brie leaped. Landing in his arms, she wrapped her legs around his sides.

"We're going to have puppies!" She covered his face with kisses before ending at his lips.

He went from zero to sixty in no time. Inside him, heat exploded. Her firm legs wrapped around him, he held her up with her very female backside resting in his hands.

Brie pulled away and dropped to her feet, turning in a happy circle. He leaned against the counter, trying to recover and enjoying the show.

He hadn't known puppies were so important to her. "You sure?"

"Of course I'm sure. What makes you ask that?" She stopped dancing, but was still grinning as she poured the wine in the two glasses.

"Well, they're...discreet."

"Goldie is *not* discreet." She handed him a glass.

"How do you know Goldie's the dad?" He smiled now.

She took a long sip. "Are you saying my dog sleeps around?"

"No. I'm saying that she's free to...see whatever dog she wants. No commitment there."

Brie looked up at him through her lashes. "What if she's not interested in any other dog?"

"Guess that depends on if we're still talking about the dogs." He set down his glass.

The corners of her mouth lifted as she bit her bottom lip. Brie set down her glass and coiled one of her legs around the back of his.

He gripped her hips and pressed her into him. The moss green gaze dropped to his mouth as the blood drained from his head.

It was she who fisted his hair in her hands and closed the distance between their lips. Hers were full, her mouth soft, firm. She tasted of wine and woman. Intoxicating. Their lips moved together as their breath quickened. He probably had hold of her harder than he should have as he traveled a hand from her hip to her lower back. Wanting, he used the hand to pull her closer.

Lips moved, teeth grazed. His other hand traveled up her waist. His thumb brushed along the side of her breast. He drifted over her shoulder on his way up to braid his fingers through the back of her hair.

A sexy female moan escaped, making sparks ignite on his tongue. Her nails sunk into his back. Lightly, she bit down on his bottom lip, then opened her green eyes to him. He broke free for a few short seconds, and they gasped for air.

Bodies twining, they rotated until Brie was up against her kitchen counter with it rammed into her back. She would worry about the bruises later. His lips trailed painfully slow across her cheek, under her ear, down her neck, across her collar bone to the void in her throat and back up again. She was gloriously losing control in the moment only to have him repeat the path once more. He stopped when she purred his name.

"Say it again," Nathan choked.

She grabbed hold of his shoulders. "Nathan."

A car door shut. Nathan's eyes shot open, and he pulled away.

With determination, she yanked him back to her, turning this time with his back against the counter. She leaned into him, body to body.

"There's someone in your drive—"

The front door opened. Together, they broke apart and picked up their glasses. Desperately, they tried to catch their breath.

"Hello!" Liz called out. "You'll never guess what I heard after work today—oh, excuse me. What am I interrupting? Ha. That sounded inappropriate." She chuckled as she took off her coat and tossed it over a kitchen chair. Stepping between the two of them to reach for a glass, she said, "Sorry, Nathan. You're out of luck in that department. Once my sister makes a decision, no one can break her resolve."

Brie crammed the back of her hand against her mouth in an attempt to keep from choking on her wine. She straightened just in time when Liz turned to her.

"What is the matter with you?"

"We're having puppies!"

"You and who? The stud retriever?"

"Who? No. With Goldie. With Nathan's dog."

"How do you know they're his?"

"Does everyone think my dog is a slut?" She tilted her head

back, laughed and then filled a glass for her sister.

She finished hers in a third, long, deep drink. "I'll have to buy 'we're expecting' chocolate bars. Pink and blue." Brie twirled in a circle. "I'm going to go change. Drink some wine, Liz."

As soon as Brie went upstairs, Liz asked, "How much has she had?"

Nathan held up his hands in defense. "Just the one glass."

"Well, keep her going. She hasn't let loose since...anyway. She's been happier than I can remember for a while now. I expect that's thanks to you." Liz picked up her glass, rotating it in her fingers. "You hurt her and I'll hunt you down and kill you with a shovel," she added with a warm smile.

His brows lowered as he looked to her. "Noted."

The next day was a Thursday and Brie stopped over to tell Lucy the good news before heading to work. She brought her a pink-wrapped chocolate bar. They ate scones and drank coffee in the dawn of the morning.

"They'd just better not dig in my petunias. I work hard in my flowers and don't need a bunch of yapping puppies digging and pooping in them."

She rolled past the comment. "When will Molly be back? If you talk to her, tell her I'm taking her out for a celebratory drink. She can bring Roger with her if she'd like."

"He's long gone. Says she's sworn off men. Again." Lucy sipped her coffee. "I'll tell her anyway. You run along and make sure that Macey is comfortable. She'll need extra rest. None of that running her for miles every morning."

"Spring break's next week. I'll have plenty of time to take care of her." Brie jumped up and kissed Lucy on the cheek. "I'll see you soon. I'm going to tell Amanda before she's off to her temp job."

"Bring Clifford some of these." Lucy held out a box Brie noticed was already packed and sealed.

As she walked around the cul-de-sac sidewalk, she thought of how good she felt. She hadn't had the dream in weeks. The grass was turning green, and she knew that underneath the dead leaves would be the beginnings of new life. Rose answered when she knocked. "Morning, Rose. Is your mom up yet?"

"She's in the shower." Rose pleaded with Brie. "Gweatgwanddad is making me wead books. I already know how to wead books."

"I bet you are a great reader. Give these to your granddad, will you, and tell—"

"I'm out. I'm out." Amanda made her way down the stairs in a white terry-cloth robe.

"Hmm. Late night?" She smirked.

"So?"

"With the cop?"

Rose opened the baked goods.

"You'd better get those to your great-granddad or Mrs. Melbourne will have our hides."

Looking thoughtful at that idea, Rose turned and headed for the kitchen.

"Things still going on between the two of you?"

"They aren't really *going on*. We didn't end up in bed that night we sort of doubled if that's what you're getting at. He was paged and had to bail. I decided it was best not to wait around. I've been holding out on him since. I don't really know why. He may decide to give up on me. I think I like him. He gets called off all the time. Has to cancel half the time, but I don't mind. It'll make it easier when I get called abroad."

Brie listened. She couldn't ever remember hearing Amanda speak more than a few sentences about any man, even Rose's father.

"So, what brings you here to interrupt my morning after a late night of no sex?"

"Macey's going to have puppies. Look, I have chocolate bars wrapped in blue and in pink. I'm not sure what color to give. Hopefully, I'll need both."

"That retriever come of age?"

"No. I keep forgetting about him. The puppies are Nathan's dog's."

"At least someone's getting some," Amanda said as she led her to the kitchen.

Chocolate was shared at Bloom and congratulations offered. By the next day, she left the extras on the workroom table. Susie Phillips had found a greeting card made just for the owners of expecting pets. They made cards for anything these days; Brie laughed as she read it while she walked down the hall.

She entered her classroom as the bell rang from lunch and the children started making their way down the hallways from the playground. Her teacher's aide took afternoon attendance while she walked around listening to the recess news each child had to share. Andy played with his markers, balancing them along his supply box.

The class quieted as they'd learned to do when they heard the tone coming from the announcement speaker. "May I have your attention please?" Sandy spoke through the intercom. "Teachers and staff, we are moving into a lockdown. Please secure your classrooms until further notice."

She looked over and walked toward her door as she addressed her aide. "This is the drill where we pull in any children from the hallways, lock the doors and move our students away from the windows. You gather them by the coat hooks, and I'll check the hallways."

As she was trained to do, she locked the door as she stuck her head out to look both ways for any children that needed to be pulled in from the hall. She noticed Mr. Babb as he walked around the corner. It took her a fraction of a second to figure out the call was not a drill and that Mr. Babb was headed for her room. Instinctively, she stepped out and shut the door behind her, placing herself between it and Aaron's father.

"This won't help you. You know that," Brie said with arms stretched pleadingly outward.

"I want my boy." She could see Mr. Babb as he shook beads of sweat along his forehead. "Nobody's gonna fucking tell me when I can fucking see my boy."

Repeating what he said was all her brain could think of. "You want your boy. I can see that. He is your boy. Getting him this way will only make it so you can never see him again. Please, Mr. Babb." He kept inching toward her. She tried not to back up. She was too close to her classroom.

"Don't talk down to me, woman." Still walking, he pulled a gun from the back of his pants.

She nearly vomited.

"I know what you social worker people are like. Think you're better shit than the rest of us. Think you can fucking tell me how to discipline my own boy." He spoke using his hands, causing the gun to point erratically in response. "I knew you people would try to stop me. You made me do this. Made me. Bring. This. Gun." And he stopped, pointing it steady at her.

She willed herself to keep calm. Lie, she told herself. "I'm not those people, Mr. Babb. I'm not a social worker. I want to help you. I want to help you see your son, but I know taking him this way will make it so you'll never get him back." Through her peripheral vision, Brie could see a police officer round the corner. She made herself keep eye contact with Aaron's dad.

"Lying bitch! You know they won't let me have him after this. Get out of my way before I put a bullet between your lying bitch eyes—" The officer jumped him from behind. Within seconds, he'd wrestled the gun out of his hand and had dug his knee dug into the back of Babb's back, his arms were stretched unnaturally behind him.

She leaned against the nearest wall, clutching her stomach. Another officer came up behind her and hauled her down the opposite hall. She couldn't remember what happened next.

Finding herself sitting in an office chair, she waited for someone to tell her what to do. Mr. Babb was actually very quiet, his chin buried in his chest as the officers maneuvered him through the hallway toward the exit.

Sandy stood in the doorway glaring at her. No, grinning at her. "You've done it this time, Miss Chapman. You get all the union representation you want. You've broken protocol."

She looked crazed, her voice shaking, her eyes red and opened wide.

"Nothing to say? That's okay. I'll say it." Her voice was getting louder.

Heads around them started to turn.

"You broke protocol during a lockdown. Not a drill. An actual lockdown. You left your class without trained, certified staff. Went out to the hallway instead of staying in your locked room." She was yelling now, maybe screaming.

Babb and the two officers escorting him had made it to the foyer. One of them turned and headed toward Sandy with arms up like he was trying to calm a wild horse.

"You. Are. Suspended. Suspended! Until further notice. Pack your bags. You're not coming back. You think just because you played saint and reported Aaron's abuse—"

Babb exploded. Hands cuffed behind him, he butted heads with the remaining officer and lunged in Brie's direction.

The officer near Sandy pushed the principal out of harm's way, sending her to the floor in front of Mrs. Seward's desk. He closelined Babb, caught him before he fell, and pressed him against the plate glass of the office.

With his faced smashed against the window, Babb stared at her. She sat frozen in the same chair she had been in all along. "I'll kill you," he mouthed before the officers joined again to drag him out and into the squad car.

"Get her out of here." A third officer pointed to Sandy who was standing and adjusting her designer skirt. "We'll interview her in another room."

Brie sipped water while waiting for her turn. She was in the conference room adjacent to Sandy's office, listening to her boss berate her for breaking the rules. The press and cameras were here now. She swore the woman was enjoying this. The police finished with Sandy, then ordered her home.

The questioning seemed to take hours. They reassured her a number of times that her class was safe and honestly didn't know what had gone on. She remembered every detail and went over it again and again. The officers were gentle and patient and repeatedly explained that the questions were procedure. The interview process hadn't changed in the last six years, she thought, and this was nothing compared to what she went through back then. When they were done with her, they asked if she'd like a ride home.

"No. I can drive. Thank you, officers." She took a deep breath, lifted her chin and asked if it was all right for her to leave.

She didn't think to pack her bag before she left. She didn't remember the drive home. Without opening the garage door, she pulled up to her house, put her truck in park and leaned her head against the back of the seat. Turning her eyes to her rearview mirror she tried to make sense of the day. She wouldn't have done anything differently. Babb would have gone ballistic if he'd seen her lock him out. It would've been wrong to put the children through the fear of having an abusive father pounding on the door, shooting at the door. Now, she'd lost her job.

Pack your bags. You're not coming back.

She could hear Macey whining and made herself get out of her pickup to unlock the front door. Macey ran past Brie without so much as a greeting and around to the back. Plopping on her porch, she leaned against one of the white pillars.

It was all over the news. "Teacher suspended for breaking procedure during lockdown." "Gunman apprehended outside suspended teacher's classroom." Standing between houses wasn't wise at this time of day, but the excitement of seeing Brie's trauma was too much to resist. It was time to get intimate.

Pretending to stroll along the creek had been easy. No one could have noticed the raw hamburger that was dropped in the tall grasses along the backside of Brie's neurotically manicured yard. Standing here, watching the dog eat the poisoned meat, was more exciting than gutting the rabbit.

The excitement turned to arousal when Brie came around the side of her house. She must be looking for the mutt. Sort of dragging her feet. Poor baby. Poor, poor fucking baby. This is what happens when you mess with people. Arousal turned erotic when Brie saw the dog stumble and fall.

Brie's legs froze. Macey lay on her side in the yard back by the field next to some winter-brown tall grasses. She battled the molasses feeling as she tried to make her way through a dizzying mental fog to her lifeless dog. When she reached Macey, she noticed the raw meat mixed with white powder lying on the ground next to her. She could hear someone yelling her name. Her eyes rolled back and Nathan caught her as she vomited violently in the damp grass.

CHAPTER 15

Nathan took Brie by the shoulders and shook her once, hard. "Listen to me. You are not going to pass out. Listen to me, Brie." He grabbed her face in his hands and forced her eyes to his. "I am going to carry Macey to your truck. You are going to walk. We are going to get her help. Walk with me now, Brie."

McKinney came running from around the front of Brie's house.

Nathan looked at him from the corner of his eye, considering.

"What happened?" McKinney yelled as he jogged to them.

Nathan already had Macey in his arms. "Find a bag or something. It looks like the dog ate some laced meat. It's in the grass by—"

"I'll get it," Brie interrupted. "I'm okay. Drive her to Dr. Lanter. Please, go. Corner of Brookfield and James streets. I'll come with Brian and the meat."

"She's breathing, baby. We can fix this." He walked around to the drive, gently placed the dog in the front seat and took off in Brie's pickup.

The three of them sat in chairs in the front waiting room of the vet's office. It was a small area with cold linoleum floors and shelves filled with prescription dog and cat food. Brian noticed some of the Pet World magazines on the small tables between the chairs were dated years ago. No one spoke.

He felt relieved Brie wasn't leaning on the new guy the same way she would never lean on him. He watched as she sat, leaning forward between the two of them with her forearms resting on her thighs and her head drooped almost between her knees. The new guy leaned back in his chair watching her, too. Damn it, he missed her.

The doc walked out and Brie stood. He had a gray beard and mustache, pooch belly. Her back was straight. Chin up. Just like Brie.

"She's unconscious, but stable. You can see her now."

Both men knew enough that this part was Brie's to deal with. Neither tried to follow her.

Dr. Lanter took her to the same room they had been in a few days before. Wall-to-wall cabinets filled most of the space and hanging metal instruments filled the rest. Macey lay on the tall, stainless steel table with a long plastic tube deep in her mouth.

The doctor's youthful assistant stood behind Macey with a wooden clipboard in her hand. She wore a light blue smock covered with pictures of cartoon dogs and cats. Macey's tongue dangled out and to the side farther than what Brie thought was natural. An IV was stuck into her front leg. Her underside was shaved with a long line of dark pink stitches starting near her tail and along her belly.

"She has a good chance of pulling through this. Your friend got her here fast. Brie, I had to remove her uterus. I'm so sorry." He placed his hand on her shoulder in a way that reminded her of her father. "I'll need to keep her at least a few days."

He reached in his pocket and pulled out a business card. Turning it over, he wrote down a phone number and handed it to her. "This is my private number. Call if you need anything or think of any questions. There's nothing you can do now. Let her rest. I'm going to stay a while."

"Can I sit with her for a minute?"

"Of course. I'll be in my office. Stop in before you leave." He gave her shoulder a gentle squeeze and left them.

As he waited, Nathan made arrangements with his folks. They agreed to keep Duncan and Andy for the time being. He sat back and quietly sighed.

McKinney stood, his chest expanding. "You can go on and take Brie's truck back. She needs me now. We've been friends for a very long time."

Nathan didn't get up or even move his head, only turned his eyes up to meet McKinney's. "This isn't the time to have a pissing contest over a girl," he said quietly, "and I have no insecurities about what's mine. I *will* ask how you happened to be there today."

"Just what the fuck are you getting at?"

"Probably just what you think I'm getting at."

"You think I hurt her dog? You're sick. How did *you* happen to be there?"

Nathan heard Brie say her goodbyes to the vet. He leaned back and pulled a leg up, resting an ankle on his knee.

Dark rings had formed under her eyes; her skin was pale and lifeless. This was the first time he had seen her look entirely defeated.

"Dr. Lanter thinks she's going to be okay. She's still unconscious and will be here for at least a few days." She walked up to McKinney. "I didn't have a chance to ask why you stopped by today. I'll just say thank you. Thank you for your help." She wrapped her arms around him.

Nathan refused to let it show the way his heart tightened and almost strangled him from the inside out. He stood and put his thumbs in his pockets, but kept his distance.

Brie patted McKinney's arm twice, then turned to him. She walked over, pressing her forehead on his chest. "Take me home," she whispered into his shirt.

He wrapped an arm around her waist, kissed the top of her head and steered her toward the door. His staggering relief mixed with guilt from thinking of himself. They didn't speak on the way to her house.

Brie sat in the middle of the bench seat of her truck, closed her eyes and rested her head on Nathan's outstretched arm. Linking her fingers with his hand, she rolled her head to the side to look at him as he drove. He'd stuck. She wouldn't forget it. One side of her heart was broken. The other wanted to run away with this man. He seemed to always be there for her without ever suffocating her.

They pulled into her garage, and he turned off her truck. He opened her door for her before she could gather the energy to do it herself. As they walked through the quiet, she felt his hand on the small of her back. Small gestures. She took a seat at the kitchen table, folded her hands in her lap. Without asking, he pulled down some glasses and an already opened bottle of wine and was pouring them both a half-glass when the phone rang.

Brie didn't move and Nathan answered while handing her a glass. She could hear Liz's voice.

She appreciated that Nathan read her enough to know she wasn't in the mood to talk and didn't try to hand her the phone. She listened to Nathan as she drank her wine, going over the story of the surreal evening and reassuring her sister that she was okay.

"She says she's glad to know you're not alone and will call in the morning." He sat next to her at the table and took her free hand, holding it in both of his.

"Don't leave." She lifted her hand with one of his and laced their fingers together.

Softly, he answered, "I'm not going anywhere."

Brie set her wine down and moved over to sit on his lap with her legs dropped one on each side. "No. I mean *don't leave*. Stay with me, Nathan." She kept her eyes on his. "I don't want to think tonight. Touch me." She slowly pressed her lips against his. "Take me." Kissing him again, she let her lids drop and sighed.

Oh, shit. His pulse flew. He could feel hers mimic his as she leaned her body over him, mouths moving together. Not now, not now..."Not now." Reluctantly, he pulled back and took her shoulders in his hands. "Not like this."

Brie sat looking at him with deep, needy eyes. "From where I'm sitting, I can tell not all of you agrees with that." She moved just enough to make his eyes cross. "I want you. I've never said this to anyone before, but I need you."

"I'm in this for the long haul, Brianna. I'll be here for you, but when I make love to you the first time it's going to be because it's time and not like this. It's getting late." She looked tired and worn. Leaving the glasses on the kitchen table, he picked her up and carried her to her bedroom.

She still had on her work clothes. He wondered if the news reports were right and if she would be wearing them again anytime soon. He undressed her down to her lacey camisole and panties, then pulled the pins from her hair. He remembered from New Year's Eve that her pajamas were in her top drawer, and he dressed her in the first set he found. He tucked her in much like he would Duncan or Andy and lay next to her on top of her covers.

She rested her head on his shoulder. "Nathan." Her eyes were closed. "I'll behave. You don't have to sleep in your jeans. Come under here with me."

He didn't know if *he* could handle it, but he undressed down to his boxers and crawled in with her. She pulled herself partially on top of him, resting her head on his chest and was asleep in seconds. He thought of how they fit. Lying awake for a long time, he combed his fingers through her mass of hair, thinking of what had to be done next and how he'd have to push her. He would give her some time, then he would have to push.

She woke to thunder and noisy drops of rain on her windows. It took Brie a minute to remember Macey wasn't in her corner bed. Lying on her side facing the windows, she also remembered she wasn't alone. He'd stuck. She kept her eyes closed, willing herself back to the sleep that wasn't going to come.

Nathan must have sensed she woke. Although no movement came from behind her, he whispered, "Hey."

She still didn't open her eyes. "Hey, back."

"How about I make us some coffee?" He kissed the back of her head, sat up and pulled on his jeans.

She pushed her side of the covers away and stood, pulling her robe off the hook from her closet door.

He walked toward the hall. "You need anything?"

"Just the coffee. The grinder is to the left of the stove. Thank you. For everything."

He left and she sat back down. Yes, she thought, he stuck. And he gave her room. It would be difficult to push him away to survive the next several days. She hoped it wouldn't push him over the edge. Taking a deep breath, she headed for the bathroom.

The hot shower and the smell of the coffee almost made her feel human again. Fully dressed and anxious to check on her dog, she knew she needed to wrap things up with Nathan first. She picked up the paper, kindly wrapped in plastic, from her porch and tucked it under her arm. Leaning against her kitchen counter, Nathan held her phone. He looked worn as he ran his fingers through his messy black hair.

"She's here." He held it out for her. "It's your sister." Handing it to her, he walked away and stood looking out the glass doors at the down-pour of rain.

She tossed the paper on the kitchen table as she took the call. "It's me. I'm really okay... No, don't. I'm just going to go sit with Macey anyway... I will. I'll deal with that next week. Love you, too."

She wasn't sure where to start. She poured coffee and joined Nathan. Facing him, she rested a shoulder on the glass. The steady thumping of the rain thrummed on her arm.

"A gun. He had a gun. Liz said pointed at you." Nathan rubbed a hand over his face. "Aren't you supposed to see some kind of trauma somebody when that happens?" He turned and faced her but didn't come closer.

"I'm more worried about what happened to my dog right now."

"That's what your sister said you would say. I know the dog means a lot to you, but-"

"I'm talking about what *happened* to my dog. Someone knew where to hurt me, Nathan. Knew she was pregnant. The vet said the drug used is meant to induce abortion. Only whoever did this used so much it could have killed her. Would have if we weren't there, if you weren't there. This isn't random and it isn't a disgruntled parent. This is personal."

"I want you to come and stay with me."

She pushed away from the glass. "And bring this to Duncan and Andy? I know how to lock my doors, Nathan, and I need to ask you to give me some room." She held up a hand before he could interrupt. "Just a few days, Nathan. I need to think. I'm going to write up that list for Dave and I'd like it if you would come with me to file the police report. Right now, I need to spend some time with my dog and wrap my head around all of this. Sandy told me not to come back. She said I'm suspended." He didn't look surprised.

"I'll agree only if I install dead bolts and locking bars for the basement and first floor windows. I can get it done today."

"I can agree to that." She stepped forward and took his hand, placing his warm palm to her cheek. Closing her eyes, she asked, "How is Andy?"

"Worried. Worried, but okay. He doesn't really know what was going on in the hallway except there were men yelling. The boys are also distracted. My folks have been planning a trip to—"

"Niagara Falls." She took the newspaper from her table and pulled the rubber band off. "I've been hearing about it all week. The weather isn't any better up north. Thank you for staying. I won't forget it."

CHAPTER 16

Brie pulled up to Dr. Lanter's building a few minutes before it opened for the day. Through the dark clouds, torrents of rain fell onto her windshield. She planned to stay as long as they would allow. So, she'd packed a bag of things to work on. Slinging it over her shoulder, she trudged through the rain and into the lobby. The receptionist pecked away at her computer. She wore the same type of smock as the doctor's assistant from the night before, light blue and covered with cartoon animals. Dripping across the linoleum, she walked to the front desk, where the receptionist nodded in recognition.

"Good morning, Miss Chapman. Macey will be so happy to see you." She led her to the room of kennels reserved for injured or recovering patients.

When she saw Macey was conscious, she dropped her bag at her feet. Groggy, her dog didn't lift her head, but her tail thumped on the concrete floor of the kennel.

"Hey, girl."

Brie sat on the hard, cold floor next to the kennel and opened the door. Macey didn't get up, but she lifted her brows and made eye contact. Brie figured she should be worrying about her students, worrying about her job, but the overwhelming relief left little room for anything else.

As she scratched around her ears, Macey's chest expanded deeply in a cleansing breath, then she sighed like a human. They sat like that until her beloved friend fell back into sleep.

Leaning against the empty cage next to her, Brie pulled out a yellow notepad and started making notes for Dave, starting chronologically from the first incident. The dead mouse. She knew it took place before the first time her windows had been shot out, but how was she supposed to remember dates? She tried to associate the events with days of the week or weather conditions. The people that were around at the time of each incident were listed to the side in a different color. Writing the names of friends and family felt like a heavy betrayal.

Dr. Lanter came in and crouched down near Brie. "She's doing well. Vitals look strong and the poison is flushing from her system. We're going to try and get her up before night."

Nathan sat in his truck in the gravel parking lot of his father's shop. He remembered the years he'd worked here in junior high and high school with his brother. The smells of sawdust and plastics glue came back quickly. He and his brother used to argue over who would start the fire when the scrap particle boards filled the enormous metal garbage can.

He parked several spaces from the front door and walked around the rain puddles. His dad had four employees who'd worked for him for years. Sylvester Reed was a great boss. Nathan didn't inherit that trait. The shop was large and open. Through a door to the left, he knew, were the offices where he would likely find him.

"Hey, Dad. You busy?" He walked in and stood next to his father, who was analyzing a set of drawings.

"Not too busy. You came at a good time. Take a look at these." He pushed the prints closer to a swivel chair on rollers where he gestured for Nathan to sit. "This is more up your alley. I never get when people spend money to have a custom kitchen made from plastic."

Nathan leaned over. "Looks like they chose plastic because of the curves you see here. Makes more sense to bend the plastic, although I could get wood to do that. You'll want to waterfall the backsplash and counter lip. Maybe suggest some glass fronts on the ends there and there. How's business?"

"Hmm," Sylvester said, nodding his head while still looking at the plans. "Business is good. I've got more orders than I do time.

I guess they'll have to wait or go somewhere else. There's an important trip to Niagara Falls I need to get to. We postponed it with the weather and all that's going on with Andy's teacher, but I suppose you know about that. How is the girl?"

"Resilient. I can keep an eye on her out my back door. That makes it easier. I wanted to talk to you about something. You've scaled back a lot over the years."

"Yes."

"I guess you're only using about sixty percent of your space here."

"Fifty percent," Sylvester interrupted. "But go on."

He recognized his father's skeptical tone. Smart man. "I need a place to build. My garage hardly works for my house projects. My little spray room is a pain in the ass."

"Is that all? Bring your tools over. You can use the empty half anytime you want. You still have a key?"

"I still have a key, but that's not exactly what I mean. I need a place to do business."

"Whoa." Sylvester held up his arms palms out.

"Nothing like what I had. I didn't move the kids all the way up here just to put them into the same situation they were in back in South Carolina. I'm scaling back, too, but I need a place. And I need you."

"Son of a bitch, Nathan. I'm just a small-time plastics guy. You're an artist... Don't give me that look. You're paid like an artist. How could you possibly need me?"

"I know how to create and design and build. That's it. I suck at the business end. I don't know how to keep guys busy when I don't need them, and I don't do well managing time or the bookwork. That's all stuff you're good at. I'd give you fifty percent."

"You do suck at the business end. Give me ten percent, and we have a deal."

"Thirty percent and we shake right now." He held out his hand.

His dad reciprocated, and they shook. "Thirty percent. You're a sap. Where did I go wrong?" He pulled his son in with the hand they clasped and hugged him with the other. "It's great to have you and the boys back. You're filling a hole that's long since been empty."

* * *

Nathan drove by the vet's on his way to meet Dave. He saw Brie's truck and pulled in. The lobby smelled like an odd combination of cleaning solution and wet dog. Behind the receptionist, on a padded office chair, lay a sleeping brown and white beagle.

"Can I help you?"

"I'm looking for Brianna Chapman."

The receptionist stood and walked around her counter. "She's in back. I'll show you the way." He followed. "We're about to close. I think she's almost ready to leave, too."

"I'll only be a minute, thank you."

"You're a man of your word." Brie sat on the floor next to a wall cage with the door open. She started to stand, but instead he sat down on the concrete next to her.

Macey whimpered at the sight of him and licked the back of his outstretched hand. "Hey girl." He scratched the top of her head between her eyes. "Goldie's out of his mind. You get better soon."

He looked at Brie while still scratching Macey's head, thinking she looked better, too. "I brought you these." He handed her a set of keys. "Same key fits the front, back and garage knob and deadbolts. Each window in the basement and first floor has a locking bar. You can't see it from the outside and barely can from the inside. How are you holding up?" He placed the keys in her outstretched hand, then brushed his fingers from the top of her hair to her shoulder.

She smiled. "Better now. They got her up for a walk. She looked a little drunk, but made it all the way outside. Dr. Lanter thinks one or two more nights and she'll be able to come home."

"We'll be waiting for you." He reached over, placing his hand on the back of her hair, and kissed her forehead before standing and walking out.

Sitting in the pub, Nathan ordered burgers and fries for the two of them. He'd chosen a ridiculously small table in the restaurant side of Mikey's, then drank his beer thinking about how Brie, indeed, looked better even though pale and tired yet.

"Anybody home?" Dave said, waving his hand in front of Nathan's face. He pulled up a chair and motioned to the waitress. "You're miles away, man."

"I need to do something. Anything. Did you read the paper? Shit. I need you to tell me what to do."

"I figured that from the sound of your call. How is she?"

"Actually pretty good. Too good. And there's more than just the lockdown at her job." He took a long drink and sat back. "I ordered you a burger."

"Just a burger? I'm starved." Dave signaled for the waitress. "I'll have what he's drinking and two pounds of wings, hot."

She nodded and took his menu.

"What more?"

"She got home later than usual. Someone left poisoned meat in her yard for her dog to find. She found her dog. I found her. The dog's going to make it, but it was pregnant and lost the pups."

"Son of a bitch. That's a bad day." The waitress came back with Dave's beer. "You don't think it's a coincidence." He took a drink and leaned back in the wooden chair. "Is she going to file a report this time?"

"Yes. She says she needs a few days to wrap her head around it. She's organizing notes for you, wants me to go with her to the station. And, no, I don't think it's a coincidence and neither does she. Someone knew her dog was having puppies and we only found out a few days ago. They knew which buttons to push that would hurt her the most and knew when she was the most vulnerable."

"The scene will be compromised in a few days. Probably already is."

"We've got a few hours of daylight left. Let's finish here and go check it out."

"Unofficial."

"Better than nothing."

They ate and switched to water. Dave went over what he was legally allowed to and what he'd found out in the past few weeks. He'd made a list of all of the employees at Bloom six years ago that were still employed there now. He did the same with the neighbors in a half-mile radius. Most of the neighbors had stayed the same; he couldn't say the same about the turnover at the school.

"No wonder. The principal's a piece of work." Nathan

finished up the crunchy corners of fries left on his plate.

"I heard something about that. The officers on duty mentioned she may be the one to be fired. They've got Brie's back and are saying she kept the parent from reaching the classroom. That the principal snapped—not the first time— breaking confidentiality by alerting the parent Brie was the one who reported his abuse. Everyone heard her." Dave took a last bite. "Don't say anything to Brie. It might not work out that way."

They threw some bills on the table before heading for the door.

They parked at Nathan's house.

"Where have your parents taken Duncan and Andy this time?"

"To the library. They'll be back soon. They're trying for a few days at Niagara Falls and a trip to Colorado when school's out for summer. Pike's Peak. Let's walk from here." The rain had let up, but the creek was high and the floodplain was a black mud hole, so they took the long way around.

"I was thinking about talking to Lucy Melbourne and Amanda Piper. See what they remember. They might recall which neighbors were home that night," Nathan said as he walked in the street.

"I've already talked to Amanda," Dave said. "She can't remember much of anything about who she saw, just that someone was walking when she passed a window."

"That's convenient. I mean the talking to Amanda part. You still seeing her?"

"Yup. We're getting married. She doesn't know it yet."

Nathan choked on air. "Shit, that's quick."

"I know and I don't care. I'm in love with her. She's perfect. Her little girl is perfect. You know Rose can speak fluent Spanish? Cutest kid I've ever seen. She loves me back. Both of them. They just don't know that yet either." Dave stopped and put a hand out to stop Nathan. "Look, there." He pointed between two houses.

CHAPTER 17

"What am I looking at?" Nathan asked.

"Footprints. Let's walk around."

"Someone walking in their own yard?"

"Probably, but not as likely in this weather."

They walked around in the drizzle, then made their way to where the homes' backyards met. Walking up to the edge of the property, Dave pointed again.

"There. Look at how the ground has deep prints in that spot. Looks like someone stood here for a long time. Could be a good spot to watch Brie's backyard, to watch Brie find her dog. Damn it, I wish she would step this up so I could come out, knock on doors and take pictures. Let's go back to her place."

Brie was worn even though she'd spent most of the day sitting. The longer she thought, the more names she added to the list for Dave. Sandy Finley and Susie Phillips were early to work the day of the rifle shooting and rock throwing practice. Sandy would be just the person for all of this, but sweet Susie? How ridiculous. She wrote it anyway.

Walking in her socks with her denim shirt untucked, she ate a toasted bagel as she went through her house, locking up to silently please Nathan. The bolts were smooth and she had to admit it was very handy to have the single key that fit them all.

She added to the list neighbors she knew were on vacation during any incident and ones she was sure weren't. The Morleys, two doors down, never liked Brie. But the Morleys didn't like anyone. They had told her four different times they didn't want Macey in their yard when Brie had first gotten her. Not exactly a tire-slashing disagreement.

She laid the yellow notepad on her nightstand and perched on the edge of her bed. The room felt lonely. Conceding that it was missing Macey was obvious, but she found herself wishing Nathan were with her, too. She couldn't remember ever sitting on the side of her bed thinking of any man. In it for the long haul, he'd said. Regardless, sleep took her quickly as she pulled the sheets up, falling almost immediately into the dream.

She didn't feel completely asleep, although it was as vivid as ever. The musty cigarette smell of the cab, the dampness of the balmy night on her skin. Despair crept up her back and into her heart, but she refused to let it take her. She forced herself this time to focus on the walking couple. As she rode past in the backseat, she turned her head and stared at them from the window. Familiarity. Damn, she knew them. Both of them.

The shock jolted her awake before the dream ever reached her parents' drive. Breathing heavily, sweat beaded on Brie's upper lip and along the back of her neck. She couldn't get the faces of the pair to come to her but was certain it was someone she knew. In the dark she wrote the word *familiar* on her notepad and went back to sleep.

The clinic wasn't open on Sundays, but Dr. Lanter agreed to let her in when he came to check on the animals. Brie sat in the parking lot, again watching the rain fall in smooth sheets down her windshield. She had her large yellow writing pad with all of her notes in the form of a timeline tucked away in her bag. Macey stood and did her happy dance when she saw her. She was slow, but today Brie was truly convinced she was going to be okay. They pressed foreheads together and she rubbed her cheeks. They worked on simple commands like sit, lay and stay. Macey loved the practice, but tired quickly.

"I'd like to see her eat a little more throughout the day before we let her go home, but it may be this afternoon." Dr. Lanter crouched down next to Brie. "You should know that Mr. Reed gave us his credit card number. He asked us to charge the bill to him. What would you like me to do?"

Shaking her head, she rubbed her hands over her face and looked up. "Do you have a copy of the bill I could take a look at?"

"Of course. I'll make sure the receptionist prints one when she comes in tomorrow."

She pulled her knees up and rested her cheek on one of them. She knew she wouldn't have the money to pay for this, would need to make payments for who knew how long. Smiling, she had an idea of how to deal with Nathan Reed and pulled out a gray binder from her bag.

A few peaceful days later, Brie had barely gotten Macey settled at home when her doorbell rang. Brie opened to a frowning Liz.

"I'm glad to see your door is locked, but I want you to know it's annoying. I grew up here, you know," Liz said.

Walking casually past her, Liz dropped her jacket on the newel post on her way to the kitchen. "With Nathan Reed as a boyfriend, I would think you would have more furniture around here by now."

She recognized Liz's attempt to keep it casual. "Since when is he my boyfriend?" Brie followed, then pulled down a bag of pretzels and a bowl.

"Honey, he's been your boyfriend for a long time now. Where's the patient?" Liz sat in a chair at the kitchen table and folded her hands on her lap.

"She's sleeping on her rug, and you scare me when you sit like that." She walked over to Liz with the bowl of pretzels and set it on the table.

"Sit like what? Have a seat, will you?" She kept her hands folded, but moved them up on the table and leaned forward. "Good news first or bad?"

"Bad."

"Figures. Your suspension will go to a sort of trial. The union lawyer thinks it's ridiculous, but honestly is a little worried about the break in lockdown procedure, especially considering the extent of it."

"Good news?" Brie leaned back and picked up a pretzel.

"Your suspension will be paid. There will be some talks and a decision by the next board meeting, the second Wednesday of this month. This should all be over soon. The charges are not worthy of termination, Brie. The best news is she's gone."

"Who's gone?"

"Sandy." Liz mimicked Brie and leaned back in her chair, picking up a pretzel. "Fired. Done. Apparently she's the one that let Babb in. Even gave him a visitor's pass before she bothered to check out who he was. Then there was the thing about her blabbing all over the front office and foyer that you were the one to make the confidential hotline call. I hear there's more, but the rest is under lock and key." Liz tossed the pretzel in her mouth.

She looked out the windows, then back to Liz.

"Your buddy, the assistant super, is coming in to interim until they find a replacement. Can you believe it?" Liz tapped the next pretzel to hers in a toast before taking another bite.

Brie sat on her heels with her knee pads dug in the mulch. She had several yards to prepare for spring. Ornamental grasses were cut back before setting the leftover stubs on fire, allowing fertile room for new life. The smell of decaying leaves and fresh mulch mixed nicely with the overturned soil and burned reeds of grass. It helped her feel her own kind of awakening.

The introverted side of her could have spent much more than a few days working like this. Cutting back the winter brown, making room for sprouting plants, her arms were covered with scratches down to where her gloves stopped below the elbow. She left the roses and hydrangeas untouched for now and tucked new mulch around the emerging green to protect it from the last few freezes that were sure to come. An efficient system in place, she could clear an average-sized yard in less than five hours. This was a much better workout than any gym. Her muscles ached and her undershirt was damp with sweat even in the chill of spring.

Stopping at home to check on Macey between customers meant it took her all of two days and the morning of a third to finish with the first group of houses on her list. The hot water from her shower was like therapy running over her shoulders. She stood in it until the water ran cold.

Dr. Lanter warned her about walking Macey too soon. So, early the next afternoon, Brie decided to drive the short way to

Nathan's house. She pulled in his drive and found another batch of pickup trucks and this time a full-sized van. There were rectangular boxes scattered across his roof and a crew busily working to secure architectural shingles. So much for keeping her dog calm. Macey jumped and whined on the seat.

As she stepped out, Nathan opened his front door to let out his yelping dog. Macey plowed through her, and the two dogs had a reunion in the grass. Nathan swaggered out to meet her. The scene reminded her of the first day he meandered down his drive in the snow to greet her. He had on the same work boots and another faded pair of jeans. His unshaven face wasn't annoying this time, just sexy. He wore that damned crooked smile that made her knees weak as he picked her up and set her on the hood of her truck, wrapped her legs around him, then stopped his face inches from hers.

"Good to see you. You look better. Both of you."

"I feel better." Her eyes dropped to his mouth. "Kiss me, Reed."

"I can't resist when you wear your hair down like this." Tucking a side behind her ear, he laced his fingers just above the back of her neck. The kiss was deep, slow. The world around her erased. He could do that to her.

"The boys will be glad to see you. Come in." Nathan slid her down from the truck and linked their fingers together.

As the dogs followed them to the front door, she carried her bag over her shoulder.

"Watch your step. I'm replacing the rotted boards on the porch, and they're not all secured."

Guided through the front, she looked around at the transformation. "It looks so different." The walls were straight and smooth and painted a light color of subtle brown. The open dining room had a darker brownish color along the bottom half. Brie guessed a chair rail would be going up in there. The curved stairway was stained and finished and looked amazing against the slick, painted walls. The floors were still a mess and the walls were without trim, but she noticed that the doors to the closets, the family room, and what she knew would be a library were in place and had the same straight-lined style as the rest of the house.

Her obvious interest in his work always humbled him. "Let's

go back and sit. You can catch me up on Macey's progress." In what would eventually be his kitchen, Nathan pulled out a folding chair for her. "Soda? Water?"

"Do you have diet?"

"Definitely not."

"Water then. What's all this?"

She was looking in the paper sack he set at the side of the folding table. It was full to the top with the written requests for his work. "Oh, that. It's nothing. People wanting furniture pieces."

She looked back in the bag. "All of them?"

"Yeah. I'm not open for business yet." He hesitated for only a second and pulled out a bottle of water from the fridge. He could hear young footsteps coming down the stairs and leaned against a wall near Brie. He could tell it was Andy.

Brie turned to see him. Andy rocked up on the balls of his feet when he saw her. "Miss Chapman!" He ran to her and surprised Nathan at the easy way he sat on one of her legs. "How is Macey? Is she better? Goldie missed her. Are you coming back to school? The newsman said you're not coming back to school."

Nathan stood with the water in one hand and his thumb in his pocket with the other. He'd forgotten how Brie had spent more time with Andy during the week than he did these past few months.

Placing her hand on his back, she looked down at him. "Macey is around here somewhere reminiscing with your dog. She is much better, and I'm afraid the newsman was right." She looked thoughtful before she continued, "I broke a rule and my bosses are going to decide on my punishment."

"Are you in time out?" he asked with a sincere look.

Nathan noticed Brie pressing her lips together. "You could say that, yes." She held onto him with one arm as she reached in her bag. "I brought you something."

"Really? What is it?" Andy strained his neck to see what she was pulling out of her bag.

"It's not much." She pulled out several decks of cards and handed them to him.

Confused, Nathan tilted his head and lowered his eyebrows.

Andy took the decks and bolted for the stairs, yelling,

"Thanks!" as he ran.

"He's likely to make a mess. So, sorry." She pulled out a gray binder and set it on his table.

He pushed off from the wall and walked toward her. "Ah. Card castle." He set the water down on the folding table. "Is this a *binder* full of notes for Dave?"

"No, I'm still working on that. I have a proposition for you."

CHAPTER 18

Nathan sat on the single empty chair, leaned back and crossed his ankles. "I'm listening."

"The binder is for my landscaping business. I threw some sketches together yesterday at the vet's. I would need to do more accurate measurements and to learn more of your personal tastes." She turned the binder to face him and flipped through pages, stopping at a sketch of his house. "I was surprised at how much I remembered of what your house looks like. Of course, I could easily picture the northwest corner since I see it every day, but I could picture the other sides, too."

He sat forward, looking at the first sketch. It was an excellent rendering of the front of his house with curvy lines of buried brick sectioning an array of plants and shrubs. He tried not to look smug that his procrastination ate at her. "You can draw."

She smiled bigger now. "I wouldn't say that with Duncan in the house." She leaned closer to him, turning the pages. She smelled amazing. "These are different angles of your home and what I recommend, but you can change whatever you want, of course. Basically, more color means more maintenance. See, this is an aerial view of the back and the corners that could be dug out at the ends of your land. Tiered is what I would recommend with the slope back there."

"Speak of the devil." He took the binder and set it on his lap, flipping through pages. He recognized Duncan's footsteps on the stairs.

When Duncan made the turn at the bottom of the stairs, Nathan noticed he had his own binder tucked under his arm.

"Hi, Miss Chapman. Andy said you were here. Macey and Goldie are crashed in the foyer. She looks better."

"It's good to see you, Duncan. What do you have there?"

"You said at lunch last week you wanted to see my latest drawings." Duncan shrugged a shoulder and handed his binder to Brie.

"Let's let your dad look through his pictures, and we'll go in the next room."

Everyone hesitated at Brie's reference to him as Duncan's dad, then Duncan looked up to her.

They seemed to exchange some sort of an understanding before she went on. "I saw a lot of clean wall space for us to lean on in the dining room." Brie took a box of drawing chalks from her bag along with Duncan's leather binder and walked with him to the next room.

Nathan flipped through the pages of Brie's plans for his yard. The trees, plants and shrubs were organized, yet arranged to look natural and casual. Honestly, he was more interested in Brie's sketches of his house. Looking at it through her eyes gave him some ideas.

He pulled out his notebook, worn and curved from the confines of his back pocket, and slid the pencil from behind his ear. He decided to add some arches to the porch that would accent the curves of the border she had planned. He also decided on some brick for the front of the house that would bring out some of the color she'd chosen. Won't the outside painters be happy with that, he imagined sarcastically.

Finished, he set the book on the table and walked toward the dogs. He stopped short when he reached Brie and Duncan. They sat close with Brie's arm around him and his head resting on her shoulder. They flipped through pages and commented on each. Absently, she fixed the tag on the back of his shirt. It was that simple gesture that caused his heart to fall out of his chest and land soundly at her feet.

It wasn't until he walked her to her truck that she explained the point of her visit. "I'll do your yard for you under one condition."

He lifted an eyebrow to her. "Condition?"

"You pay for the materials, and the labor will be my way to work off the vet bill."

He opened his mouth and took a breath.

Brie lifted a hand. "It's my only condition. Take it or leave it."

He stood and looked around, considering. He wanted to refuse, but the thought of having her here almost daily was too tempting. Instead he held out his hand and they shook on it.

A Bonneville pulled up the gravel drive. Nathan noticed her pull at her ear. His dad stepped out of the car first as Nathan opened the door for his mother. They both wore blue jeans and sneakers like a young couple.

"Is this her?" His dad gestured to Brie. "I'm Sylvester Reed and this is my wife, Mackenzie. It's good to finally meet you."

Brie held out her hand.

Nathan spoke up. "Yes, this is Brie, Brie Chapman."

His dad took hold of Brie's hand and pulled her into a hug just as he had done with him a few days before. He gestured with his thumb over his shoulder in Nathan's direction. "He'd better be taking care of you."

"I'm tucked away nice and safe."

"Well, a shave would be nice." Mackenzie reached up on her toes to kiss him on the cheek. She turned to face Brie. "We've heard so much about you, dear. I just want you to know we didn't raise our boys this way." There was silence at the mention of Nathan's older brother. His dad breezed over it.

"We've got cans to shoot and boxes of BBs to burn through. Where are those grandkids when you're looking for them?" His dad kissed the top of his moms head and patted her behind.

"I really should take my dog home before we go downtown, Nathan. It was very nice to meet you, Mr. and Mrs. Reed."

They waved and Brie blew two whistles for her dog. Macey bolted out a little faster than she should have and paused to make a quick circle around his parents before jumping into the cab of Brie's truck.

Macey lay sleeping in the middle of her oval rug. At the sound of the door, she scrambled to her feet. "You have a key," Brie said as she opened it.

Nathan smiled at her. "I'm being polite."

Anxious, she didn't step aside for him.

"Can I take a look at what you've got before we leave?"

"I made a copy for you to keep." She slipped her hand in his arm and urged him out the front door. The rain had stopped but the air was still damp. Most people didn't care for the smell, but she felt it was soothing, nearly as soothing as the man climbing in her truck.

As he drove, she caught him up on what her sister had found out regarding her suspension. Not-so-subtly, Nathan led the subject to something lighter. He spoke about Goldie's morning ritual of whining at his front door, expecting her and Macey to run by.

"Thank you for giving me some space. I do feel better, much more together and ready for this." She nodded her head toward the police station as they passed.

A spot was free on the first level of the parking garage. They dodged puddles and spring potholes as they crossed the street to the station.

"Is he expecting us? I didn't think to call ahead." She was surprised at how the feelings of anxiety and despair crept back as she walked toward the building, like they had never been suppressed.

"Yes."

"And he will be in charge of looking into this? I really hope so."

"He won't be *in charge*. He'll be working under a senior detective."

She felt the warmth of Nathan's hand on her lower back as he opened the glass door for her. They checked in and the officer behind the front desk pointed the way to the stairs. Dave met them as they reached the top.

She noted how clean it was in the station. And empty. She always expected dirty people sitting on benches, waiting to be questioned or arrested. Television. Metal desks were pushed together next to clusters of chairs with arm rests. It didn't smell soiled, but she sensed coffee that had likely been on a burner all day.

"Glad you could make it." Dave shook hands with her first, then Nathan.

"Come on back to my office." He gestured and followed

behind them.

"Office?" Nathan asked. "You moving up? What happened to the desk stuck next to your partner?"

Dave spoke as they walked. "One of the detectives took early retirement. Offices moved around. I got the small one. They're finding a new partner for him. He's not too happy right now. They're phasing me out for the next few months. I still have beat time. Would you like something to drink? Coffee? Water?"

"No, thank you." She clutched her bag with two hands.

"Well, please sit down, and we'll make this as painless as possible."

"I know how this goes. You ask a lot of questions and don't tell me anything about what you think and very little about what you know. I'm not trying to be rude. I just know."

"I'll be up front with you, Brie. I do have questions and you're right, I can't tell you anything that would compromise an investigation. I can tell you that I take a personal interest in this case and will do everything in my power to find out who's after you."

Dave motioned toward two wooden chairs that sat opposite his desk. His chair scraped along the floor tiles as he pulled it around to sit with them. "Tell me what you've got."

She handed Dave a copy of the list he'd asked for. She went through, explaining as she pointed to different pages. There were several. The first was a visual timeline covering each incident to the closest date and location she could remember. Each subsequent page listed individual incidents with more details, starting with the dead mouse. Everyone she could think of was listed. Each page following covered another episode.

"Impressive," Dave commented. "The only question I have, for now, is who you told that your dog was pregnant?"

She rested back in the chair, considering, and went through the list in her mind chronologically. "My sister, Mrs. Melbourne, Amanda Piper and, well, everyone at work."

When she stopped, Dave finished taking notes, then explained he would canvas her neighborhood and the houses around the school asking what people heard or saw during the time of each incident.

"I need to tell you I'm going to be questioning some Bloom staff, too." He reached in his shirt pocket and took out a business card. "You also need to understand I'm only second in command here, Brie. If you have something to add, you can contact me." He held out the business card for her to take. "Or you can contact Officer Tanner. I'll be in touch with—"

She stood up from the chair and took a large step back, clutching her copy of the folder to her chest. "Why is Tanner involved?"

"Well...it made sense since he was lead detective after the fire."

She felt the color drain from her face as he stepped forward to take her arm. She pulled back.

"I thought you knew." Dave turned to look at Nathan. "Didn't you tell her we're looking at putting these together?"

She turned and stormed out, speed-walking to the stairs.

She paced back and forth in front of his truck. She could see Nathan from the corner of her eye walking with that damned swagger toward her.

"Take me home, Nathan. I want you to take me home."

He unlocked her door and opened it. They drove slowly in silence for the first half of the way to her house. "Do you think it's a coincidence someone would have an unsolved case of arson to their home and then have a random, disturbed vandal after them?"

"What I think is that you didn't tell me. Do you think I didn't try to put all of this together? There are no similarities. You didn't tell me," she repeated and clutched her bag closer.

She opened the door before he came to a complete stop in her drive.

Nathan reached over her and shut it before she could step out.

He looked out his windshield as he spoke.

"I don't know why I didn't tell you other than I couldn't stand the look on your face at your party when you talked to your parents' friends or when you look in your empty family room. I have a need to protect you. I can try to do it without smothering you, but you're going to have to deal with it."

He pulled the latch on her door and pushed it open for her.

She sat with her eyes closed before slowly getting out and walking to her porch.

She cut back butterfly bushes with a vengeance. Brie was angry with Nathan for not being open with her. She was angry with herself for turning off like she always did. She wasn't cut out for relationships, but he knew that and he stuck anyway. Mostly, she was angry that he was making her feel things she'd never felt before. She had gotten along just fine on her own until now.

The fragrance of the early blooming tulips helped her focus. She closed her eyes and took two slow breaths in through her nose and out through her mouth. She'd worked late, long after dark. The brilliant moonlight was better than anywhere inside. She hauled the cut butterfly bush branches and stalks from a set of autumn joy sedums in her double wheelbarrow out to her truck and tossed them in the back. She would stop at the clean landfill spot to dump her cuttings before she drove back home.

In this for the long haul, she remembered as she drove through the night. Why? Parking in the garage, she let Macey out as she walked down her drive, enjoying the night air. There was a load of mail. Had she gotten it the day before? Flipping through bills and ads, she walked back up her driveway as Macey sniffed around in the grass. Her legs jerked to a stop when she uncovered a blank manila envelope. No address. No return address. Uneasiness bubbled through her.

"Macey, heel."

The dog responded to the urgency in her voice, galloped over and sat at her left side. Brie looked around as she walked deliberately and casually to her garage. Her heartbeat quickened as she checked her surroundings before closing the overhead door. The mix of frustration and fear unsettled her. She went around checking doors before mindlessly setting her keys and bag down on her kitchen table. Unhooking the metal clasp on the envelope, she peered inside.

Brie decided it was better not to walk in uninvited this time. It was late and she wasn't sure where things stood between them. She knocked with Macey sitting at her left side and waited for Nathan to answer. When he opened his front door, she stood uncomfortable and somewhat speechless. He must have been working out, because he wore gray sweats with a white, no-sleeved undershirt that was damp with perspiration.

"I know it's late," she stuttered.

He pulled off the undershirt and replaced it with a gray

sweatshirt as he moved back from the open door.

She stepped in behind her dog, and they walked to the back of the quiet house to the only three chairs available. Nathan flipped his chair around backward and sat.

Folding her hands, she set them on his card table. She felt like Liz.

"I was wrong," she said. There. Not so hard. "I can say I won't close you out like that again, but I probably will." She shut her eyes and shook her head. "But you already know that." She took a deep breath. "I can also live with you having a need to protect me. You've never smothered me."

"Are you sure? Because I need to know that up front."

Nathan looked at her in silence with eyes half open long enough to make her feel insecure. "My ex left when I had a need to protect Duncan and Andy. I'm not going to start comparing, but it brings back memories."

Distracted, she forgot about the manila envelope tucked under her arm.

"Yes. Duncan told me that."

"He did. Well." He looked at her, maybe through her. "You know, they've gone through more than the death of their parents. They've also lived through a divorce and having an inexperienced dad."

Nathan turned his chair around. "She and I became godparents when Duncan was born and again for Andy." He leaned back. "When my brother died, we took them in. She was supportive at first, but it didn't last. She couldn't handle being thrown into motherhood.

"The studio was taking off. I started getting more orders. Orders from significant people. We were invited to stuffy parties, rubbed noses with politicians and CEOs. I wanted a balance with the boys. She wanted to embrace where our lives were headed. My folks offered to take Duncan and Andy. I needed to keep the promise we made to my brother and to the boys. I loved them. Love them. I couldn't let them lose two dads. We made our choices."

"Whatever happened to for better or for worse?"

"I don't blame her. She married the governor's personal assistant."

"She moves fast."

"Yes." He leaned toward her. "Are you going to tell me what's in that envelope?"

She took one deep, cleansing breath. "I was wrong. Twice. This time about the connections to the fire."

As she suspected, his eyes turned intense, the bold blue making them look all the more intimidating.

"Before I show you these, I want you to know I'm really okay, and there are pictures in here that might not sit well with you." Handing him the envelope, she sat back. She turned her head but kept her eyes on his, wanting to read his reaction.

Cautiously, Nathan turned the envelope upside down and shook the contents into his hand. Dozens of photos spilled around his fingers and onto the small table. Some were close-ups, some far away, all different sizes and each a picture of Brie. His eyes darted to hers, back to the pictures and again to her. She kept her face composed. Spreading them out hurriedly on the table, he straightened the ones that had landed upside down. Most of the pictures were of her with different men. One on a small rowboat. One taken through a window at a restaurant. Another sitting with Liz and Tim, all with the word SLUT written in red letters across the front.

CHAPTER 19

"What the hell is this?" Nathan asked.

"I don't know. They were in my mailbox tonight when I got home." She picked up a specific picture. "Look at this, Nathan."

He took it from her. "Is this you?"

"Yes. I used to be heavier. Do you know who these people are next to the man I'm with?"

He looked closer and recognized them from pictures over her mantle. "Your parents. That makes these six, no seven years old."

"Eight. That's an old boyfriend. Marketing major. I met him at grad school when I was taking night classes. I was twenty-two years old in that picture. Nathan, I've never seen these before."

The photo she pointed to was of her eating corn on the cob at a table that was clearly in her parents' backyard. The deck was different and there was no patio, but it was definitely her house. Next to her was the boyfriend with his arm draped over her shoulder.

Pushing through the dozens of pictures, he noticed one with him in it. He was in Brie's kitchen nook by the glass doors with Brie's leg wrapped around him and his hands dug in her hair. There was one of Brie as she sat suggestively on his lap, and even one from a few days ago when they were tangled on the hood of her truck. It must have been taken from the road because he could see the painters working on the siding in the background. Written on the bottom of the pictures of the two of them were the words, "A present for the Board of Education."

He sat back and ran his fingers through his hair. "I can't leave Duncan and Andy. You need to take these to the station."

"It's late. Can't we just call Dave and see what he thinks?" She put her elbows on the table and ran her hands along her ponytail.

Nathan turned his head contemplating. "All right." He lifted from his chair and dialed.

Dave was still at the station and said he would come by.

"See you in a few," he said before hanging up.

"Okay. Late night," Brie said.

"You can catch up on sleep tomorrow," he said curtly while leafing through pictures.

She spoke up again. "Tell me about the house."

"Hmm? Oh. Show work this week."

"Show work?" He heard her voice crack.

He looked at the picture of her when she was on his lap, trying to figure out the angle it would have been taken from. "Show work. Work that's faster and just for show. Upstairs is done and most of the down." He lifted his focus to her. She was sheet white. He piled the photos together and took her hand. "Let's walk while we wait."

They toured the house. He pointed out examples of show work as a means to distract her, and it seemed to work.

The change from the week before was big. He'd trimmed out every upstairs window and door. All the trim except the baseboards was finished. Purposely, he kept the design the same, just modified the color depending on the room. Mission style he explained to her.

When they reached Duncan's room they found Andy had wandered there. They put a blanket over him as he slept and shut the door.

Dave wasn't long. The three of them sat in the folding chairs as Brie explained what Dave was looking at and how she'd found the photos. Nathan noted the way she could stuff her fears and suspicions whenever she needed to and supposed he should feel relief that she could let loose when they were alone.

Dave took in a deep breath and let out a heavy sigh. "Trouble is there's no threat here. I can get a patrol to pick up the neighborhood canvas, but I can't get a squad car to sit at your house just because someone thinks you're a slut."

For the first time in a very long time, Nathan lost it. "No threat? Are you joking? She's had some, some*maniac* taking pictures of her for almost a decade! He set fire to her home, broke into her garage."

Brie intervened. "You're going to wake up Duncan and Andy, Nathan. He's right. There's no proof to say any of this is connected."

"Can I take these?" Dave motioned to the pictures.

"Sure," Brie offered.

Nathan turned to Brie. "You're not going home."

"Nathan," she spoke softly.

"Damn it. You heard me."

Brie turned to Dave. "Do something. I can't bring this to a home with two children."

"By the looks of the pictures, it already is. It's late. I'll let myself out and the two of you can duke this out." He stood. "Stop by the station tomorrow. I'll see what we can do about extra patrols," and headed for the door.

"Where will I sleep? I need my stuff. Oh, hell."

"I have a mattress, and I have an extra toothbrush."

"Goes to show what you know about women. I need a lot more than a toothbrush. I can bring Macey with me to at least get some things."

"Not tonight, and I can't come with you and leave the kids here."

She folded her arms across her chest. "I'm tired, Reed. Show me where you are putting me."

Brie woke to the smell of fresh coffee and the sound of an air compressor. Dogs barked out back. Reluctantly, she lifted the arm with her watch and looked at the time with one eye. Holy crap. She hadn't slept this late in years.

Yesterday's clothes would have to do. She buttoned her jeans while walking toward the glorious smell. Her head did a double take when she passed the room Nathan designated as his temporary work-out room. Stopping in the doorway, she stared at the side wall.

Hanging was a fair-sized piece of cork board with note cards stuck to it using white push pins. One name was written on each card, the cards were lined in columns. In the first, there seemed to be what looked like a short list of suspects that included Sandy Finley and Brian McKinney. The long list must be the middle column. It contained Susie Phillips, Elizabeth Whittier, Isabel Seward, Mr. and Mrs. Moreley, and Mr. and Mrs. Novick.

Brie slowly made her way to the board before she sensed she wasn't alone. After reading the final column, which included Clifford and Amanda Piper, Lucy and Molly Melbourne, and Tim and Liz Brownley, she turned to face Nathan.

"What's this?" He looked tired.

"I'm making a case board." He stepped next to her, looking at the names. "Good morning."

"No, I mean this last list of people. Good morning back." She tapped the column of names that included her sister's.

"People to talk to. I've already spoken with Lucy Melbourne a few times. Dave seems to have Amanda covered."

"When did you speak to Lucy? How did you get her to let you in her house? No, to open her *door* for you? She doesn't like you, you know."

"That's not true. She loves me." He reached around and gave her a quick kiss on the mouth. "I invited Dave and Amanda over tonight. I guess I should've asked you. Will you stay?"

"For the evening, yes. For the night, I'd better not. I'll stay with Liz."

"I figured. Tell me what you think." He nodded toward the board.

She turned her head to the side, keeping her eyes on the names. "I think Sandy is in the right spot. I would have never believed it, but as I look back, she's perfect. I didn't meet Brian until after the fire. Or during the fire, I should say."

"He could have known you. I've looked over your notes. The timing is too perfect. Recent incidents started right after you starting seeing each other seriously, worse when you broke it off."

"He broke it off. Nathan, he's a...softie."

"He put his hands on you at your party. Has he tried to contact you?"

She took a deep breath. "He drank too much at my party

143

and...has driven by a couple of times. I spoke with him briefly. We don't have to talk about this if it makes you uncomfortable."

"I'm not uncomfortable, especially about anyone my girl calls a softie."

"Susie Phillips is too sweet. Elizabeth Whittier is too old. I could shoot you for even having Isabel Seward on your list. Moreleys, again too old, and the Novicks were on their cruise the day I found the dead rabbit. Remember? I was putting up their lights."

She walked over and pulled the pin out of the Novicks note card and moved it over to the third column. "My bet is on Sandy. Have the police questioned her yet? She was there when I started working at Bloom. I moved up too quickly, worked with the assistant superintendent, offered higher positions. That's what Liz says.

"She was always trying to make things difficult for me and wouldn't support me if I had an unreasonable parent or a student that needed accommodations. She was sent home long before me the day of the lockdown, would have had plenty of time to set out poison for Macey. And she was there both mornings my windows were shot out. Huh. It makes even more sense when I say it out loud like that."

She walked over and looked through the window, noticing the crew had already arrived to start cutting down the dead trees. "I overslept. I need to get out there."

His long arms wrapped around her waist making her eyelids drop. He kissed her on her bare neck, sending chills down to her feet.

"Dun-can!" Andy yelled from the doorway. "Dad is kissing Miss Chapman."

"Shit." Nathan left his hands on Brie's waist and turned to squint at Andy.

"Gross," Duncan yelled back from his room.

Andy stood and grinned from ear to ear.

Nathan was determined to finish the base cabinets for the kitchen. It was the last thing to do before he could start finishing the floors. They'd been without furniture in the house long enough. The high from being so close kept him moving. After drilling the first cabinet in the corner of the kitchen, he stopped for a short water break.

The bottle he'd half-emptied dangled between his thumb and forefinger as he rested his arm up on the window frame. Eventually, a double-deep kitchen sink would be centered beneath the window. He imagined standing at the sink, looking out at the breathtaking view of the lake morning after morning. The lake was calm, then, and looked like an enormous mirror framed in green. The reflections of the homes lay in the water and looked like an underwater city. The wild flowers that bloomed along the floodplain were an acre's wide patchwork quilt.

He spotted Brie with her large yellow notepad. She looked efficient in ugly boots and sexy golden thighs. He couldn't believe how much she'd gotten done in the past few days, or how different the yard looked.

She must have gotten too warm because she'd taken off her sweatshirt, exposing the tank underneath. It was damp with sweat and clung to her slightly. He could see the outline of muscles in her back that were long and sexy. He remembered the feel of her firm legs when they'd wrapped around him in her kitchen.

The bright color of the wildflowers created a backdrop for her female shape, and he imagined how she would look lying underneath him in all that color. Her mass of hair tossed around her oval face, over her shoulders, over her naked body. He could nearly feel his hands trail across her smooth skin and up her golden thighs as he lifted them, moving into her until they lost each other in the heat.

"Nathan?"

"Son of a bitch!" His arm slipped from the window, and he dropped his water. "Ma," he said, slowly closing his eyes.

"Watch your language around..." Realization filled her face and she stopped. "Oh, good grief, Nathan. This is like walking into your high school bedroom. Is she out back?" His mother walked casually to the fridge and set down her wicker basket as she opened the door.

He rubbed both hands over his face and picked up his half-empty water bottle. "Ma."

"That's it. Your father and I are taking Duncan and Andy for the night." She unloaded small plastic containers of mostaccioli bake.

"Ma." This was not happening. "It's not...she's not...we're not like that."

She reached in her basket and pulled out a bag of garlic bread. "Obviously."

"I'm not having this conversation with my mother." He turned toward the door to the garage pulling his headphones over his ears. "I'll be in my spray room."

"Thank you for seeing me, Mrs. Melbourne." Nathan walked in as Lucy opened her door.

"Please call me Lucy. Come in and sit down. I heard about Brianna."

They walked back to the kitchen.

He followed and propped one leg on a stool. "You look lovely today."

She wore turquoise slacks and a matching blazer with her hair up high.

"How well did you know Brie's parents?"

Lucy hesitated. She stood at her coffee pot and sighed. "We were very close. My husband and I moved in a few years before we had MollyAnne. We raised them together, you know. MollyAnne, Elizabeth and Brianna were like triplets."

She sat on her stool, gazing at a china dish filled with potpourri. "I remember when the boys would run after the girls with frogs they'd pulled from the creek. MollyAnne and Elizabeth ran away squealing, and Brie snatched them from the boys and put them back into the water. What is being done, Nathan? That girl has been through enough if you ask me," she said gruffly.

"The police are keeping an eye on her place. Do you remember the night of the fire?"

"Of course I remember the night of the fire." She stood. "Why would you ask me something like that? Do they think all this has something to do with the night of the fire?" Lucy clutched a fisted hand to her chest.

He took her free hand in his and patted it softly. "Amanda's friend. The police officer? He's looking at everything. He may want to talk to you. And to Molly. Tell me what you remember. Please, Lucy."

She sat again with empty cups and a full pot of coffee. "I was sleeping. It was late. June. A hot night for June. I heard the explosion. No, felt the explosion. I remember what time it was, because my clock was the first thing I saw when my eyes flew open. It was eleven-forty. I was too scared to do anything except pick up the phone and call the police.

"It seemed like a long time before they arrived, but they told me it was just under ten minutes. My husband had passed away a few years before. I'm just now becoming accustomed to being alone. I rocked on the edge of my bed until I heard the wail of the sirens and collected the courage to walk down the hall to look out a window.

"The whole other side of their house was engulfed in flames. Two fire trucks were pulling up, and I could see the lights from police cars coming around the back way from over by the old farm...by your house. There was a loud knock on my door. I stood in my housecoat in the heat while they asked me the same questions over and over again. Everyone moved so fast. It looked like chaos to me, but they pulled Brianna out quickly. They didn't bring out her parents. They were too..." She stopped and moved her closed fist to her lips. "Please keep her safe. She's like a daughter to me."

"Do you know how I can get a hold of Molly? I know Brie would like to see her." He put his hand on her shoulder.

Lucy nodded. "She told me she's on a buying trip out of the country. It's what she does. Buys clothes from shows and brings them to stores around the state. She has a condo downtown. I'll write down her number for you."

They sat together, sharing coffee and cranberry-orange scones. Nathan took his time asking her about childhood stories and bringing her back from her painful memory.

"I'm glad she's staying with Elizabeth for now, but you'll send her back when this is over?"

"The police hope to wrap this up as soon as possible."

Nathan returned to find Brie in his backyard wearing snug blue jeans and old sneakers. She was speaking loudly to two men he hadn't met over the roar of several, extremely noisy machines.

She motioned for him to follow her back to the front. "We'll never hear each other with the chainsaws and mulcher running at the same time."

He followed, thinking about the different hats she wore, each with its own personality, yet all very Brie. Mostly, each would serve as an effective distraction of the night before. This hat was an intriguing mixture of tomboy and site boss. "What are you doing to my trees?" he asked.

"Dead trees. You have six of them back here. Arnie there owes me a favor. Well, a lot of favors. We may be even after this. He's almost done." Reaching the front, she turned and put her hands on her hips, thumbs facing forward.

"How do you know they're dead?" He was more interested in hearing her boss voice than he was about the trees.

"No bend to the branches. No green on the inside. And I live behind you, remember? I've watched them die. Four died when Dutch elm disease came through. Two are poplar, which is a blessing if you ask me. You work with wood and you don't know trees?"

"I know them when they're cut and dried."

"Listen, if I'm going to be off work for a while, I'd like to use the time to get this done." She looked around at his property. "Can you hold off your outside guys for a few days? Maybe a week? Or two? I was hoping to have sod delivered the day after tomorrow. It can't be walked on for a while after that."

Brie handed her sister another suitcase and her pillow. "I appreciate this."

Liz maneuvered them down Brie's stairs. "I still don't know why you don't just bring Macey with you. Tim wouldn't mind."

"She'll be happier with Nathan's dog."

"I hope the pictures of him and me don't seal the suspension." She stood with her eyes closed rechecking her mental list of everything she would need.

They made their way to the garage to hook up the trailer she used for hauling her landscaping equipment. After getting the mail and her newspaper, she stopped in front of Liz, who stood in the garage. "Why aren't you saying very much?"

"Because you're an idiot." Liz dropped to the step that led into the mudroom. "Who cares about your job? Who cares about where you're sleeping and what pillow you have? You are in danger." Tears fell down her stony face. "Someone's been watching you."

Brie plopped on the step next to her. "It's my defense mechanism. Laugh or cry. We've already been through hell, Liz. This is nothing." Brie leaned over, and they rested the sides of their heads together.

CHAPTER 20

Brie left Liz's a few mornings later frustrated that Liz lived so far away, didn't drink coffee and that Brie had broken her last hair tie and had to wear it down. Parking her truck out of the way of Nathan's crews, Brie decided to take the dogs over the creek to pick up yesterday's mail and newspaper. How could the man start work without first reading the newspaper? The short walk was just enough to give her time to sort through her day. Macey and Goldie ran without leashes and used the log without hesitation. She looked at her empty house and thought about the damned hair ties.

She kept her promise to Nathan and went only to the mailbox. Tucking the mail and paper under her arm, she whistled for the dogs and started back.

As she balanced across the fallen log, she noticed the creek was receding. What happened to April showers? As soon as she stepped down on the other side, she started flipping through her mail while the dogs scattered noisy mallards. She stopped when she noticed a thick manila envelope. Pavlov's dog. Her shaking hands calmed when she read the return address. Bloom Elementary. Opening the clasp, she peered inside cautiously, much like she did with the photos. In it were letters written on school paper. Dozens of them.

Right in the cold field, she plopped down, crisscrossed her legs and started going through the letters. Curiously, the dogs pressed their cold noses against her cheek. The letters were from her students. From more than just her current students. Sean Spencer wrote several pages of misspelled words asking what she'd been doing and when she would be back. Others filled her in on the sub, giving the retired teacher a reluctant thumbs-up. She suspected the package was exactly something Liz would have put together.

It might all work out after all.

Brie held the phone between her head and shoulder speaking with Mrs. Seward as she took a diet soda from Nathan's fridge. "It's nice to speak with you, too. Thank you for asking. Can you find Liz for me? Her students have PE at this time. Thank you. You, too."

As she waited on hold, Nathan meandered in. His tool belt hung low on his hips. Why did women find that so sexy? Because it was.

The weather had turned cold again and she saw the thermal wear sticking up from under his Henley. She looked over and smiled at him before turning back to the phone as Liz answered.

"The letters are perfect. Just what I needed. Thanks."

"How'd you know it was me?" Liz asked. Brie could hear papers rustling on the other end of the receiver.

"I know you."

"You're welcome but don't get too excited just yet. I found out Mrs. Whittier got her backstabbing hands on copies of your pictures and put some choice ones up in the workroom before Tyman got hold of them. Half the lunch hours saw them before she took them down."

Brie squeezed her eyes shut at the visual flashing through her head.

"If it makes you feel any better, she's in Tyman's office as we speak."

"That helps. Check on Duncan and Andy for me, will you?"

She hung up and sat thinking.

"What happened?" Nathan leaned up against a base cabinet with his thumbs in his pockets.

"Nothing really. Liz had some students write me letters. They were heartwarming. I miss it."

"Mmm. And?"

"You are observant. A teacher got her hands on copies of the pictures. Our pictures. And pinned some up in the workroom. If they let me back, I'm not sure exactly what I'll be going back to."

"Ouch. And?"

Brie turned around to look at him. "I can't stay at Liz's forever. Whoever these people are could wait another six years before they decide to come after me."

"Let's go out."

"Out?"

"On a date. Tonight." He didn't approach her. "We'll go to your place. That way I can check through your house while you get ready. I just need to make sure my folks are free to keep the boys."

Brie dried her hair until every strand was straight. She hadn't asked where they were going and hoped slacks and heels with a buttoned cashmere sweater would be appropriate. The pants were pinstriped gray and the sweater matched the color of her eyes. She nodded with approval in the mirror as she clicked off the hair dryer. Down the hall, she could hear Nathan pleading with the dogs.

She walked to them and leaned against the jamb of the door to her room. He had on black pants and a crisp gray shirt. He was trying to pull the dogs from her bed. They thought he wanted to play. Reluctantly, Brie whistled for them to jump down. The show was almost worth any rips in her comforter.

He pulled at the crumpled cover. "They don't listen to me."

As she watched him, it occurred to her she wasn't hungry anymore. "Nathan."

"Hmm?" He walked around to the other side and picked up a pillow that had been tossed.

"Macey's okay."

"I'll say."

"I'm okay."

He stopped and looked up. "All right," he said slowly.

She slithered around to him and placed her hand on his chest. "I want you." She smiled at the feel of his heart as it picked up speed.

Shit, shit, shit. He took her wrist and pulled her hand from his chest. "You'll get your job back." Was she trying to throw him into cardiac arrest? "The board meeting is coming up."

"The pictures, Nathan. I think the cat is out of the bag to anyone that matters." She unbuttoned the top of her sweater with her free hand. "How many more times do you think I'm going to try and seduce you if you keep rejecting me?"

He stepped forward and closed the distance between them. "Point taken."

When she reached for the next button, he took both of her hands and caged them within his, shaking his head.

"Me," Nathan said and pressed their foreheads together.

A shallow, throaty purr rumbled low in her throat enough to sink him into a deep puddle of want.

He took his time traveling his hands up her arms, over her shoulders, along her neck before braiding his fingers through the back of her silky hair. Keeping the narrow distance between their mouths, he looked into the soft green. He wanted to remember every second of this, every second of her.

Brushing his lips to hers once, twice, he then dipped into the warm and moist. She tasted like raspberries. As he finished with the buttons of her sweater, he traveled his lips along her jaw and settled at the spot on her neck just below her ear.

Taking a wrist in each hand, he held them out, keeping hold as he stepped back, looking at the glimpse of cleavage and smooth stomach through the spread of cashmere. His gaze met hers as he lowered her arms and used both hands to spread her sweater, exposing lace and the generous swell of flesh above. For a painstaking moment, he closed his eyes and took a deep breath.

When he opened his deep blue to her, Brie saw a new determination. She bit her bottom lip and braced. Nathan grabbed both the back of her hip and behind her head, breaking their fall.

Their lips crashed. Their teeth grazed. The taste of him. The feel of him. His weight, his warmth, his need.

She tugged with the buttons of his shirt before giving up and yanking it over his head. Running her hands inside, she found his back strong and lean. Grappling with skin and muscle, she ran her hands around to the planes of his stomach.

Possessive lips trailed a line of warmth down her neck and over shoulder, taking her straps with him as he went and spilling flesh into his hands. She combed her fingers through his thick, black hair and guided him to her. Her head flew back as he took her in, moving his tongue to circle before carefully using teeth to pull.

Grappling with the rest of his clothes she ran her hands up to find him. Nathan clasped her wrist. "Not yet.' They rolled, flesh on flesh, gasping and exploring until she found herself over him. His eyes were glossy with a drunken blue haze. The awe was humbling.

She sat over him, heat to heat, with her long waves of auburn draping over her shoulders. Nathan released the button at the top of her slacks. Her gaze became sincere and focused as she trembled. He ran his fingertips inside the exposed stringy lace. A small, female whimper escaped.

He understood that her utter pliancy beneath his touch was more than physical. The protective bubble she kept so carefully tucked around her melted away, leaving him with great responsibility. Her head rolled back as she shuddered, invited. He lifted to her and used his teeth to graze the line of her jaw. Taking her by the waist, he slipped her around and beneath him, tossing the rest of her clothes to the side.

He lifted her arms above her head before traveling his hands down the soft of her inner arms, down the sides of her breasts and down her flat stomach, learning every inch of this complicated woman.

He groaned when he found her. Her hands flew to his shoulders and he felt her nails as they dug in. Pushing her to the edge, Nathan whispered, "Let go."

The release was more than Brie was prepared for. She cried out as she hung onto his shoulders. Nathan dipped his head to her neck as she trembled and gasped. Moving her lips close to his ear, she pleaded, "Now, Nathan."

He slid over her body, damped with sweat. His eyes tightened as they joined before they came back to her. Brie and Nathan moved together, racing, flying, desperate to get closer. Refusing to lose eye contact, she held his face as she went over to a place she'd never been before. Of heart, of body, of mind.

She watched the blue haze turn opaque as he held on and released, holding, savoring. Dropping his head into her hair, Brie linked the backs of her feet together. Nathan collapsed lifelessly over her, the weight of him keeping her on this planet.

While their bodies twined, they came back to the present and her stomach growled.

She felt his cheeks swell next to her face.

"I'm crushing you," he said.

"You're not. Don't move." The feel of his warmth and of his weight left her staggered.

He shifted next to her, pulling her partially over him as he recovered. She looked up at him. He must have sensed her gaze because he opened one eye and smiled. He took her hand and kissed it before laying it on his chest. "You're hungry."

She lifted on an elbow. "I'm not that hungry." She looked at his mouth and bit her bottom lip.

"And I'm not nearly done with you, but we should get up and find something to eat first. Our reservations are long gone."

They spent the next evening eating Chinese delivery with Dave and Amanda, Rose and the boys. Brie thought about how she didn't feel any day-after jitters. She did spend the day, however, feeling wonderfully weak and unhinged.

They played an entire Uno tournament, Amanda keeping meticulous score. Brie lost. Duncan won. Brie squinted at him playfully.

"You have to say 'uno' when you have one card," he told her.

"So you keep reminding me." She mussed his head as he maneuvered the deck back into the box.

Dave and Nathan helped the kids clean up and took Rose with them to read stories before bed. Amanda and Brie hauled paper plates to the kitchen.

"I'd help you with the dishes, but there's no kitchen sink." Amanda looked around.

"I heard that, and I'm working on it," Nathan yelled from the stairs.

"They live in paper and plastic around here, and you're having sex," Brie said while tying a garbage sack.

"Just." Amanda turned and put her hands on her hips. "How the hell can you tell? We haven't so much as brushed up against each other all night."

Brie walked out the mudroom door to toss the garbage in Nathan's dumpster. She came back with the dogs and answered, "I'm a woman. I can tell. You move differently around each

155

other, even without touching. So, are you happy?"

"For someone who *never* kisses and tells, you're nosy." Amanda smiled when Brie lifted a brow. "Let's just say he can walk and chew gum at the same time."

Brie stopped what she was doing. "I meant are you happy to be dating him."

"Oh. This is embarrassing." Amanda stood for a minute. "So happy that I'm afraid whether or not he'll still be here when I get back from an assignment."

"Have you talked to him about it?"

"I think it's too early for that."

"He's planning a trip with you and Rose to Disney World, and you think it's too early to talk about it?"

Amanda sighed. "I'm tired of leaving, of having no place to call home. It was great when I was younger, but Rose is putting down roots here. She's making friends at school, loves Duncan and Andy. I told him I'm going to get a place. I'm looking for a steady job, then Rose and I are getting a place of our own. Scary, huh?" She clasped her hands on top of her head. "What?"

"You've changed. I guess we both have."

Nathan walked in and looked back and forth between the two of them. "I hope I'm not interrupting anything too important, but he wants *Mooncake* and he wants you to read it," he said to Brie.

"Which means Rose is still up there," Amanda said. "That's one of her favorites."

Nathan nodded. "Duncan is just glad he didn't have to share his bed with two little kids. He's sound asleep."

When she walked into Andy's room, he and Rose were sleeping, too. The book was stuck between them and their mouths were hanging open.

She laughed to herself and put the book on Andy's desk. Picking up Rose, her miniature body snuggled into Brie's shoulder.

"No story?" Dave asked as he took Rose from her at the bottom of the stairs.

"They didn't make it. Sleeping like a rock," she said.

Waving as the content trio pulled down the drive, Brie leaned against the jamb of the front door, then turned to Nathan. "I need to get going, too, if I'm going to make it here bright and early. I want to take the dogs for a short walk before I get started, before we get started."

He shut the door and wrapped his arms around her. "I like the sound of that."

CHAPTER 21

"Hmm?" Nathan was completely confused by the stranger in his doorway.

"I said I'm here to grade your yard." The man pulled out an order invoice. It had Brie's name on it.

"Oh, right. Sure. What is it you're going to do?"

"I'm going to make a really big mess," the man said as he headed to his white box truck and lowered a ramp out the end. He backed out what looked like a combination of an end-loader and a small tank. Another man with tripods circled the yard and house, shining lasers at the ground.

He barely had time to comprehend before Brie pulled up in her truck. He noticed her look at the men, then wince. She jerked her head up once to the crew as she lowered her tailgate and pushed up her wheelbarrow, the dogs running at her side, toward the porch.

Site boss hat.

When she was close, she smiled at him like she'd discovered something secret. "You have puffy sleep eyes. Very cute."

Girlfriend hat.

Speaking louder, she offered introductions, then explained. "These guys are here to survey and grade the yard. They make sure the water travels away from your house, even during a hundred-year rain. Depending on the lasers, the tiller there will grind up and move the soil around to prepare for the sod." She kissed him on the mouth. "And all at a wholesale price. Pull out your checkbook, Reed. They'll be done in a few hours."

Whistling for the dogs, she walked past him toward the house. "First, I'm going to make you some puffy, sleep eyes coffee."

The girlfriend hat was definitely his favorite.

Nathan worked on sanding down the floors, preparing them for stain. Most of the floors still had the original wood. Even through his custom-fitted dust mask, he recognized the rich, clean smell from the boards that had to be from at least the 1950s. Hardwood floors hadn't been made with fine old growth wood for decades. Some boards needed to be replaced, but Nathan was pleased there weren't many. The previous owners had laid carpet in most of the rooms, and it served as handy protection.

He wanted to get the house to a basic, finished state. Then, he could start work on the projects he really enjoyed, like wall-to-wall, floor-to-ceiling bookcases in the would-be library and wainscoting under the stairs.

He would check on his landscaper at break time.

Brie had the sod delivered early the next day. It was warm already that morning. Odd for early April. She stood next to the scattered pallets in her favorite rubber boots that reached her knees, a pair of denim shorts and a tattered NYU sweatshirt. Her hair was tied in a tail and stuck through the clasp of her worn Giants' cap. She felt rested and where she belonged.

Using spools of thick orange yarn, she created a pattern where the line of brick edgers would frame the landscaping plots. She placed the yarn in a curved, flowing pattern, walked back to look at it, moved it and looked at it again. Sitting on the ground with legs crossed, her bare thighs rested on the sun-warmed soil.

While Brie contemplated the northwest corner of the house, Nathan came out carrying two steaming mugs.

He handed her the one with the cover.

"Is that coffee? You are the man of my dreams."

"And you are sitting in dirt." He stood with his free hand in his front pocket. "The dogs don't like being stuck inside."

"They'll have to live for now. I'd invite you down, but it's dirty." She stood instead, brushing the dirt from the backs of her legs.

Nathan's gaze dropped to her bare thighs.

"I'm thinking of adding tiered plots at this corner and under your bedroom window." She waved her hand in front of his face. "My eyes are up here, Reed."

"Yeah, but your legs are down there."

She tried her best wise-ass smile. "You keep telling me to decide what to do back here. I need you to tell me what *you* want."

"That's like you telling me what color to stain the dining table. Not your thing. I trust you."

"There's no small something you'd like for your own yard?"

"A pond." He tucked a lose piece of hair behind her ear.

"A pond? That's not a small something."

"A pond with those jumbo goldfish and a waterfall I can hear from my bedroom window."

"That won't work."

"See? Not my thing. Why not?"

"Great Blue Herons."

He lifted an eyebrow. "Not following you."

"We have Great Blue Herons that would think of your pond as a food dish. If they didn't get to your goldfish, there is plenty of wildlife around the creek that would. Fox, raccoon, muskrat."

"I would notice a heron. I've only seen a million Canadian geese and a few dozen mallard ducks."

"They'll be migrating back here any time now. You won't miss them. How about a small pond with floating plants and a waterfall up here under your window so it's close enough to hear at night?"

"See? Your thing."

"It will attract frogs," she warned. "They're noisy."

"I like noisy frogs. I'm a camper."

Interesting. "Me, too."

"There's a lot I don't know about you." He reached down and kissed her under her ear.

In her head, Brie had a small argument with herself about work first, then play, before she came to her senses. "The first thing is I'm on a roll, and I need to go to my house and pick up extra sprinklers from my garage."

"I'll get them." His face was set.

She shook her head. "Okay, I need the timers for them that are on the shelves next to the back door."

She watched him meander toward the creek sipping his coffee and wondered how he ever got anything done moving at that pace all the time.

After Nathan finished spraying the last of the base cabinets, he found Brie sitting on his workbench, her legs crisscrossed, waiting for him.

"I thought you'd never come out of there. Where are your boys?"

"Why do you always ask me that?" Before she could answer, he told her. "At my folks for the night making homemade pizza."

"The last set of pallets will be here first thing in the morning. I'll have to use seed that will tolerate the shade under your trees and along your drive."

He thought she looked amazing sitting there covered in dirt on his workbench. "There's Italian in the fridge, and I've got a bottle of Chardonnay. Microwave and a card table?"

"I have a better idea. Give me fifteen minutes. I've got a change of clothes in the car. I just need to clean up."

They brought the dogs and a paper bag full of food his mother had left and they had warmed. They sat in Brie's Adirondack chairs on her brick patio. The fire pit blazed in front of them. Nathan added treated pinecones that caused shoots of flames in brilliant greens and blues. The air was chilly, but the wind was calm and the night was clear. Smells of spring mixed with the smoke. Ducks and geese made an occasional noise from the lake and from Black Creek. They ate and talked of growing up in Northridge.

"Birthday?"

"July."

"Mmm. Older woman. I'm September. What day in July?"

"The fifth."

"My brother's was the fourteenth. We still celebrate. My folks decided not to commemorate their deaths, but their birthdates."

She rotated her head against the tall back of the chair and faced him. "That's smart. I've never known how to ask about how they died."

Nathan watched her face flicker in the light of the flames. "Just ask. You know it was a plane crash. There was no foul play." Their feet rested together on the only wooden foot stool. "Andy acted out for a while without completely understanding why. Duncan didn't understand at all for a long time. We sat on our couch one evening, and Duncan asked for the thousandth time when his parents were coming home. I tried to be gentle. I don't know if I did it right, but I explained for the thousandth time they weren't coming home. Out of the blue that night on the couch it hit him. He screamed and tossed the room around until he fell asleep in my arms from exhaustion."

A single tear spilled down Brie's face. Nathan assumed the story must have felt familiar.

He brushed the side of his boot against her sneaker. They traded happier stories about family before he decided to change the subject altogether. "You must have run track."

"I was tired of being the fat kid no one wanted to date."

He left his eyes closed but lifted the corners of his mouth. "There was enough of a variety in your anonymous pictures."

"I told you the photos might not sit well with you." She pulled on her ear. "You must have been one of the jocks."

"Nope. My brother and I worked for my dad. It was all about the money back then. The jocks impressed the girls, but I had the funds to take them out. And the chick magnet car, of course."

"And now you drive a pickup."

"Mmm hmm. I have a car in storage with the rest of my furniture."

"A chick magnet car?"

"Saab 9000 Turbo. Black. Leather interior. I miss her."

The next morning, Brie lost herself in rolls of sod, while dodging sprinklers. Pallets of brick edgers were coming, and she wanted to finish with the sod before they arrived. She cut each piece carefully to fit next to the orange lines she had sprayed in the smooth soil, marking where the edgers would be placed.

She fit the rolls on pre-dampened soil tightly next to each other, making sure the seams buckled slightly to give room for shrinkage. A myriad of hoses, hose splitters, sprinklers and timers made Nathan's yard look like a well-organized road map. The sprinklers were set to soak the new grass in regular intervals without neglecting any corners.

She glanced up when she saw movement from the corner of her eye. Nathan walked with Andy on his shoulders and Duncan at his side. Over their shoulders were chairs, a tackle box and fishing poles. She stood as they walked toward her.

"Come fishing with us, Miss Chapman. We are really good fishers." Andy balanced his fishing pole in one arm and his chair in the other.

"Next time, guys. The boss is a bear around here."

"That's okay," Nathan interjected. "Now we can make man noises and smoke cigars." He winked at her as they walked toward the lake.

"Coooool." Andy rode on Nathan's shoulders with his feet tucked under his arms.

Brie was glad she'd worked the yard front to back. She was close enough to hear the three of them talking and felt only a tiny bit guilty for eavesdropping. Andy didn't want to lace the worm on his hook. Duncan had his line out before any of them. Nathan tried to explain to Andy how the bobber worked.

Brie butted sod up next to the corner she planned for a wall of ornamental grasses. She wanted a frothy green to give a backdrop of solid color that would allow the effect of the flowers to show more brilliantly. Unrolling and cutting, she adjusted the sod, imagining a cluster of tall purple cone flowers behind bushes of knee-high Early Sunrise coreopsis. There would be variety without looking like a botanical garden. The corners would be crowned with autumn joy sedums for fall blooming.

When she heard Andy yell excitedly, "Dad, I've a big one!" she turned her head to watch the fun.

Except it wasn't Andy. Duncan held onto his awkwardly bent pole as he obviously realized he'd addressed Nathan as his dad. He jerked his head to look at Brie. Nathan stood composed with his thumbs in his pockets, but with eyes shut. Brie and Duncan stared for only a fraction of a second in silent understanding before Duncan continued.

"Get the net, Dad," he addressed Nathan again. "We're eating this one."

And they did. They ate together using Brie's kitchen. In real chairs. At a real table. Brie silently decided this would turn into an evening habit until Nathan's kitchen was finished. She thought of how long it had been since she'd cooked. She liked to cook, was actually good at it, but living alone left her rushing out often with a yogurt in one hand and her keys in the other.

No, she corrected her thoughts. Nathan was right. She'd avoided anything that took extra time in the house that once belonged to her parents. She decided to work to change that.

"You coming back from that daydream anytime soon?" Nathan tucked some loose strands of hair behind her ear as he sat down with drinks for the kids.

Blinking a few times, she sat. "It smells delicious. Let's eat."

After their late meal of breaded catfish and garlic bread, compliments of Mackenzie, Brie sat in a tiny red chair next to Andy's bed, reading him a story about bears and moons.

"What will she look like?"

Brie sighed with frustration that their first substitute teacher couldn't handle the job. Or didn't want to. "She's about your grandma's age and is very nice. I think she'll do a great job as a sub and that you will like her."

Andy nodded politely. "Will you be here before I leave?"

"I'll make sure of it."

He nodded again. "Will you make me lunch?"

Now she laughed. "Lunch? Why?"

"It's cheeseburger day tomorrow and the cheeseburgers are gross. Dad is just going to tell me to choose the peanut butter and jelly instead, but it's gross, too."

"I'll see what I can come up with. Go to sleep." She pulled up his covers and kissed the top of his head. She tried to keep her deep frustration of her suspension hidden, but suspected Andy could sense her reservations as they discussed her newest replacement. Her expression remained tight as she turned out his light.

She walked out and shut Andy's door gently just as Nathan shut Duncan's. They stood there awkwardly. The scene felt so right, it unnerved her. Quietly, they walked down the stairs together and out the front door to her car. After a few comfortable minutes laughing about worms and the look on Andy's face when he tried the catfish, she headed to Liz's for the night.

Detective Tanner and Officer Dave Nolan stood before the case board first thing Monday morning. Over the smell of strong coffee, they went over open files and their plan for the day. Tanner was a big man with skin the color of coffee. Not in shape like Dave, just large. It was easy to tell Tanner had been off beat patrol for several years, but he was still efficient, meticulous and brilliant. When they reached the Chapman section, Tanner opened the floor to Dave.

"What've you got?"

CHAPTER 22

"Finley is still missing. Looks like she cashed in her savings and disappeared," Dave said. "Didn't cancel her accounts though, and kept some in checking. We're watching for credit card activity, but so far nothing. I've got someone checking out-of-town transportation after the date of the lockdown, but she's come up empty so far. The old boyfriend has been seen driving by at least two times and was said to have grabbed her during a party on New Year's Eve."

Dave tapped at a picture of Susie. "Susie Phillips. Works in Chapman's building. Started the year before she did." He sat a hip on the edge of the desk, flipping through his notes. "Possible motive? Brie was offered the administration position Phillips applied for. Twice it looks like, and Brie turned down both offers. Hardly a reason to burn someone's house down."

"Stranger things have happened," Tanner interjected. Make sure you approach that one as someone who could help Brie. Don't let on that she's a person of interest."

Tanner looked at the pictures as he spoke. "The case is just as frustrating now as it was six years ago. No forced entry. No prints. Precise backdraft. No activity post arson until recently. It feels as much of a loss now as it did then. Is that all?"

"No, there's Elizabeth Whittier. She was Chapman's teacher when Brie went to school there. Got a hold of the photos meant for the Board of Education and pinned them up in their workroom. Says she found them in her office box."

Tanner wrote on the board and in his file as he continued. "Neighbors?"

"Lucy Melbourne is the only one known to have been home during each incident."

"She's the one who made the 911 call six years ago."

"Yes, and she's also *always* home. So, not much help there," Dave said.

"Okay. Get the ex-boyfriend in here. Let's see what he's got to say. Shake that one up. See what happens when someone pushes his buttons. And line up interviews with the staff who was at the school six years ago. Looks like a short list there. Oh, and call the vet to find out the drug used on the dog. I want to know how easy it would be to get it and in that amount."

Dave finished writing down Tanner's instructions, flipped his notebook closed and started to walk to his office.

"Nolan."

"Yeah?"

"I want this one wrapped up. Whatever you need. Keep me posted."

Brie had already taken the dogs for a run. She was able to get Macey to stay at her left and Goldie at her right now, no matter the speed or terrain. Training dogs was one of her most treasured parts of life. She'd showered in one of Nathan's guest showers that morning and didn't kick his gorgeous cabinet when she realized she'd forgotten her brush at Liz's.

The three males in the morning were a sight to see. Socks that didn't match, bed-head hair and favorite hats that had gone missing. She had to admit that they'd found a comfortable system and it warmed her heart.

She noticed that Nathan had taken her advice and laid out backpacks and clothes the night before. Andy gave Nathan throat-choking hugs and Duncan one armed chest humps. The boys walked to the bus stop and Nathan to his garage. Brie sensed he wanted to give them some growing up room while still keeping an eye on them.

It was no accident that he waited to put on his headphones until after the bus arrived. That morning he said he was working on installing the slides to the kitchen drawers. She brought the dogs with her to say goodbye to the boys.

Andy bent down and rubbed cheeks with Goldie as his lips moved a mile a minute. Duncan spoke of the new friends who'd asked him for drawing lessons during recess.

When the boys spotted her brown, paper lunch bags, they stood straight and turned their backs to the house. She slipped a bag to each of them, then glanced over her shoulder. Nathan revved his drill and was concentrating on his work.

After waving goodbye through the high windows, Brie headed to his garage before going to get her mail and newspaper. She knew Nathan would think of some excuse to come with her.

He picked up the steaming mug that sat at the end of his workbench and took a sip as she noticed he had another. She could get used to this routine and this man. And she was getting all too used to him escorting her to her own home. This time, he assured her it was time to do a thorough walk-through.

It had actually been a long time since she felt this good about coming into her own home.

Nathan stood in his work jeans, looking in Brie's fridge. "You have nothing in here."

"I haven't been living here, remember?" She walked over to look out the glass of the doors. "There's no rain in the forecast. We've been without a nor'easter all spring. I'm going to focus on finishing the edging and your pond and put off the plants for a rainy week." She turned to face him. "What do you think about a patio?"

"Come away with me for the weekend."

"Away? Where? Are you serious?"

He took her face in his rough hands. "Yes, away. Camping. Very serious."

She shuttered. "I have work to do."

He pulled back and curled one side of his mouth. "All you've done is work for weeks. And there's no rain coming for your...for my plants."

"*This* weekend?"

"Yep." Nathan meandered over and searched the empty cabinets. "My folks think the weather looks good for Niagara Falls and the kids have Friday off. I think Dave is taking Amanda and Rose to Florida."

Brie tried to pinpoint the moment from last December when her life turned upside down and realized she didn't care. "Yes. Yes, I'll do it. Wow. I have a lot to get done before then." She headed upstairs to pick up an extra brush before getting started. Pausing, she thought and turned back, kissing him long and hard.

Standing with knees locked, Brie stood in the dry, chilly air judging the look of the curved edging. The earthy red color blended with the slate gray of the house. Each brick lay on a layer of sand to prevent movement. They were evenly buried so two inches remained exposed and lined nicely with the tops of the new grass. There was plenty of room for the river rock.

Slowly, she rotated while resting her hands on her hips. She'd used an assortment of fitted, limestone and granite rocks of all different shades for the three tiered spots, the two back corners of the property and the northwest corner of the house. The short, staggered walls were easy to stack once she used sand, string and a level to lay the first layer flat. The areas still needed to be filled with black soil before she could start on the fishless pond and trickling waterfall.

She looked forward to each day working in the fresh air and each night spent with Nathan and his kids. As her mind wandered, she looked at the space for the deck, the empty tiered corners and back again. She made a decision and picked up her shovel.

The tile guy finished the grout in the kitchen. Intricate and complicated patterns framed the base cabinets and the imaginary kitchen island Nathan had drawn on the kitchen floor. He chose several colors of tile, all that would enhance the cherry color of the kitchen cabinets. He let him finish in peace and walked around to his backyard and found Brie neatly digging up some of the sod she'd laid just the week before.

"What are you doing?" Nathan asked.

Brie didn't stop or look up, but he could see her smile as she slid her shovel under the green, loosening it from the soil. "Patio."

"Really? It's so big."

She pulled up heavy squares of wet sod and tossed them in her wheelbarrow. "Round will accent the radius of the edging, but it's not too late to change if you would rather have a different shape. I know you've worked mostly with straight lines inside." They looked mutually at the red brick that curved the entire length around the house before Brie finished filling the wheelbarrow with clumps of grass.

"No. Don't change it. Your thing, remember?"

Nathan moved his weights and the mattress he'd been using for the past several months into Andy's room. The boys' rooms were the only two that wouldn't need stain and finish the following day. He stopped to look out his window and check on them.

Brie had them walking on the patches of exposed Black Creek soil with their sneakers. She would point, turn over a submerged rock and then pick up what looked to him to be a wiggling crawfish. Explaining animatedly, she then put it down and Duncan grabbed at it. He held on and cheered as he held it out at arm's length.

Nathan leaned against the window frame as Andy took a turn. Brie pointed. Andy turned over a dirty rock. It took him several tries of reaching in, pulling his hand back and reaching in again before he gathered enough courage to grab at the pinching creature. Brie and Duncan applauded as Andy held up his prize for a split second before tossing it back in the water.

"I brought you something for your trip." Brie sat at the desk chair in Duncan's room as Andy brushed his teeth for the night. She pulled out a compact, collapsible tripod.

"Uh. Thanks." He scrunched his brows. "What is it?"

"It's an easel that folds up and will fit in your case. I thought you might want to start a sketching of the falls this weekend."

"Cool," he said. "Thanks." After trying it out, Duncan lifted his drawing case, opened it and slid the easel easily along the side next to his colored pencils. "Will you be here in the morning?"

"Sure." She sat next to him and covered him up. "Andy tells me lunch is way gross. I'll bring you something."

"Dad says no one can walk on the floors for a while and it will smell bad, too," Andy interjected as he walked in the room. "He says you guys are going away. Are you dad's girlfriend?"

Duncan rolled his eyes and as soon as Andy climbed in,

pushed on the side of his little brother's head.

Brie took a deep breath. "Yes. I suppose I am. Go to sleep." She covered them up and kissed the tops of their heads. "I packed an instant camera in your bag, Andy. Your job is to use all of the pictures. I'll be back in the morning and see you off before you catch the bus."

She found Nathan folding up the card table and hauling it and the chairs to the garage. He stopped when he saw her, grabbed his half-empty bottle of beer and walked with her to her pickup.

Before opening her door, she paused and turned, noticing him watching her. "You're staring at me."

Self-consciously, she reached up to tuck a few stray hairs out of her face. He stepped closer, causing her to lean back against her door. He placed the fingers from one of his calloused hands on the side of her neck, then brushed his thumb across her lips.

"You're stunning." His other hand trailed up her arm to just above her elbow. "I should tell you I'm going to take advantage of you this weekend." He ran his thumb along the line of her jaw.

The corners of her mouth turned and she rested a hand on the center of his chest. She thought of how he so often managed to blanket her with calm.

He pressed his forehead to hers. "I should also tell you I'm in love with you."

In a knee-jerk reaction, she used the hand on his chest to push him. "Oh, boy," she said out loud and started pacing back and forth in a small line in front of him. "Let me think, let me think." The palms of her hands pressed absently on her temples.

Nathan turned and leaned against the side of her truck, sticking his legs out and casually placing a thumb in one of his pockets. She could see his brow lift as she paced.

"You see." She moved her hands to the backs of her hips but kept pacing. "I really like you—"

"This isn't high school, Brie," he said. "I don't need the same."

"But everything is so good *now*. You'll jinx it. We'll be going along just fine and then you'll think I'm too detached, and—"

He grabbed an arm and pulled her up against him, using his other hand to place a finger on her lips. He inclined her weight along the length of his. "Let go, Brianna."

She laid one side of her head on his chest and listened to the slow, steady beat of his heart. It made her want to lean on him.

Brie lay in the dark, trying not to worry about what Nathan had confessed to her. How could she help it considering her terrible track record with men? Pulling the covers close around her neck, she realized she'd never stressed about a man before. It was also the first time she could remember ever having these feelings about a man.

The phone rang and she rolled over, appreciating the interruption from her anxiety. She had enough to worry about without the man, and much to look forward to, like a big-budget landscaping project complete with a circular patio.

"Hello?"

The phone was silent. Again. She could tell there was a connection. "Hello?" She hung up hoping it was wrong number.

CHAPTER 23

Most of the next morning was spent digging the hole for the patio. The sky was completely clear and a striking blue. It reminded Brie of the color of Nathan's eyes. Good grief. She was acting like she was in high school. It was actually nice and exciting. She filled the spaces between the tiers of rocks below Nathan's window with the displaced soil from the patio hole. The extra was wheeled down to fill tiers around the pond corner. A leveled layer of road gravel, followed by a thin layer of sand and she would be ready to set the patio bricks.

Days were longer now and the spring flowers were in full bloom. She could see the red tulips and purple hyacinths around her deck all the way from Nathan's yard. She worried how the lack of rain might affect finishing this project.

Nathan wore his lacquer mask as he spread the finish on the stained floors. He started from the back of the upstairs rooms toward the front, then down and around to the back again, careful not to paint himself into a corner. He'd already packed his truck for the long weekend with Brie. He figured he would finish long before she would, and he was right.

He watched out the window in the back of the garage as he made a phone call to the movers to see if he could get them to bring the rest of his things earlier than next Thursday. He noticed Brie covered in dirt again and that she was completely in her element when she was like that. He worked on spraying the kitchen's upper cabinets while she finished. When he came out of his spray room, she was sitting on his workbench, again, with her legs crisscrossed and, again, in shorts and a tank.

"I'm at a good stopping point. How about you?"

He wrapped a spray hose around his forearm. "Yes, and I'm stuck out of my house now. You hungry?"

"Starved. How do you feel about a giant Mikey's tenderloin?" She slid down and picked up the spray can, placing it on the shelf where it belonged. "Liz asked if we'd like to get a drink with her and Tim, and we kind of owe them for keeping the dogs while we're gone."

"I'll follow you to your place, and we can take my truck from there."

The dogs rode in the back of Brie's pickup, running circles and lifting their snouts high in the air.

He let the dogs out for her as Brie parked in the garage and opened the house. He thought it was a long shot, but did as Brie suggested, speaking with authority, yet not frightening.

"Macey, Goldie come." Goldie hesitated. Traitor. But Macey trotted over to him and sat. Goldie wasn't far behind. "Well, I'll be damned," he muttered. He rubbed their heads. "Good dogs. Good frigging dogs."

He found her inside, facing her unused fireplace in her family room, holding her unopened mail at her side. She looked up toward the photos of her parents and family arranged over the mantle.

"I'm going to buy a couch," she said like she'd had an epiphany.

He smiled with one side of his mouth.

"A couch *and* a loveseat. Will you come with me?"

"Mmm hmm."

Brie picked up the phone. "I need to call Liz and see·what time she wants to meet. I only have the one shower. Do you want to go ahead and go first?"

"I'd rather wait for you."

Looking up at him, she put the phone back down. "I can call later."

He scooped her up and headed for the stairs. "Not that I'm not glad, but I still can't believe you didn't put in another shower."

They stood in the bathroom together. Nathan dressed slowly, feeling weak and spent. Clean, definitely, but weak and spent. Slipping on his worn black jeans, he left the top button undone and stood at the mirror, shaving with bare feet and a bare chest.

Brie was next to him, dragging something hot through her hair.

Their eyes met in the mirror. "We still have an hour," he said, wiping left-over shaving cream from his face with her hand towel.

"Jeez, Nathan." She grinned. "I'm not a machine."

Lifting one side of his mouth, he said, "I meant for couch shopping."

They pulled up to Mikey's with the bed of his pickup filled with a sable green couch and matching loveseat packed into Nathan's eight-foot bed.

"I can't believe how much money I just spent. I feel sick."

"You're just hungry."

He tucked a piece of hair behind her ear as he pulled up to park across the street where they would be able to keep an eye on his truck from the windows. It was busy for a Thursday night. People were coming out of their burrows in the traditional reaction to spring and warmer weather. The beer garden was open and a band made up of two people sang off-key about margaritas.

Liz and Tim were already in a bar booth with oblong plates full of wings and nachos. He and Brie took a bite as they said their hellos.

Liz took a long time catching Brie up on the latest from their work. "Apparently, Mrs. Whittier wasn't in as tight with Dr. Tyman as she was with Sandy Finley," she said.

The fifth-graders were anxious to graduate and, in his opinion, sounded like healthy fifth-graders should be acting. Nothing was said about next week's board meeting, at least not around Brie.

He played with a piece of her hair as he and Tim kept to easier topics such as the Yankees' early stats.

He turned his eyes to Brie when he sensed her chin lift and her shoulders stiffen. He followed her gaze to the other side of the room. GI Joe and baldy leaned against the bar, facing their booth. Buzz cut held a glass of what looked like whiskey on the rocks. Cue ball had a draft.

Liz must have caught on, too. "They've been here a while. Some of their buddies were in the beer garden but left. What's his deal?"

"My yard's one very large, complicated mess." Nathan changed the subject. "No one's been able to touch it for over a week now. Brie's making me a waterfall under my bedroom window with lavender around it so I can hear and smell while I sleep."

"You were listening."

Diversion successful. "Of course I was listening. I'm a guy," he said sarcastically. "You've planned blue chip junipers for in front of my porch because they only grow eighteen inches and won't cover up the railings I'll be making there. You said you would add some purple salvia and blue palace for color. A third grader could finish my yard from the detail you have mapped out in that binder of yours."

"Blue *salvia* and purple *palace*, but I'm still impressed."

They spoke of the house inside and out and Amanda's changes in lifestyle since she met Dave. After the best tenderloins in town, they sat back to relax and finish their last beer.

"Why do they always go to the bathroom together?" Tim looked to Nathan as he stretched out his feet on the wooden bar booth.

"Don't know, but are they always gone for so long? I think I'll take a walk myself."

Nathan headed toward the bathrooms and noticed Brie and GI Joe through the glass in the door leading out to the crowded beer garden. He shrugged it off until he saw McKinney backing her up.

With Tim on his heels, he pushed open the door in time to hear what the little prick had to say.

Grabbing hold of Brie's upper arm, McKinney spoke through his teeth. "...and then jump into bed with the first guy you come across."

Nathan made it to the two of them in a three long strides. Taking McKinney's fingers, he bent them back unnaturally. Using his other hand, he moved Brie out of the way, let go of buzz cut's fingers and shoved him out the parking lot door.

McKinney stumbled and fell on his ass. "I bet you know all about the police coming to question me." He bounced back up to his feet. "At my work. Who the fuck do you think you are?"

"I told you not to put your hands on her again."

Satisfied, Nathan started to turn and head back into the bar. He saw the sucker punch from the corner of his eye but not fast enough. It clipped the side of his temple as he dodged, but not hard enough to keep him from dancing around the next swing.

Nathan blocked an uppercut, then landed a vicious hook to McKinney's left eye, dropping him where he stood. He walked back to the beer garden with McKinney mumbling and holding his eye while sprawled out on the concrete. He passed baldy on his way to Brie.

Rob gestured to Nathan's eye and smirked.

"You might want to check on your friend." Nathan jerked his head toward the parking lot before turning to Brie. "And we might want to get out of here."

"You're bleeding."

"Not really." He took her arm and walked briskly with Tim and Liz on their heels. The crowd was growing in the beer garden and the noise picked up.

"Why is it kind of sexy?" she added.

"In that case, I'm hurt really bad." He turned back to Tim and Liz as they walked out the front door. "Sorry about all that."

"I've never liked him," Tim interjected. "He gives me the creeps the way he paws around Brie."

"I've never flown first-class before." Brie stretched out, enjoying the room.

Nathan was resting his head back with his eyes closed. "You'll have to choose the spot next time." He was massaging her hand with his thumb.

She hadn't noticed how sore her hands were from carrying bricks. Her eyes nearly crossed from the feel. She shifted her body to face him, careful not to displace her hand from his. "There are camping sites in New York. And we didn't bring any gear," she said. How did he find all the tight knots?

"Just wait and see."

She pulled on her ear with her free hand. "Have you brought other women here?"

"I've never been here. My folks came last winter. I've seen pictures."

"You didn't bring any camping gear," Brie repeated.

He opened one eye and smiled. Leaning over, he used his thumb and forefinger to clasp Brie's lips together. The corners of her lips turned up and she leaned her head back, let her lids drop and took a deep breath.

"Alone on a romantic fucking weekend."

Without bothering with a glass, the swig of whiskey went down smooth and eased one side of the rage while lighting another.

Copies of photos lined the walls of the tiny room. Pictures of Brie walking with her precious wheelbarrow, running with the two mutts, shopping for a couch with the latest flavor-of-the-day.

"I am going to get off watching you squirm." The bottle was tipped to the photos in a kind of a toast.

"Watching you afraid, watching you bleed."

CHAPTER 24

Brie decided not to ask him why he rented a convertible to drive to a campsite. Instead, she sat, enjoying the cool breeze and bright sunshine. The air smelled of pine needles and fertile earth. The enormous Douglas firs and Sycamore trees lined the roads and grew bigger as they drove farther back into the woods.

"Redwoods." Nathan must have noticed the puzzled look on her face.

"I thought you didn't know trees."

"Farther west are trees big enough to drive cars through the trunks."

She'd never known anything like this existed. They pulled up to about a dozen tiny cottages nestled high in the air, each in their own tree. Actually around each tree. Nathan checked in as she stood leaning against the convertible that looked all the more out of place in this remote gravel parking lot.

She cocked her head at the one that was connected to the main lodge by a drawstring bridge. It also had access through a tall and winding staircase around the trunk of its towering Sycamore. Trying to imagine the visual of his parents staying here wasn't much of a stretch. They seemed like teenagers to her. Suddenly, she thought a little too much about them staying there. TMI.

Nathan came out with a few brochures in one hand and keys in the other. "We're down the road a ways." He kissed her as he set the papers in the center console of the rental.

"You call this camping?" she asked as she got in the passenger seat in her jeans and flannel shirt.

"Point taken, but before you get too cozy, know there's no Jacuzzi or even a tub. I assume the structure of the cottage can only handle a shower stall fifty feet up in the air."

"Fifty feet? What were you going to do if I was scared of heights?"

"Distract you." He kissed her once more before putting the car in gear.

The cabin was absolutely amazing. The floor was hardwood laid in a hexagonal pattern that grew out from the center around the trunk of the tree. A colorful patchwork quilt covered the enormous bed that was centered in the single-area and was piled with matching pillows. Smoothed tree branches littered with knots created the arms and legs of the chairs and couch.

The curtains were sheer. Brie assumed privacy wasn't a priority this far up. There was a mini-fridge and the smallest sink she'd ever seen. No table or desk, only a single chair, which meant no cooking or working. Perfect. A tiny loft that fit only a cot-sized bed looked out over the rest of the cabin.

She stepped onto a shallow porch that wrapped around the entire circumference of the cottage and was scattered with chairs covered in outdoor cushions and surrounded by the same bare-branch-looking railing. The air was clear and dry and felt amazing on her face. It smelled...clean. Turkey vultures and hawks circled the trees. The view was a breathtaking sea of brown and green needles littered with straight, brown trunks.

She stopped when she came back in and noticed him watching her. He was leaning against the tree trunk with one ankle crossed over the other and thumbs in his pockets. So cute. She would never tire of the stance.

He pushed off. "Are you up for a hike, or do you need some time to rest up after the flight?"

"I'm anxious to get out there. Come. You can see where the trails lead from up here."

She pulled him out to the skinny porch feeling like an excited child and tucked her arm in his. They compared the maps of the trails he'd picked up from the lodge with what they could see.

She turned to him, wrapping her arms around his waist.

"I'm glad we're here. I didn't know how much I wanted this, needed this." She looked in his eyes and smiled.

He took her face in his hands and rubbed his thumbs across her cheeks. "I love you."

She closed her eyes and felt his thumbs and the love he had given her. She could lose herself in this man without ever feeling lost.

They walked through oceans of Douglas firs. The quiet was peaceful and only disturbed by snapping twigs under their feet and an occasional call from a bird. Brie stopped every few hundred yards to study a plant that was completely new or somewhat similar to what she worked with.

"I want to find a native plant guide before we come out again. I know these are Penstemon, but I've never seen this variety. And look, these are bleeding hearts. You'll have these in your corner, back by the pond."

By the time they made it to dinner, both were starved. At the main lodge, they ate prime rib with garlic sauce and twice-baked potatoes. Brie wore her second flannel shirt, a clean pair of dark blue jeans and hiking boots.

"I wish you would have told me what kind of camping to pack for."

They shared a piece of carrot cake and experimented with the Oregon craft beers.

Far too much experimenting made hiking up the trail a challenge. Her thighs burned as they climbed the stairs to their cabin. She headed straight for the huge bed.

Nathan sat and loosened the strings of his shoes before kicking them off.

And she was sound asleep, fully dressed, boots and all.

Sunlight slanted through the sheer curtains. Brie opened her eyes to see Nathan inches from her. She sighed frustratingly and closed them again, kicking herself for falling asleep early.

Feelings that stirred deep were new to her. His hair curled just at the ends when it was messy like this, much like it did when wet. She'd expected to feel fear attached to this kind of intense desire for someone. She thought how he looked sitting at the bottom of the stairs in his dilapidated house with his notebook in his hand. How careless and sexy he looked when she opened her door to him on New Year's Eve. That mind-numbing first kiss. With perfect clarity, she could picture him hiking Andy up onto his shoulders and how tightly he'd closed his eyes when Duncan first called him *dad*. No, there was no fear and for the first time in her life, Brie knew what it felt like to be in love.

Carefully, she crawled out of bed and headed for the shower. The water was hot even if it was only a trickle. She stood there with the heat dripping down her back, feeling more relaxed than she could remember in a very long time. As she dressed, he slept. So, she decided to go out and pick up something to eat from the lodge.

The scene seemed surreal. She walked through the towering woods over the damp leaves. Webs hung with droplets of dew, giving away the hiding places of spiders. She returned with egg muffins, bagels and coffee to find him toweling his hair dry.

"I brought breakfast as a peace offering. Why didn't you wake me? We only have two nights together. You should have woken me."

"Yes, but we have two days, too. Anyway, you're a light weight. I think you were passed out, not sleeping." He took the bag from her and peeked inside.

She bit her bottom lip as he reached for the coffee. When he took it, she gave him a tiny push in the center of his chest, landing him in the chair behind him. Standing in front of him, she reached for the top button of her blue, cotton blouse. The look on his face was one she hoped she'd never forget.

In that one small gesture, Nathan felt his IQ drop thirty points. Reaching for her, Brie shook her head at him and continued painfully slow down the buttons of her shirt. Brilliant morning sunlight shone on the side of her. She was just as irresistible in her cotton and jeans as she was in her cashmere. The wind whistled through the trees from the windows behind her. And he was lost.

Pulling the unfastened shirt over just her shoulders, she left it covering her chest and toed off her shoes. As she pulled it down her arms, her fingers brushed over herself before exposing the matching, blue lace underneath. The shirt dropped as did her hands down the center of her stomach ending at the top of her jeans. Was she trying to make him crazy?

His grip was firm where he held onto the arms of the chair. Rotating her back to him, she pooled her jeans around her ankles, then stepped out, a perfect mixture of lightly bronzed muscle and feminine curves. Reaching behind, she released the clasp of the lace and slipped it from her shoulders. She added the rest to the growing pile at her feet and turned. His breath caught. She stood unashamed and all woman.

Taking a step toward him, Brie stopped just out of arm's reach from his chair. Taken with intensity of both the physical and of his heart, he slid to the floor. Sitting on his heels, he pulled her to him. Pulled the most complex, amazing woman he'd ever known close to him. Burying his face in her stomach, he took hold of her ankles.

Brie felt rough, possessive hands explore from the back of her heels, over her calves, behind her knees and up her thighs to her backside. As he stood, his lips followed a similar path.

"You're beautiful," he whispered in her ear. "I found you. How did I ever find you?"

Her legs trembled and caused her insides to ignite and her legs to weaken. He simply scooped her up and carried her to the messy bed. They rolled, joining lips and tongues and grazing teeth. Together they pulled his shirt from his shoulders.

His fingers ran up to her throat, circling her neck before making his way to the back of her head and lacing his fingers through her hair. She felt needed and loved. She felt her breathing become short and ragged. She pulled off the rest of his clothes and swam in his awe as he trailed his fingers along the length of her arms. He reached her breasts. Holding each in his hands, he sunk to her.

Grabbing hold of the back of his hair, she tried to pull him closer. She lay tucked under him, his mouth feasting. The palm of his hand pressed along her as he traveled to her center. She gasped as he pressed her over the glorious edge.

Their bodies slid dampened with sweat. Trembling with aftershocks, she found him and sent him into his own growling moan. He moved his lips under her jaw, teeth grazing along her collar bone up to just below her ear. He took hold of her lobe with his teeth as she touched him.

He clamped his hand to her, taking her back up and over. She cried out and grabbed his back. Rolling on top of him, she lifted and guided him to her. Her head turned slightly as he held onto her hips, pulling her against him until they both shook with need. She arched and, together, they cried out in release. Joined. Loved. Trusted. Spent. They fell back wrapped in a tangled mass.

Nathan didn't know what way was up. He just knew their bodies were slicked together Brie was still trembling. He turned his head, placing his lips on her cheek before she rolled and collapsed next to him. "The coffee will be cold."

"Coffee who?" She laid an arm over her eyes for a full minute before rolling off the side of the bed.

He lifted on his elbow enough to watch her walk to the tiny sink. She took a sip of the tepid caffeine as she walked back with it to him. Watching her had him already feeling aroused. She handed him the covered paper cup. It was when she crawled back up to the pillows that he lost it and set the cup on the side table to take her again.

Nathan analyzed his work. The three days since they'd been back had been spent entirely on laying the base trim that now sat on smooth, finished and sealed hardwood. To him, the house was still missing a beamed ceiling at the top of the open, two-story foyer and a wooden arched entryway to the dining room. But it looked finished to anyone who didn't have access to the worn notebook resting comfortably in the back pocket of his faded jeans.

Brie made no mention of the evening's board meeting. He knew she missed her students, missed her job. Liz's confidence in the outcome was helpful, but he didn't know that much about those kinds of things.

The moving van would arrive in the morning and the house would become a home. He still had months of work to do with the kitchen, front door, deck, porch, shutters and all of the extras he had planned.

He wondered if Brie would want him with her at the meeting. He would let her decide and if she didn't want him there, he would leave it at that.

They both heard the squeal of the brakes from the bus. Brie came around the side of the house and met Nathan coming out the front door. They paused and locked eyes before continuing down the drive to meet Duncan and Andy.

"Hey, Dad, Miss Chapman. Mrs. Whittier says good luck tonight."

Duncan was incredibly mature for his age, Nathan thought, recognizing the taste of sarcasm in his voice.

Brie winked at him. "Piece of cake."

Andy took Brie's hand as they all walked up the gravel. "Will you come back tomorrow? Sean says you'll be back tomorrow. It's not fun without you."

"I'm not sure how this works. How about I let you know as soon as I know?"

"Are grandma and grandpa coming here? Are we going to their house?" Andy continued with his rapid fire questions.

All eyes looked to Nathan for an answer.

"Why don't you two go find something to snack on and we'll be just a minute."

He tried to be casual, leaning back against her truck and pulling her to him. "I didn't know if you wanted me there. I should have asked."

He felt her chest expand and release as he ran his hands over the back of her hair.

"I've tried to picture it both ways," she said. "The board thought we were having a heady affair long before we were, but they're likely to stare and judge anyway. The thought of being without you tonight feels unsettling. I've never been in love before."

CHAPTER 25

He pulled her by the shoulders to an arm's length away and looked at her. "Say it again." He ran his hands over her shoulders, along her neck and held her face tightly.

She smiled warmly at him. "I'm in love with you, Nathan."

He pulled her forehead against his and closed his eyes tight before bringing their lips together.

"Stop spying," Duncan yelled from the fridge with a banana in his mouth. He leaned in the doorway. "What're they doing?"

"Kissing." Andy didn't turn to his brother but smiled wide.

"Gross," Duncan said as he pulled out some lunchmeat and bread.

They took Nathan's truck, but would have opted for Brie's shorter pickup if he had known it would be so difficult to find a parking spot.

"They decide this kind of thing in executive session," Brie said to him. "I have to tell you that regardless of the outcome, I need to move back home, Nathan." She looked like she was expecting an argument.

"I figured." He knew it was coming and actually thought it would happen long before now.

Taking a deep breath, Brie opened her mouth, then got the strangest expression before closing it again. She remained somber and quiet as they parked.

There was a crowd hanging outside the back of the brick building adjacent to the parking lot. He took her hand as they walked closer. He could tell that she recognized people in the crowd. Her hand tightened around his.

"These are parents of students I've had," she whispered. "Nathan, they look angry."

"Not just parents. Look." He tilted his head to the right. Two cops were in the mix.

Back straight, chin up, Brie walked to the edge of the crowd, excusing herself as she stepped through them. The crowd soon noticed her and started clapping. Slow at first, but soon they were a loud mass of bodies.

A man walked through the crowd toward them. "We gave them an earful on their way into the building, Miss Chapman. We support you and let them know it." He shook her hand. "You kept our kids safe."

The first officer approached her and also held out his hand. "Every situation is different and sometimes you have to use common sense. That's what you did, and that's what we told each of them on their way in." He shook gingerly. "When administration starts reprimanding staff for using their heads, we have to stick together. We'll go to the press if this goes badly tonight."

"Thank you." She cleared her throat and spoke a little louder. "Thank you, everyone, for your support. It's...overwhelming."

Nathan led her through the crowd into the building, but not without him noticing the stares at his hand on the lower part of her back. Brie was visibly relieved when they spotted her sister.

As they hugged in greeting, Liz explained, "They have to publicly announce what they decided in executive session. It's first on the agenda after the motioning of approval for the minutes of last month's meeting."

Liz led them to skinny metal chairs with blue-gray cushions. The board members sat around a huge kidney-shaped table covered in a white drop cloth that reminded him of a wedding party table. Each member, plus the superintendent, assistant superintendents and the press had a shiny name plate and a microphone at their seat.

Odd, for such a compact area, Nathan thought.

Brie looked glazed over as they listened to corrections to the board minutes from the last meeting. He didn't get all of it. All he knew was that his girl needed to get back to work.

"Second the motion?" Brie jerked to attention. In response to the raise of a hand from a rather hefty board member in a floral dress, the president continued, "Note the second motion was from Alisha Harris, and let's move on to other business."

The board president was easy to distinguish, wooden gavel and all.

"Meeting in executive session, the board, in cooperation with the Northridge Education Association, has made a decision regarding the lockdown procedure that took place March eighteen of this year at Bloom Elementary. Principal Sandy Finley was dismissed and teacher Brianna Chapman will retain her teaching position with a letter of reprimand placed in her permanent file. Next business is to recognize our winter athletes..."

He hadn't noticed she'd been holding her breath until it came out all at once. Her eyes went first to his. Warm and glowing, she had the prettiest smile he'd ever seen.

Next, Brie's eyes turned to her other side to Liz, who didn't look as relieved.

"We'll fight the reprimand," Liz mouthed.

Brie ignored Liz's comment and looked like she might bounce out of her seat. "I do go back tomorrow, right?"

"Yes. Aren't you at all mad? Did you see the crowd out back? And they're still going to write you up?"

Brie didn't seem to be listening. She kissed her sister on the cheek, slid her arm through his and looked back up at him. "Take me home, Reed."

As they drove, Brie looked out the window. "I had no idea how relieved I would feel. Relieved and alive."

"I need to swing by my folks to get the kids." He played with the hair that escaped her pins and danced around her neck.

"I've never seen your parents' home. I can't wait to tell Andy about all the work he's going to have in the morning," she said mischievously. "You dress up well, Reed. I'm in love with you."

His hand tightened on the wheel, but his eyes stayed straight. He moved his other hand down to join with hers.

They celebrated with a game of Uno before tucking the kids in their beds.

"The moving van comes tomorrow." Brie thought Nathan's eyes lit as she said so. "You'll be surprised at how much we have. I hope to have most of it out and the extra boxes hidden before you get back from work."

"You sound like Mr. Mom."

"That's not an insult."

"I'll walk myself home tonight. You stay with the kids."

"Take my truck."

"Just around the corner? On this gorgeous night? I'll walk across the creek. You can watch me."

And she knew he would.

Brie stopped when she reached her yard, the usual unsettling feeling crept up her back. Macey stood panting comfortably and Brie smiled. Unlocking the back door to the garage, she went in that way.

She let Macey out the front and headed to the mailbox in the dark. She paused at the faint lilac smell of the arrowhead viburnum, enjoying the scents of spring. She stood with Macey at her feet looking at her mother's dianthus that were turning green with the warming temperatures. Checking the locks behind her, she grabbed a granola bar before heading up for bed.

The phone rang as she lay in the dark. She almost didn't answer. The only calls she's gotten this late were silent.

"Hello?"

"You aren't as sneaky as you think you are."

"Nathan."

"You sound shaky. You okay?"

"Of course. Locked up nice and tight."

"After your stroll around the front in the dark, alone?"

"How do you know?"

"Again, you're not as sneaky as you think you are. Macey wouldn't have let you go to bed without letting her out and your back light never went on."

"That's just a little creepy, Reed."

"I also know you slip the kids' lunches in their backpacks every day except pepperoni pizza day."

"Wow."

"Did I wake you? Where are you?"

Brie grinned while cozied up in her sheets in the dark. "I'm standing at my lingerie drawer deciding between a sheer, silk teddy or black lace for bed."

She heard something thump through the receiver.

"You're killing me. I've never seen the black."

"I'm a little top heavy for that one and sometimes fall right out of it." She bit her bottom lip, stifling a laugh.

"I could come over and help you choose."

"Sleep, Nathan. Big day tomorrow."

She barely had time to roll over after hanging up before the phone rang again. "That's all the phone sex I can offer for one night, Reed. Go to bed." But there was no answer. She could hear breathing. "Nathan?" More breathing, then disconnect. She broke her own rule and whistled for Macey to come up and sleep at her feet.

The morning was crisp and the ground dry. Brie stopped by to pick up Nathan's anxious dog and ran with Macey on her left and Goldie on her right. They had worked up to a mile and a half, but Brie still cut their usual route short and ran along the floodplain. The ground was rock hard and the wild flowers stunted. One good rain would bring them all to life, Brie thought as they ran.

She chuckled to herself at the four-wheeler in the field. It was a sure sign of spring when the snowmobiles were gone and the four-wheelers came out. She didn't completely trust Goldie yet to control himself around a vehicle that drove much like a spunky rabbit, and she guided him over to Macey's side. Brie thought about the materials she would need to prepare for her first day back. She felt amazing running her lover's dog with hers and thinking of what to pack for the boys' lunches.

The sensation at the back of her head was confusing. She wasn't sure what happened. Just that one minute she was running and the next she was rolling down the floodplain, tangled in leashes and landed halfway in the cold water. The back of her head felt warm, wet. And then there was pain. Sheering, mind-numbing pain. She couldn't move and the sky grew darker before it blackened all together.

Duncan stood at the kitchen window in shock.

He'd been watching Miss Chapman and the dogs. They'd almost made it back to the house. He noticed the four-wheeler and thought it might be following them, but he was too preoccupied with the idea that she might have forgotten about making his lunch to pay close attention.

Then, he saw the bat. So badly he wanted to yell out to her, but nothing came out of his mouth, just like now. He watched the dogs bark hysterically. Goldie tried to wrestle free of his leash. He jerked her around in the mud like a rag doll. Macey lay next to her limp body, setting her snout on Miss Chapman's shoulder.

No, Duncan thought. No, no, no, no! He'd already lost a mom.

He watched Goldie flip around in panic, then pull her farther into the frigid water. Eventually, the dog wrestled his leash free and raced toward home. Using his teeth to turn the mudroom door knob, Duncan heard him come in, barking madly and leaving muddy prints throughout the house. He remained like a statue as he heard an ear-piercing scream. Then he realized it was coming from him.

CHAPTER 26

Nathan was upstairs when he heard Duncan and the dog. He could tell it wasn't a simple scuffle between the boys or a skinned knee. He passed Andy in the hall while wiping shaving cream from his face. Throwing the hand towel over the banister, he took the stairs two at a time.

When he reached the kitchen, the situation was easy to analyze and threw him into overdrive. Duncan was standing, intact, looking out the kitchen window that faced out back. He was still screaming at the top of his lungs. Goldie dangled his leash from his neck as he barked like mad, jumping and spreading black mud all over the kitchen floor. He didn't bother to look out the window at what Duncan could see. He knew it had to be Brie and that it was bad.

He darted for the garage with Andy on his heels. His mind raced, when he saw the yellow of her fleece jacket.

Brie was lifeless, half in the cold creek water with Macey's snout lying across her. He couldn't breathe. He used the adrenaline from the slap of grief and grabbed a nearby packing blanket as he turned to Andy. He spoke loudly over Duncan who was still screaming in the kitchen. "Call nine-one-one. Can you do that, son?" Andy nodded and went for the phone as Nathan sprinted out the back door.

As he ran, he heard himself yelling *no* over and over again. Frantically, he watched for movement. There was only Macey whimpering with her head resting protectively on Brie.

He skimmed clumsily down the cracked floodplain, sliding across the dried green of the wildflowers. Ignoring the fallen log, he splashed his boots through what was left of the creek water to reach her and skidded onto his knees.

"Baby, no," he said aloud as he felt deep under her jaw for a pulse. He found it and desperately began pulling her out of the cold water. She didn't have gloves and her fingers were a ghostly white.

It was when he was untangling Macey's leash from around her that he noticed the blood. He remembered something about not moving accident victims until help came, but it was cold and she was wet. He tried to feel if she had broken bones and decided he had to get her warm. Working on autopilot, he wrapped her cautiously in the rough blanket and carried her toward his house. He could feel blood warming the crook of his arm as he ran with her up the hill.

"Did you call?" he yelled as he entered the back door to the kitchen.

Andy nodded and handed him the phone. Duncan had stopped screaming and dropped to his knees next to them, the corners of his mouth trembling. Andy hid his face behind his brother's shoulder.

Nathan took a towel and tried to wrap it tightly around her head as he spoke to the rescue operator. "Wait, wait. She's awake." He held the phone between his head and his shoulder, leaning closer to her.

"Nathan," Brie said quietly with her eyes closed.

Sticking his head close to her face, he answered, "I'm here, baby. The ambulance is on its way."

"Nathan." A tear fell from her still face and down her temple. "It hurts."

He stuck his forehead gently to hers. "I know. We're going to fix it. I can hear the rescue. Just be still now. I love you." He squeezed his eyes shut and propped the phone between his ear and shoulder.

Slowly, the group in the waiting room grew. Nathan had tried to get Duncan and Andy to go with his folks. He thought school might take their minds off this, but Duncan had a tantrum

Nathan didn't know he was capable of. So, his folks came to sit with them instead. They sat quietly in rows of cushioned chairs that were attached side-to-side. His parents had contacted Liz, who came with her kids, followed soon after by Dave and Amanda.

"We're waiting," he said. "They don't think there are any broken bones, but she's got a gash on the back of her head, and they won't know how bad it is until the test results come back. She might lose some fingers from frostbite." His patience thinned. If he had to explain her condition one more time, he was going to punch something.

He pulled Dave aside. "Where's McKinney, damn it? Find him and you'll likely find him with Black Creek mud on his boots."

"He's actually in the parking lot."

Nathan exploded for the door before Dave's giant hand caught the back of his LL Bean shirt. Dave quickly and smoothly twisted his arm uncomfortably behind his back and whispered in his ear, "Not here. Not now. Think."

Defeated and feeling helpless, Nathan slumped down in the chair next to him, set his forearms on his thighs and put his face in his hands. "He did it. I know he fucking did it. He set the fire. He's always conveniently around when this shit happens. Here he is again. Can't you do something?"

Dave shook his head. "Listen, patrols are at the scene and CSU is on their way. We'll wrap this up, man. I swear."

They waited long enough to make him think the worst. When the doctor finally came out, he and Liz approached him away from the others.

He was a small man that looked to be in his sixties and walked toward them like he'd done this hundreds of times. "She's unconscious. We were able to get some response from her and test results look good, but she needs to rest. She's lost a lot of blood. We suspect a pretty hefty concussion but will know more when she's awake. I'll check on her again in the afternoon." He stuck his hand out to shake like he was ending the conversation.

"Can we see her?" Nathan interjected before he held out a hand in response.

"Only a few at a time. She's needs to sleep and let her body heal."

* * *

"You know I need to talk to Duncan."

Dave and Nathan sat in the closest waiting room while Liz and her family took their turn to see Brie.

Nathan sighed. "I know. He's not taking this well. Be easy on him." He held onto the back of his neck and tilted his head up. "My folks are taking them for the rest of the day. You can talk to him after they go in to say goodbye to her."

Dave felt for his friend as he watched the disparity run over him. He could see McKinney pacing outside the sliding doors and wanted to pound on him himself. He realized he was really only officially seen when the dog was poisoned. Unless you count the fire. He couldn't help but let his mind turn and contemplate. Brie swore she had never met him before the day of the fire. Shit. What a mess.

Dave shook his head. "I need to take him back to the house and have him show me what he saw and where." He winced like he was waiting for a backlash. "The area will be surrounded in yellow tape and the evidence crew might still be there."

"Shit, Dave." Nathan rubbed both hands over his face. "Okay. It makes sense. I'm going to be with him. Let me talk to my folks."

Dave spotted Amanda and made his way to her. She looked like she was analyzing him, then buried her head in his chest as he sat.

"I hate this. It's like six years ago all over again."

"I'm taking Nathan and his kids to his house while the scene is still fresh in their minds."

Amanda looked up. "You have on your cop face." She leaned back in the chair. "I'll stay with Brie."

He pulled her back to him as Nathan made his way over to his parents and the boys. Andy was curled up in Mackenzie's lap. She stroked his hair as he lay quiet. Duncan sat in a chair by himself next to Sylvester. He had his arms wrapped around his legs in a tight ball, staring at the floor. Liz and her kids walked out and everyone stood up.

"I'm going to get the dogs and see if they'll let me check on her house. Then, I'll take care of things at school for both of us. I'll stop back later." Liz's eyes and nose were puffy and red. "You'll call if she wakes up?" She kissed Nathan on the cheek and rubbed the tops of Duncan and Andy's heads. "Sylvester. Mackenzie." She nodded politely to them before she left.

It looked like chaos to Duncan. The moving van drivers waited at the end of his drive. A squad car sat at Brie's house and two at his house, one was plain with a light stuck crookedly on top. People were there taking pictures. A big man with a small, gold name tag that read Detective Tanner said he was there to hear his story.

He did as he was told. He stood right where he was when he first saw Brie and the dogs. "She came from that way." He pointed across the creek along the lake. "She was jogging with the dogs. She doesn't usually go that way, but Macey isn't supposed to go far yet."

"Then what did you see?" Dave stood back from him.

He crossed his arms tightly as he spoke. "The lady on the four-wheeler came the same way as Miss Chapman."

He saw both Dave and Nathan jerk their heads to each other from the corner of his eyes.

Duncan turned. "Miss Chapman moved Goldie around to the side with Macey. I think she heard the four-wheeler coming." He swayed back and forth, holding himself closely with his arms wrapped around his sides.

His voice started to get louder. He could hear it crack. "I saw the lady hold out the bat." He stopped to keep himself from crying. He wanted so much to get this over with. "She swung it at...at Miss Chapman. At her head as she passed her." He put his hands over his face and muffled into his palms. "She fell down the hilly part to the water. Macey lay on top of her. Goldie tried to get free from his leash. He, he pulled her around in the mud for a long time, then into the water. He got free and came into the house barking. Then Dad came down." He turned and looked at Nathan. "Can I go now?"

The man named Detective Tanner spoke up first. "Not yet, son." He placed a hand on his shoulder. Duncan yanked it off. Tanner put his hand up and shook his head like he was trying to signal it was okay. How could this be okay?

"Do you remember how many people were on the four-wheeler?"

"One."

"Are you sure?"

"Yes."

"What makes you think it was a woman? Did you see the person from way up here? Could you describe her?"

"Yeah, I could see from here."

"Do you know who it is?"

"I couldn't see her that good."

"So, you're not sure if it was a lady."

"I, I...yes, it was a lady." He sighed and squeezed his eyes shut.

His uncle walked up to him and put both hands on his shaking shoulders. Duncan turned and buried his face in Nathan's stomach. He looked up at him pleading.

"It's okay, Dunc."

He yelled into Nathan's shirt, "She held the bat like a girl. She was small. She wore all black. She had on a cap. The four-wheeler was black. It was new and shiny."

He sobbed in Nathan's arms, and Nathan cut a hand across his neck to signal they were done.

Dave stood in his uniform as the walkie on his shoulder buzzed. He turned his body and took a few steps from them to take the call. He looked up and met Tanner's eyes, motioning his head toward the front room. Duncan heard them.

"They got a hit on Finley's phone. Someone's at her house. There's a patrol on the way out there."

Nathan walked in with a duffel bag. Amanda sat in a chair on the other side of Brie. She was mumbling to herself, talking on the phone and writing on a napkin.

A nurse took vitals and pricked Brie with a pin at the ends of her fingers. Brie jerked her finger and moved her head slightly in response. Overtly, the nurse looked down at his bag. "We don't have accommodations for overnight guests, sir."

The doctor walked in at that moment and added, "But we can probably find a recliner somewhere. How is the patient?" He turned to the nurse.

"Still responsive, but hasn't awakened yet. Vitals are normal. Looks like she's going to keep her fingers."

"Good, good." He lifted Brie's eyelids.

It was difficult to watch them handle her so casually. Nathan interrupted them. "She's been asleep for going on six hours.

How do you know she's not in a coma?"

"She's responsive. Prognosis is good. We just won't know until she wakes up." The doctor wrote on the clipboard that hung at the base of Brie's bed before letting it swing loosely. "I'll be back in the morning." He turned to the nurse. "Call me if she wakes before then."

"Listen, Nathan," Amanda said to him. "Dave told me about the moving van. I'll be gathering folks together to unpack and move furniture for you. We can come back later and adjust whatever you don't like. I'll make sure the dogs have a place and check on the houses; get the mail and papers for tomorrow, and however long you need." She looked at her napkin as she spoke. "I'm assuming your mom and dad will take care of Duncan and Andy, but I'll give them a call and check."

"What's all this?"

"It's what I do. Boss people around in emergencies. This doesn't qualify as a hurricane or drought, but it feels as bad in some ways. Personal. Ya know? I'll get in touch with Brie's boss before she goes home for the day. Does she keep files on her landscaping jobs?"

He told her about the gray binder and where he saw it last. He gave her Liz's phone number and where to find the dog food before she blew out of there.

He sat alone listening to the machines and watching Brie for a long time. The pain and feeling of helplessness nearly choked him. To keep from going crazy, he pulled out his notebook from his back pocket, and sketched a small, trickling waterfall at the corner of his house. The hell if he knew one plant from another. He only knew what tulips were and what they looked like, so he drew them around the falling water and stones.

Liz came back with Tim and her kids before dark. Nathan's parents and the boys were already there. Duncan sat in a chair away from Brie. Andy was back in his grandmother's lap. "The dogs are fine," Liz told Nathan. "I gave them both a bath."

"Amanda is—"

"A whirlwind, we know. She's already had your folks and Tim working on your boxes and called Zach and Chase. They'll be here first thing in the morning."

"Damn. I didn't think to call them," he said.

"We've got it." Liz looked at Brie. "Nothing?"

He shook his head.

"You look awful. Will you sleep?"

He nodded. "I'll be all right."

Exhausted, he finally laid the side of his head on her white sheets and fell asleep holding her hand. His dreams were a fast-motion picture of flashes of memories: Macey chasing Brie in the snow; Brie reading by her fire pit, walking in snowshoes and hauling his dirty dog back to his house. The look of her sleeping in a tall cottage in the forests of Oregon. The first time she told him she loved him. He could hear her across the field calling the dogs over the fallen log. She sounded closer than across the field.

"Nathan. Where are the dogs?" He felt the tips of fingers tap his cheek. "Are they okay? Wake up, Nathan."

He turned his head to her. Overwhelming relief flooded him. Was she really asking about the damned dogs? He smiled and took her hand from his face, kissing her palm. "How do you feel?" he asked, lifting his head.

"The dogs?"

He shook his head and closed his eyes. "Heroes. Liz has them. How do you feel?" he repeated.

She closed her eyes and whispered, "Like some asshole hit me on the back of my head."

CHAPTER 27

"Did they get him this time?" Brie mumbled, squinting at Nathan. "I guess that's a no."

"I love you. We will." He pressed her call button.

They came and asked Brie a myriad of questions and completed a battery of tests, including trying to get her to sit up, which didn't work well. He tried not to push his after-hours-visitor's luck and kept quiet in the corner chair. He heard them conclude she had lost her sense of smell and that her equilibrium was off.

The doctor on call turned to him. "She'll likely be here for at least a few days."

"A few days? What's wrong?"

"It looks like the concussion is a grade three. We'll want to keep an eye on her."

"How many grades are there?" he asked.

"Well, just the three. I'll be back later to check on her head. She'll be tired and the dizziness may take some time to dissipate. That's normal. Don't be alarmed. It should get better. Has she ever had a head injury before?"

Nathan nodded his head. "Concussion. Six years ago, yes."

Indeed, she was out cold again. Almost twenty-four hours of sleep and she was back out after twenty minutes. He grabbed a shower and politely ate the rubber eggs and cold toast the nurse brought him.

Trying to keep his mind together, he worked his seventh Sudoku puzzle when Amanda showed up with Dave.

"How is she?" Amanda asked before she was all the way in the room.

"She woke up. Not for long. Well, long enough to ask about the dogs."

"You look like shit." Dave sat in the empty chair while Amanda sat at the foot of Brie's bed. "What's the prognosis?"

"They want her here for a few days. She's not going to be happy about that."

"Damn right she's not going to happy about that." Brie opened her eyes but kept her head still as she slurred, "I just got my job back. Did you tell them I just got my job back?" She patted around her hospital bed with one hand.

"What do you need?"

"I need to sit up, and I could use some coffee and some real clothes and a toothbrush and a cab."

He pressed the button to raise the top half of her bed as he spoke. "Nothing wrong with your head, it sounds like."

"There's always been something wrong with her head," Amanda said playfully as tears rolled down her cheeks.

Relief flooded him. He handed her a white paper cup of coffee and kissed her forehead. "Your brothers are due in this morning."

"This morning? How...what day is it?"

"It's Thursday."

"Who has my class?"

Amanda piped in. "The same sub you had before. Liz is at work getting things ready for her and her own sub. She's taking the rest of the week off. I ran the dogs this morning, or maybe the dogs ran themselves. You have them trained well. I have your mail in my bag. Nathan's parents are lined up to clean up the mess the movers left in his garage and foyer. I'm stopping over to..." She took out Brie's gray binder. "...wrestle with the landscaping fabric for Nathan's yard. Do you always keep such detailed plans? A third-grader could follow this binder."

Dave raised his eyebrows toward Brie. "She's a machine. I wouldn't get in her way if I were you."

Brie lifted the cup to her lips and took a sip.

"What's the matter?" Nathan asked in response to the look on her face.

"I can't taste this. I can't smell this." She handed it back to him and used the side rails to pull herself up. "What is the matter with me?"

He noticed the dried, brown stain left on her pillow. It nearly choked him as he reached for her call button again.

"The doctor said you have a concussion. He says it's not uncommon to lose your sense of taste and smell and that it will probably come back."

"Probably?" She sighed and looked over at him. "Okay. Thank you, Amanda. Nathan." They exchanged a silent conversation, and he kissed her knuckles as the nurse walked in.

He tried not to sound as desperate as he felt. "When does she get her head dressing changed? And she needs a new pillow."

"The doctor will do rounds after lunch. I'll ask him then." The nurse walked to the closet.

Brie turned to Dave. "What do you know?"

"We've got a mold of the tire print and are running it. Duncan believes he saw one person and that it was a woman—"

"Duncan?" she asked, wincing.

Nathan nodded. "He saw from the kitchen window."

"Oh, no." She took a shallow breath. "Oh, no." She closed her eyes and rested back on the new pillow.

Dave continued, "We're looking into the whereabouts of persons of interests—"

"Dave." Nathan shook his head at him.

She was sleeping again.

A glass of warm whiskey lifted in celebration of a job well done. The feeling of power and the adrenaline rush from swinging the bat were intense and satisfying. The three fingers of whiskey slid down in one wonderfully painful drink. The empty glass was hurled at the wall of photos. Uncontrollable laughter erupted as the shards of glass sprayed the tiny room. The yellow crime scene tape was the perfect finish to a perfect plan. It would be difficult to wait until it was time to finish her off. The edges of the dozens of photos flipped in the breeze from the twirl of the office chair. Laughter bounced off the walls as the table was swiped clear of an assortment of knives, a rifle, accelerants, wicks and lighters in one quick sweep. The chair continued to twirl and the laughter roared.

Sandy Finley sat in a small room with nothing but a metal table and four chairs. Dave sat with Tanner and watched her sweat through the one-way mirror. Her hand shook as she sucked deeply on her cigarette, trying to sit straight and poised.

Dave walked in and turned his chair to sit in it backward. He pulled out a manila file folder and glanced in, not opening it fully. "Thank you for coming in, Ms. Finley. We just have a few questions. Is there anything I can get you?"

"Out of here. What more do you need to know? I already told the officers everything on the day of the lockdown and look what that got me." She took a long drag and tapped her ashes in a battered, metal ash tray.

Dave looked up at her, judging. "Where have you been for the past several weeks?"

"What does that matter? Why is that anyone's business? Can't a woman take some time off to be by herself?"

"Where have you been for the last several weeks?" he repeated.

"Looking for a job."

"I'd like a list of the potential employers you visited. When did you get back in town?"

She looked down. "I haven't been keeping track of time. I'm unemployed. Sometime this week, I suppose."

"Do you own a four-wheeler, Ms. Finley?"

She lifted her eyes to meet Dave's. "Do I need my attorney?"

"That's your right, but I'll tell you cooperation would make things look better for you. Do you own a four-wheeler, Ms. Finley?" he repeated, allowing his eyelids to droop half way closed.

"No, I don't. And I don't own a rifle if you're going to ask me that next. You can search my house if you want. I have nothing to hide. I got back Tuesday night. I wanted to be here for the results of the board meeting. Is that what you wanted to hear? Who wouldn't? She breaks lockdown protocol and gets her job back with nothing more than a slap on the wrist. I make one accidental slip and lose my job. How would you feel, officer?" She sat back in her chair, looking him square in the eyes.

The questioning continued until he felt satisfied he'd shaken her and gotten all he was going to squeeze from Sandy Finley. She was annoyingly consistent with her story. "Don't leave town again without letting us know where you're going. We'll be in touch."

"I'll agree to taking one more day off work, but that's it." Brie sat in the guest chair, trying to look poised in her hospital gown. She knew she was acting like a spoiled child and didn't care.

She also knew Nathan kept his chair close to her. He was slick the way he was never more than a few feet away, yet looked to be casually hanging out. Why did she think that was sweet?

He sighed. "You'll have to take that up with the doctors."

"You need a break. You should go home and check on my brothers. I'm tired from the lunch time crowd and should get some sleep so I look rested when Duncan and Andy come." She stood up slowly, but steady and walked back to her crumpled white bed. She stopped to try and smell the flowers Lucy and Molly had sent her. Not yet. She looked over at Nathan. "Can't hurt to try."

Amanda flew in with a duffle bag in her arm. "I have come to save you."

"You're getting me out?"

"Shit. Not that kind of save you. I brought girl stuff." Amanda pulled out some of her waffle pants and an NYU sweatshirt. "I think we can talk the doctors into letting you wear this stuff since it's just your head they need to work with mostly."

"I could kiss you." Brie looked in the bag. "Makeup and real toothpaste? This is like Christmas."

"So, now that I've offered you gifts, you'd better sit back."

She leaned back on her inclined bed. "Okay. Hit me. What's up?"

"Your brothers are unpacking boxes," Amanda said.

Brie saw Nathan's eyebrows lift.

"I met with the Petersons and gave them your sketches and estimate. Lucy is checking on your house. Liz is taking care of the dogs. Nathan's mom and dad—"

"Go back."

"Go back where?"

"Go back to you meeting with my client. Who did you say you

were? What did you say about the estimate? Which sketches did you give them?" She felt wide awake now. "Who did you say you were?" she repeated, flustered at the thought.

"I said I work for you and that you were in the hospital and that it's nothing too serious...because it's not, and I guess now is a bad time to tell you I have all of Nathan's plants, shrubs, and trees set to be delivered in the morning."

Her face turned red.

"Fresh coffee anyone?" They ignored Nathan as he slipped out.

"You know my brothers are calling you bossy-Mandy again? It's like grade school all over. I was thinking of telling the Petersons to get someone else to do their property. How am I going to get Nathan's one-hundred-thirty-six trees, shrubs, and plants in the ground when all I do is sleep? I was going to postpone his planting to fall. I have my other customers to consider. I'll be lucky to work full days with my teaching job. And what sketches did you show the Petersons?"

"A monkey could figure out your binder. It's more detailed than a Red Cross relief report. I gave them the sketches you had labeled Peterson and the price you had ready for them, and I'm planting for you. Let me do this, Brie. It's been months since I've been on assignment. This temp job can go straight to hell."

Brie sat for a long time, carrying on a debate with herself. Why did she always feel the need to do everything herself? Because she could. Why did she push people away whenever they tried to step into her life? Because it was safer. Why did her friends and family continue to love her when she was a bitch like this?

"You'll dig the holes twice as big as the pots?"

"I can do that."

"And you'll use diluted root stimulator?"

"Okay."

"You'll mix peat with the soil from the holes you dig?"

"Your directions are easy to read, Brie."

"You'll tuck mulch around and keep the plants watered?"

"A monkey can follow this binder, remember?"

She closed her eyes and rested her head back on her pillow. "How did I get so lucky as to have such a good friend?"

"And family. And in-laws," Amanda added.

Brie could feel her damned lids drooping yet again. Amanda

lowered her bed and covered her up.

CHAPTER 28

She was able to nap, shower and eat before Duncan and Andy showed up for their evening visit. Brie felt almost human again other than the dizziness and throbbing in the back of her head. And the not being able to wash her hair. And the can't-stay-awake-for-more-than-a-few-hours-at-a-time syndrome. Oh, yeah, and her inability to smell and taste. She convinced herself she could pull this off and sat in the guest chair, the better to make a good impression. The doctor walked in just as she was getting settled in the cushioned wooden seat.

"How's the patient?" He looked surprised to see her out of bed.

His surprise made her feel better. "I'm feeling very well, actually. I'd really like to go home."

"I'll tell you what. When you can walk across the room without assistance, we'll discharge you," he said with a sincere smile as he checked her stitches. "You should be able to get your head wet tomorrow. We'll give the stitches one more day to seal." He glanced at her chart. "No rubbing the wound just yet, though."

Duncan and Andy walked in with Sylvester and Mackenzie just as the doctor finished up. Nathan followed him out to the hall.

Sylvester rested a hand on her shoulder and Mackenzie patted her arm as they exchanged warm greetings and best wishes.

Duncan offered a polite hello and sat in the chair at the

opposite side of the room. Andy absentmindedly walked to her and sat on her leg.

"The kids in class want to know when you are coming back, and Sean says we have to finish *Charlotte's Web*. And I miss the dogs and I don't like sharing grandma's guest bed with Duncan." He turned his head to her and smiled. "I miss you. You look tired. Are you tired?"

"I'm just ready to be out of here. I miss you, too." They pressed the sides of their heads together as Andy continued to catch her up on classroom happenings, and the boys' plans for their upcoming trip to Colorado with their grandparents. She was relieved when Nathan finally returned.

"Nathan, would you and Andy please get me a diet soda? I can't drink another glass of apple juice."

Nathan took Andy's hand. Sylvester and Mackenzie followed.

"I know, I know." Andy followed. "She wants to talk to Duncan about why he's all pouty."

Brie waited until they were gone before standing. She made sure she was stable before making her way to the dreaded hospital bed. "Come sit with me," she said to Duncan.

He obeyed and sat next to her. She pulled him under her arm, and they sat in silence for a few minutes. She felt his shoulders start to shudder and tears fell on her arm.

"I heard you saw it happen." She tried to be casual by crossing her legs at the ankles.

Duncan nodded in her arm.

"Thank you." She stroked his hair.

"I didn't do anything," he barked.

"You yelled for Nathan. I could have lost the fingers and toes from my right hand and foot if you hadn't done that."

"I don't remember yelling."

"Okay." She sighed, thinking...realizing.

"You know, I couldn't get my legs to move when I knew my parents' house was on fire. I wanted to yell to them, tell them to get out, but I couldn't. I blamed myself for a long time. I guess I still do, sort of."

"Oh." He sat silently before he went on. "I didn't know that. I'm sorry I didn't help you." He turned his head and buried it deeper in her shoulder. "Are you going to make me say what I saw again?"

"No. No, Nathan told me. I just want to make a deal with you. I will stop blaming myself for not helping my parents if you will stop blaming yourself. You are only eight, you know. We never know how we'll handle emergencies. It looks like we are a lot alike, you and I."

"Will you and dad break up?"

Whoa...she didn't see that one coming. "I'll be right across the creek from you." It was the best she could do.

He sighed comfortably and turned to her. "Dad says you'll be in that damned house alone over his dead damned body." He grinned. A little.

Brie's eyebrows lifted high and she tilted her head back to get a look at Duncan. She was relieved to see him smiling.

"Just sayin' what he said."

"Oh, did he?" She pulled him in and mussed his brown hair.

Brie tried threatening to check herself out. The doctor was as casual as ever.

He must have been between surgeries, because he still had on a hairnet and footies.

"How about we make a deal? You're still not steady. Mr. Reed, here, talked to me about discharging you if you'll stay in his care at least until our next appointment." He spoke while checking boxes and flipping pages on his chart.

She squinted at Nathan. She'd only missed half of the work week but already had been gone so long before that. "Where do I sign?"

Until her strength returned, she would only be able to work half days. Frustration with what she considered slow progress mixed with the worry of how she would handle twenty first-graders.

They stopped by her house first to get her things. Her plants were alive, and her mail and newspapers were piled neatly on her kitchen table. Macey's braided rug looked lonely. There was no dog hair or small clumps of dirt on it. Her leash and bag of food were missing. She moved to her couch and loveseat and remembered her agreement with Duncan. She would embrace the help from her friends and family, she vowed, and not push them away.

Pulling up in Nathan's drive took her breath away. It was all just as she had pictured it. Amanda had shoveled river rock gingerly around freshly planted flowers and shrubs. Tall, red cardinal flowers adorned the stairs leading up to the front door, and Amanda had even remembered to cluster larger stones at the corners. The blue salvia was in bloom and the upright junipers at the corners of the house brought everything together. She turned to look at Nathan. It occurred to her that he'd stuck, even still. She could see the dogs as they jumped up and down in the window.

"Welcome home." He pulled her hand to his lips and kissed her knuckles.

"I love you. I'd say thank you for this, but you're keeping me prisoner."

"Yup." He swaggered his way around the car to get her door.

Luckily, Amanda stopped what she was doing to let the dogs out before they broke something. Brie motioned her hand down, and they sat at her feet with tails wagging madly and high-pitched whining coming through their snouts. She scratched their heads, one with each hand, just as Andy came running around from the back of the house.

"Miss Chapman, Miss Chapman, you're here! Wait 'til you see the house. It's like a real house now, and the plants are real pretty, and there's a huge bird in the creek with its legs on backward." He pulled mercilessly on her arm before turning his head in Nathan's direction. "I mean...can I help you or somethin'?"

"The herons are back."

"The, huh?" Andy already forgot his manners and was pulling her toward the back of the house.

As she was drug around to the side of the house she yelled playfully to Amanda over her shoulder, "It looks great! You're hired!"

Turning to Andy, she explained, "The birds with their legs on backward are called Great Blue Herons, and they *are* huge. Almost as tall as you."

Amanda was a machine, she decided. The back was spectacular. The shrubs and bushes were spaced, clumped and arrayed nicely. Everything was new. Just as she felt. The trees stood in their burlap-covered root balls and waited over the places they would be buried.

Indeed, there was a single, three-foot-tall heron jerking its tufted head as it walked in search of a snack. Just as Andy described, its pencil legs bent backward as it walked stealthily in the hunt. The bird froze and slowly leaned its head forward.

"Watch." Brie squatted down next to Andy and pointed.

The bird stood perfectly still for several seconds before stabbing its beak lightning quick into the water and coming back up with a thrashing fish the size of its head stuck in its beak. Andy jumped up and down at the sight as the bird seemed to look side-to-side, showing off its silvery catch before shifting it long ways and eating it whole, head first.

Nathan came from behind and grabbed hold of Andy, tossing him effortlessly up on his shoulders. "Come on, champ. Duncan is waiting to show Brie his surprise."

Andy rocked back and forth on Nathan's shoulders a few times before tucking his legs underneath his arms and holding onto his chin. Before they turned to head inside, the dogs must have gotten too close to the creek for the bird's comfort. They all watched as it squatted, spread its six-foot wings and took to the air. It flew low along the length of the lake, dipping the tips of its wings in the water as it went.

When they walked in the front door, Brie looked around at the transformation. The family room was still somewhat empty, but it did have a set of end tables in it that Brie swore looked like what Chase had gone on and on about with Nathan last January. In the center of the dining room stood an exquisite table with massive clawed feet and eight high-backed chairs lined with a spray of what she thought of as square spindles. The walls displayed single, decorative tiles in elaborate frames. Under the table lay a large, complicated rug. The future library to the right was home to a leather wooden-legged recliner along with an enormous desk and some soft lamps on designer tables. Finally, her focus zeroed in on Duncan, who stood under the long arch of the stairs at the back of the massive foyer next to a canvas filled with a pencil and chalk drawing of Niagara Falls.

Mackenzie stepped forward. "He wasn't sure where you would want it, so we decided to put it here for now. He's worked on it every spare minute since your...accident."

"It's...stunning." She walked forward and kissed Duncan on the top of his head. "Thank you. Are you sure you're not twenty-two?"

"Lunch is ready!" a voice interrupted from the kitchen.
"Molly!"

Brie recognized her voice and headed back toward the kitchen, taking Duncan under her arm, she walked like a first-time home buyer. The kitchen table was big enough to hold twelve, which was nearly how many people were there to eat. She felt thankful and flattered but already weak and would have preferred her bed over a meal.

Molly wore an apron over her flared khaki slacks and brown patent leather boots. She kissed Brie once on each cheek and ordered her to sit. Lucy and Molly prepared and served glazed Cornish hens, steamed asparagus and red skinned potatoes.

Brie tried to ignore the uncomfortable looks of worry and pity. "I want to thank each of you for all you've done. I feel better already." She turned to Molly. "It smells wonderful."

Molly prepared a hot dog for each of the kids, and Nathan leaned over to Brie's ear. "Liar. You can't smell a thing." Her blinks were getting longer. Nathan slipped his arm around the back of her chair.

"It was a polite, white lie," she whispered back.

"I'll have to remember you think that way."

Smoothly, Nathan expressed both thanks for the assistance and apologies for ducking out, then took her hand. She offered no argument.

Habitually, she ran her hand along the smooth railing of the stairs, then looked in the familiar rooms of Duncan and Andy. Reluctantly, she headed for the mattress on the floor of the room she was beginning to consider hers and then stopped in the doorway.

There was no bench press. No cork board with note cards and no mattress. Instead, there was a massive bed with a towering headboard framing lines of spindles that reminded her of the backs of the dining room chairs. An ivory, eyelet-laced cover tucked into the arched side rails and was adorned with three, simple, matching pillows. A desk with tall legs and an attached mirror beside a matching dresser completed one side of the room while each side of the bed was crowned with matching nightstands. The lamps on the nightstands were made of copper and thin, stained glass.

"Those don't actually go there." He gestured to the lamps.

"Did you change this to the master bedroom?"

He shook his head a few short times.

"Oh, I see. This is your *extra* room." She sat on the edge of the bed. "It's no wonder people pay you what they do." She felt drained and would have crawled in with her clothes on if Nathan weren't there to help.

"I'll check on you after a while."

But she hardly heard him. She was already falling asleep.

In her dream, her arms and legs felt heavy. She stood at the bottom of her parents' stairs. She felt determined to keep her promise to Duncan and move on from this, but it was so hard when her parents' killers walked free and continually disrupted her life and now those around her.

Think, Brie, think. Her parents were still upstairs, yelling her name. The backdraft from her bedroom was still sucking air, the yellowish tint underneath the door. The couple. Where the hell were they?

"Mother." She squeezed her eyes shut and forced herself to leave her parents' house. Leave the scream of the smoke detectors, the warmth of seeing her mother look to her.

She walked out the front door and instantly felt the balmy, warm June night. She could smell the moist air and the green of her mother's bushes.

She forced herself to walk faster and then to run. They had to be there. Down the street.

She could see them. See the backs of them. They wore black. How cliché. They seemed to sense her footsteps and picked up their pace.

CHAPTER 29

Anxious for knowledge, Brie yelled at them to stop, to turn around. One was a woman. One a man. The woman was taller than the man, but they both had on caps so she couldn't see their faces or their hair. They ran at the sound of her calls and turned the corner at the end of the cul-de-sac.

"Stop!" she cried, dropping to her knees.

Her eyes flew open to the dark, and she sucked in three deep, fast gasps of air.

"It was just a dream, baby. It's over." Nathan sat back, giving her blessed breathing room.

She rolled over in the soft sheets to catch her breath. "You didn't wake me?"

"Was I supposed to? You were dreaming of your mother. I didn't know if you'd want me to." He sat for a minute. "You want water or something?"

"No." She rolled over to look at him. "Will you stay? Just for a while?"

He tucked in behind her, and she pulled his arms close. "I dream about the fire sometimes."

"Is that good or bad?"

"Funny you should ask that. It's both, actually. I feel ripped apart to relive it, but I can't stay away. The last thing my mother does before she dies is look at me. I relish that moment, as sick as that sounds."

"Not sick. I'm glad I didn't wake you."

"That's the thing." She rolled, being careful to lift the back of her head as she turned to him. "It's been changing lately, evolving. Ever since I met you, actually." Her eyes wandered in thought. "I see the people who murdered my parents. I saw them that night and in my dream, they're becoming more...real. I'm not sure if it's me yearning to learn who they are or if I'm waking parts of my memory, but it feels like I know them."

"You know, the police aren't leaning toward a *them*."

"I know. Maybe they're right." She rolled back over and tucked into him.

Dave finished his time as an officer and was officially Detective Nolan. He stood in brown shoes, brown pants and a long-sleeved blue shirt with his handcuffs fastened to his gun sling. He sat on the edge of his metal desk, studying his case board.

He wasn't ready to take McKinney off the short list just because an eight-year-old kid thought Brie's thug swung like a girl. He had motive, opportunity and skill with setting fires. Finley was crazy enough. She had the opportunity and a motive, in her own schizo-head. Lucy Melbourne could have done it. She's not too old for a four-wheeler. Jealousy. Pride. All good reasons for revenge.

Nolan's brainstorming was interrupted by Detective Tanner's voice. He walked up to Dave and introduced the woman walking next to him. She was average height, with straight, glossy black hair cut in a bob around her face. Thin, she looked to be in her late thirties or early forties.

"Detective, this is Dr. Tracy Li. She's a profiler on loan from the city and will be here for a few days looking into some of our cold cases. I want to show her everything we've got and give her our hunches. Get any of the persons of interest back in here. Whatever she wants." Tanner looked back to Li. "I'll be in my office. Come in anytime."

"I'm going in for a full day tomorrow. I'm feeling much better. It's just the incline of your drive that still gets me." Brie sat at the end of Nathan's brown leather couch in the room meant to be a library with her legs propped on his lap. "I'll have the weekend to recuperate if I get too tired."

Nathan sat flipping pages in a custom kitchen magazine with one hand and digging his thumb in the bottom of her foot with the other.

"Are you ever going to touch me again?"

He stopped turning pages but didn't look at her. "I am touching you."

"You know what I mean."

"You got out of the hospital less than a week ago, mostly thanks to me making a deal with the doctor." He lifted his eyes to hers.

"I'm not breakable." She sat up and crawled over to him, laying across his lap.

He gently tucked her into the crook of his arm and kissed her long and soft. "Your head says otherwise." He held her face and rubbed his thumb across her cheek. "I have a great need for you. I hope that doesn't scare you. I don't want to hurt you."

She closed her eyes and sighed. "Still not breakable, but I guess we should wait for a time when your kids aren't just up the stairs. Will you tell me what Dave's got going on?"

He shifted her to face him. "Not as much as you might like."

"Try me."

"Brian's been questioned a number of times. Duncan's sense that your attacker is female has given him a reprieve. Sandy's back in town—"

Brie sat up straight. "Sandy's been found? What did they find? Is she in jail?"

"They've questioned her...thoroughly. She offered to let the police search her home, and they came up empty. She says she took out cash and went to get away for a while to look for a new job. They're working on her. Patrols pass by regularly. A profiler was called in. They're still watching activity and checking on a number of other people, but have come up empty so far. I'm sorry."

"It's okay. I'm used to it. I meant it when I said I won't be caught off guard again."

Dave sat at his old metal desk next to Jim. Dr. Li used his office for the duration of her time, preparing reports and profiling suspects for a handful of their cold cases. He'd hoped she'd gotten a good feel for the one that was so personal to him. A grease-ringed brown napkin sat under his ignored, stale doughnut. He sipped lukewarm coffee and reviewed his files.

Detective Tanner came out of his office and motioned for him to come in. At the same time, Dr. Li came out of his new office and headed in the same direction.

Finally. Patiently and attentively, he listened and took notes regarding the case of a missing teenager from an upper-middle class family in the small town just west of Northridge and that of a decade-old murder of a forty-seven-year-old man who had been engaged to marry his fourth wife. He wouldn't give Brie's case anymore attention than the others; it would just be nice to know.

"Chapman case. I have five distinguishing characteristics I would recommend you look for regarding the assailant." She flipped through some of the pages on her full-sized yellow legal pad while tilting her head up to see through her bifocals.

"I believe the assailant is female. Due to Chapman's mostly gender specific occupation, the criminal we are looking for is statistically speaking not a male with issues regarding her success. My belief in the gender of the accused also lies in the nature of the attacks against the victim. The particular species chosen for mutilation are animals women generally think would illicit distress.

"I believe she has professional experience with fire, either through employment or an active hobby or has an accomplice thereof. The fire was precise and unique. Definitely not started by an amateur. The use of the backdraft would not be from a homegrown, self-study arsonist. The lack of evidence and of witnesses shows precision in calculations and in timing."

Dr. Li lifted from her chair as she spoke and began pacing slowly over the generous office space. "I believe the occupation of the suspect to be similar to that of the victim. However, at a lower level of pay and/or of status. Jealousy and pride are relative to one's rank. Miss Chapman's attacker struck her place of employment on a number of occasions, ending with the extensive effort to defame her reputation with the public exposure of the private photographs.

"The criminal is likely to be someone that is at least somewhat close to Miss Chapman. It seems she knows Brianna not only teaches, but works individually with the assistant superintendent, has turned down a number of administrative offers and has been chosen as keynote speaker in at least a half-dozen seminars. The criminal chose a night Miss Chapman was to be alone to set the fire, knew which room was hers and how to get in the house. The use of RU-46 on the pregnant dog points to knowledge that would likely come from a close acquaintance.

"Finally, I believe you are looking for someone that is between the ages of twenty-eight and forty-five. The suspect would be old enough to have been of a working-class age six years ago and young enough that Miss Chapman's lifestyle would be motive enough for assault and murder."

The weeks passed. The air grew warmer and Brie grew stronger. She sat in the soft grass with Nathan, Dave and Amanda as the kids played in the creek. The Forester grasses had grown tall enough that they blew in the wind and provided protection for the blooming purple Liatris. Rain was still sparse and the creek still low.

The children's small feet sunk in the exposed creek mud up to their ankles. As usual, Duncan seemed to prefer a chair and a fishing pole over walking in mud and was becoming a pro at hooking the catfish from the lake. Andy and Rose were too impatient for sitting and chose to explore the creek.

She leaned back against Nathan's legs, wearing her denim shorts and tank as they watched. Amanda twisted open a beer to share with Dave while she and Nathan sipped on Zinfandel.

Andy taught Rose how to catch crawfish. It was a sight. He pointed. She pushed. At one time they stood nose to nose with their arms straight and pointing behind them looking ready for battle. It was Amanda's turn to try to intervene, and it was Nathan's turn to stick his arm out to keep her from it.

"Just wait. Give them a minute."

Before the stand-off came to a head, the kids both saw something from the corner of their eyes, pointed at the water and dug in. Each came out with a thrashing, pinching crawfish. Andy stood like it was an everyday thing, and Rose jumped up and down heroically. Each tossed their catch in their bucket of water and hugged, covering one another with mud.

Rose turned toward the adults and yelled, "Can we eat them?"

Andy made a face of great disgust as he stood behind Rose. When she turned to him for approval, he merely shrugged one shoulder, mimicking his brother.

"Sure thing," Nathan yelled back before he turned to Brie. "Anyone know how to cook crawfish—" He heard Duncan let out a whoop and saw his pole bend over and Duncan jerking it, then reeling the line. "—and catfish?"

Dave carried Rose nestled in his arms the short walk to Clifford's house. "She smells like fish," he said, and kissed the top of her head.

"You've been quiet all night. Is there anything the matter? Something I can do?"

Taking hold of her mass of strawberry blonde hair, Amanda held it behind her head and looked away. "You've always treated her like she's your...like she's special to you."

"Mmm." He nodded and tucked Rose into him like a small pillow.

"You took her with us to Florida."

"Damn straight." He thought of Disney World with a five-year-old and smiled. Smiled until he noticed Amanda rubbing her fingertips in circles against her forehead.

"There's something I should talk to you about. Can you come in for a while?"

"Yeah. There's something I need to talk to you about, too."

He waited on the brownish plaid couch that felt like burlap. There was an ancient television set with rabbit ears that stood on the floor in the corner of the room.

Amanda came back in then. She sat in the corner of the couch, crossed her legs and set her hands in her lap. The look on her face pained him, but he was patient.

"I should have told you this a long time ago. I'm sorry for not doing that." She looked everywhere but at him. "I'm okay with...no, not okay... I understand whatever you decide to do with what I'm about to tell you. I thought about telling you when we were at Disney, but it never seemed like the right time. I've never told anyone this, Dave, not even Brie. And, of course, Rose doesn't know because she's too young. And I'm not sure when or how to tell her."

She was nearly hyperventilated. He wanted so much to reach

out to her, but something told him not to.

Instead, he placed his arm across the back of the sofa, almost reaching her.

"Rose's dad," she began and looked at him with wide eyes. She closed her eyes and turned her head, taking a deep breath. "I was in Nicaragua—"

"You don't have to do this," he interrupted.

"Please." She didn't look up. "The stories of me being young and loose and not knowing who...that's not exactly true."

She stared at her hands.

"I wasn't loose. I was busy getting into more administrative positions with Red Cross, involving international aid operations." Her speech sped to a mile a minute. "He said he was there from the U.S., but now I'm not so sure. He didn't look like a local. Blond, tall, but spoke fluent Espanola."

Oh hell, why was she telling him this?

"We went out for drinks a few times, and he thought that gave him the right..."

Without thinking, he flew up from the couch.

She looked at him now and in her eyes he saw fear.

"He raped me. Rose is...is from that."

He'd never felt such anger. She never told anyone? She's gone through this by herself? His mind flew into cop mode. Date, probable time, location. Pacing, he ran his hands through his hair, grabbing chunks and holding on as he tried to think. His glare flew to the ceiling, the walls. There were questions in his mind at the edges of a dozen vivid images. The feelings were overwhelming, unbearable, and his mind raced. He would find him, find him and hurt him and everything he was.

"Where is he?" He needed information, but when he looked to her he saw something much more terrifying, much more unbearable.

Amanda sat trembling with large beads of sweat lining her forehead. And in her eyes he saw shame. His Amanda.

"I...I didn't see him after that. I s-swear. He doesn't know about Rose, I mean."

Dave dropped to the couch and sat next to her.

"Marry me."

"What? Why? What?" Amanda shook her head slowly and wiped the tears from her cheeks. "I drop this on you, and you propose? You don't have to do this. Don't do this because you feel...sorry for me...sorry for Rose. I'm just...I just thought I should—"

"Because I'm in love with you. I knew I was going to marry you the first time I walked you to your grandfather's door. This is what I had to talk to you about tonight." He moved over in front of her and lowered to one knee. "I'm in love with you. I want you to be my wife. I want Rose to be my daughter. I don't care how she got here. I want to make her little brothers and sisters." He dug in his pocket and peeled through a tissue. "I've been carrying this around with me for months. Will you marry me?"

The tears flowed freely over her beautiful chipmunk cheeks. She sat on her grandpa's old couch in his old living room perfectly still. "Yes—"

He covered her mouth with his before she could say another word. Picking her up, she wrapped her legs around his sides. He felt her cling to him as he wriggled around to get the ring on her finger. It was a single solitaire diamond and too big for her finger. She dropped her forehead to his as she held it out to see.

CHAPTER 30

Brie couldn't get used to the idea that someone at her work place might be the one responsible for the attacks against her. It made her feel both like a traitor and also rather paranoid. If not with Liz, she preferred keeping to herself.

Report cards were completed for the last time. Boxes were packed and walls were stripped. She realized this was the first time she could remember the summer feeling like a need and not a want. No summer school, no tutoring. She would work with Amanda on her landscaping jobs and work through the list of things the boys wanted to see and do.

"Hey, stranger." Susie Phillips stuck her head in Brie's classroom. "Will you be packed up today?" She walked in and looked around. "Oh, figures. You're already packed up. Is that a bulletin board for August? I hate you."

See? Brie thought. Paranoid. "After six years at the same grade level, I have a system. How much longer do you have?"

"Days. Ugh." She walked around looking at the boxes and empty walls. "It's always hard to see them off, don't you think?"

"Yes." Paranoid, paranoid.

"Especially this year, for you. How is little Andy Reed?"

"Very well, thank you."

They continued small talk until Susie looked at her watch and excused herself.

Bulletin boards were empty and extra garbage cans placed throughout the hallways. As Brie walked down the busy hallway, she thought of how Nathan maneuvered around her each time she brought up staying back at her house. Living out of a suitcase was getting old. Duncan must have sensed the tension on the subject with his nightly questioning to Brie about where she'd be staying.

"My cumulative files are finished, Mrs. Seward. Here are my report cards ready to be mailed." Brie handed her favorite school secretary her stack of envelopes, fastened together with a rubber band.

Mrs. Seward set them on her desk next to the other matching stacks. "Take care of yourself, Brianna. See you next year."

Brie offered her warmest smile on her way to say goodbye to Dr. Tyman. "I'm taking off. You've got my home numbers if you have any questions on the math curriculum alignment. Call me anytime. Have a nice summer."

The interim principal smiled and nodded. "Be careful."

Brie returned the gesture in mutual understanding before leaving Bloom. She drove her truck thinking about her students. A few would move over the summer, but most would return in the fall. Some would be in Susie's class. Brie tried to shake off the knee-jerk thought that Susie could be responsible. She decided this might make her crazy yet.

She forced herself to focus on the full bloom of summer as she drove. The new growth was both literal and metaphorical for Brie. She'd let a maniac run her life for nearly seven years, but now she was determined to move forward. She was in love with both the man and his children.

As she neared her neighborhood, she glanced at the trees lining the long drives. The leaves were dark green and full-size now. Red buds and marigold trees had finished blooming, and the hostas and Shasta daisies had flowered in their place.

Brie could see the smoke from someone's grill and wished her sense of smell would come back to her. As she rounded the corner into her neighborhood, she realized it was too much smoke for a grill and decided on a fire pit. Instinctively, a sensation woke up at the back of her neck. Uncomfortable. It was too early in the evening for a fire pit. The smoke thickened and when she saw the flash of the sirens, the uncomfortable feeling changed to mind-numbing fear.

She took the corners too fast, and when she turned onto her cul-de-sac, the relief was a mixed feeling. Her house was intact, yet a fire truck was parked between her house and her next door neighbor's.

Her brows became tighter and tighter as she reached her driveway and discovered the fire crew was behind her home. She opened the door of her pickup before she came to a complete stop, threw it into park and rushed out.

Recognizing the chief in conversation with a younger firefighter, Brie interrupted, "How many? When was the call? Why wasn't I notified?"

The chief's shoulders fell forward. "Just a brush fire. Mr. Reed talked me into holding off until we had it contained, seeing as you were at your last day and all. McKinney agreed."

She stormed around to the back before the chief was done with his lame excuses. Brush fire? Her yard was scorched a charcoal black in a neat line spreading from one end to the other. Arson brush fire was more like it. The stupid idiot didn't take into account the dry season they'd had or the brisk wind blowing *away* from her house. If they were trying to burn her house down, they should have checked the weather. Idiot.

The blaze traveled through the field as the men sprayed hoses and dug trenches to stop the spread. She noticed Brian and Rob in the mix of firemen before she noticed Nathan. He was covered in soot and soil, heading toward her with a shovel in his hand.

She picked up a spare shovel and walked toward him. It felt heavy in her trembling hands.

"Go on in, baby. You don't need to see this." Nathan reached for her shovel.

"No," she snapped automatically as she rotated her shoulders around him. "It was meant for me." Her voice cracked.

Nathan stepped in her path and pulled the shovel out of her already sweating hand. "Go. In. The. House. Macey's been going crazy. This won't help anything." He pointed his free hand toward her frantically barking dog in the window.

She hadn't heard Macey before he mentioned her. "Get out of my way, Reed. I'm going to do my part." She was yelling now. Several of the firefighters turned half of their attention to watch.

Nathan looked at her pale skin and her hands as they shook, then threw down his shovel. It clanked on top of hers before he took her by the shoulders, turning her backside to the flames. "You'll do as you're told for one damned time in your life and get your ass inside."

He caught a glimpse of Brian and Rob over her shoulder, exchanging dollar bills.

"Don't talk to me like a child. You told the chief not to call me. How dare you? And get out of my way."

"If you don't get the hell inside, I swear I'm going to carry you in and lock you in your room. Go take care of Macey and stay there until we're done here."

Brian and Rob casually covered their faces with their hands to cover their laughter.

Brie stared at him, breathing heavily for a solid minute before spinning around and walking inside.

Rob grinned as he stuffed the money inside his fire pants and into the pockets of his jeans, then went back to shoveling dirt to form a trench. Brian stared at the two of them long and hard before getting back to work.

Nathan was hot and dirty and tired. They worked until the last of the plants and grasses finished smoldering. He answered questions and described what he saw when he first noticed the flames, which was fucking nothing. Looking over the field at the charred land, he tried not to think what would have happened if the wind were blowing in the other direction, or if Brie had been home.

The person responsible was long gone, no doubt, leaving others to clean up after her as usual. Coward, he thought. When the last police car and fire truck left, he made his way right through the creek and up the hill to his house. He walked in mindlessly and headed for the shower.

He stood with the hot spray running over his face. Defeated and angry, he couldn't go on like this—or watch Brie go on like this, waiting for the next assault. He dried off, determined to get Dave's ass back over here, so the two of them could make a new plan of action.

Wrapping the towel around his waist, he decided on a beer first as he walked out of his bathroom to find Brie standing in his room. With the muscles in his jaw flaring, he purposely ignored her on his way to the built-in drawers in his closet.

"Nathan."

"I'm not ready for this talk, Brie."

He came out of his closet with clean clothes in his arms.

She was still there, still in her work slacks and blouse.

"I give you all the damned space you want. Now it's my turn. Go away."

She looked down at the towel wrapped around his waist and smiled. "There's a bit of a contradiction there."

"You don't want me like this, Brianna," he said through his teeth.

She bit her bottom lip and took a step forward.

He tossed his clothes on the floor and grabbed the mass of her hair. Wrapping it once around his hand, he pulled her head back and smashed his mouth to hers. He took his free hand and tucked his fingers around the top of the opening to her blouse. With one downward sweep, he tore open the front, sending buttons bouncing over the hardwood floor.

He pulled her shirt down over her shoulders enough to lock her arms to her sides before backing her up to the nearest wall. He stood for the longest time pressing their foreheads together, his eyes squeezed tightly shut. He let go of the torn shirt and pressed his lips to hers while using both hands to grab her face, her shoulders.

The feel of her was like a drug. He couldn't get enough. Never get close enough. Her hands were everywhere, pliant and giving.

Burying his face in the smell of her hair, he pulled open her slacks and dropped them to her feet, grabbing at flesh on the way back up to her face. His breathing raced with hers as their bodies slicked together.

He pulled back and looked at her. She moved her head to the side with her eyes closed, lost in heat.

"Look at me."

She swayed and purred—

"Look at me," he said louder.

He used his hand to gather her wrists together and pull her arms over her head. His glare was determined and focused. As the two of them looked at each other in understanding, he ran a hand down to her.

Her legs gave at his touch, as she let out an unleashed cry, releasing violently.

Her legs started slipping as her weight pulled down on her uplifted arms. Her eyes rolled around inside her closed lids as she gasped and cried out. He tightened his hold.

Brie felt dizzy and weak. She couldn't feel her legs. "Nathan, Nathan wait. Give me a minute."

He didn't give her time to recover this time.

He let go of her wrists and used his free hand to wrap around her, holding her up against the wall. "No. Again."

She let her weight fall on his arm, dug her nails into the muscles in his back and let go. The rough hands on her face, the bold blue of his eyes that saw through her. He looked tortured and conflicted. She felt his hands grasping frantically down her neck, grabbing her and traveling around to her backside. He lifted her and stared as they joined.

Moving furiously, he stuck his forehead back to hers. He grabbed onto the back of her thighs, repositioned her legs and sunk deeper.

She felt bruises coming on the backs of her legs and floated in the thrill of his intense need for this. For her. "I love you," she choked out as they went over together, standing in the bright light of the evening sun before slowly sliding to the cold, hard floor.

She lay on top of him with her dead legs still wrapped around him, slowly feeling their breath return to normal. She felt his hand lace up her mass of hair and stop his fingertips at the fresh scar at the back of her head. His chest rose quickly, then fell slowly.

"Brianna—"

"If you dare apologize for any of that, I'll find some energy somewhere and kick your ass," she mumbled into his bare chest.

"I told you to leave."

"I didn't listen."

"I don't know what to do."

She knew what he meant, but she didn't know how to soothe him.

"I feel helpless. How have you lived like this for so many years?"

"You get used to it."

He stroked her hair from the top of her head to the middle of her back as they came back to the present.

"I may not be able to move until morning," she said. The doorbell rang followed by the dogs barking. "Or not. I don't think I can walk yet."

He slipped out from under her. "I've got it." Pulling on his jeans, Nathan meandered downstairs toward the front door.

Brie heard the knocking change to an impatient pounding before Nathan could have reached the foyer. She willed herself to stand and started to dress, contemplating what to do about a shirt. She picked something from his closet and heard the visitor's voice begin to rise. Was it Dave? She went into the hallway with bare feet, buttoning one of Nathan's white cotton dress shirts.

She caught the tail end of their conversation. "...found the frigging gas can in the backseat of Finley's car. Just sitting there in fucking plain sight. They've got her in interrogation. I'm on my way, but you wouldn't answer your damned phone, so I stopped by."

Brie stood at the end of the upstairs hallway around the corner and out of sight. She leaned her back against the wall, staring mindlessly while tears fell uncontrollably over her face. There was a part of her that was scared to accept the idea that this could be over. If it was a mistake, the devastation would be too much to bear. She sunk slowly to the floor as her mind raced through images of Sandy in prison. Living in her parents' house without fear of running the dogs or simply answering the phone. She thought of Nathan and what this meant for them. The relief of wondering if the one of the boys would ever be in any kind of danger.

He came back to her as she sobbed quietly on his floor. He slid down the wall next to her and silently wrapped his arms around her shoulders. She curled up like a child and melted into him. He held her until she cried herself out.

Early morning sunlight slanted through Nathan's bedroom window, waking Brie. His fisted hand rested in the middle of her chest as he breathed deeply. The moment felt unreal.

They'd said Sandy was in custody, ranting, raving and denying everything. Her fingerprints were on a lighter found in the char from the field. Her shoes had pieces of wildflowers and grasses stuck in the treads.

Slipping her foot between the calves of Nathan's legs, she wrapped her hand around his and tried to pull him closer. She lay there for a very long time trying to file away the past seven years and look ahead to her future. She had friends and family that were there for her and loved her. And she had Nathan and his family. She took a cleansing breath, climbed out of bed and put her robe on over her pajamas. She snapped her fingers quietly at the sleeping dogs on the floor. They followed her downstairs, and she let them out the kitchen doors before she ground coffee beans.

As the coffee brewed, she dressed and went for the first run with the dogs since her attack. The morning was warm and humid and perfect. She probably went farther than she should have on her first trial run, but her legs yearned for the action, so she took an extra winding path and even dipped through her cul-de-sac.

Macey was confused when they passed their house without stopping but ran obediently at her left side. She cruised past the Melbournes' just as the front door opened. She went to raise a hand in greeting to Lucy, who was in her pajamas getting her morning paper, when she noticed Clifford standing behind her. Almost tripping over her feet, she tried to pretend like she hadn't seen them and ran on, laughing hysterically to herself.

She could faintly smell bacon and coffee when she returned. She stood for a few moments taking in the hint of lost scents and watching her lover as he leaned against his granite kitchen counter in his sexy boxers with his steaming mug in one hand and paper in the other.

"I'm going to get use out of your whirlpool this morning." She stuck a piece of bacon between her teeth as she poured a cup.

They didn't speak of Sandy or the fire as they made love in the bubbling water. Nathan knew there would be time and need for that soon enough. Instead, they went for a walk through the dewy grass and discussed his plans for the porch. He would put the boys to work gathering stones from the creek to use in the base of the posts. Sentimental pieces.

But when they wandered around to the back, the smell of wet soot and the sea of black on Brie's side of the creek were too much to ignore.

"Nature feeds on fire," she said. "It's a biological process. Many plants will thrive from the ashes. Some won't come back."

They looked over the lake and the creek. There were two Great Blue Herons walking stealthily through the reeds of grasses. He walked with her along to the end of his property. Brie stopped in front of the pond. "Told you."

He stood by one of the new white oak trees and looked over to see what she was talking about.

She bent down and gingerly picked up something small. "See? Frogs." She set it back by the pond and stood up as he pulled her into him.

He took her face in his hands. "Marry me, Brianna."

CHAPTER 31

Brie's face contorted into a bumbled and confused mess. Nathan thought it odd that with all her brains and education, all she mustered was, "Huh?"

One side of his mouth lifted as he gripped the sides of her face. "Baby, I want you to be mine. I want you forever. Marry me."

"Jeez." She pushed away from him, using his chest for purchase. "Are you crazy?" She started to pace in a short path back and forth in front of him.

The side of his mouth lifted a little farther, and he leaned back against the oak, sticking his thumbs in his front pockets. He loved watching her think.

Brie pressed the palms of her hands on her temples and paced in the grass. "Why would you do this? Everything is perfect." Her hands moved to the backs of her hips. "I can't breathe."

Nathan decided to kick back and crossed a leg over his ankle while she cycled through this.

"Nathan, I don't do relationships well. Have you been listening? Marriage? What about the houses? Have you thought about the houses? What about the kids? Have you thought about Duncan and Andy?"

"Yup."

She stopped and looked at him. Her face softened.

He knew the look in her eyes, knew everything about her. He stepped one foot back as an anchor. She ran at him and flew into his arms, wrapping her legs around him, and showered his face with kisses.

"I'll do it. Oh, my gosh, I'll do it." She held onto him. "How did I ever find someone so perfect for me? What can I ever possibly give you that you don't already have?"

He slid her to the ground and took her face in his hands. "A little girl."

"Our anniversary is coming up, Brianna."

A figure stood in the shadows between the houses, snapping high-speed photos. "I guess that will make seven of them now."

She took a close-up of Brie wrapping her leg around Nathan's calf. "Don't the lovebirds look so sweet? Do you have no frigging modesty?" She clenched her fingernails into the palms of her hands as the camera hung from her neck.

"Of course you don't. You're a slut. A bitch. A backstabbing thief. You'll pay dearly. You'll pay with what is closest to you." She tilted her head with her eyes half open. "Do you really think I would be so stupid? So sloppy as to set that amateur gas-can fire? I have my own little professional at the snap of my fingers."

She clicked a few more shots before slinking away down the street.

Nathan sat in Dave's office for a celebration, except he didn't feel much like celebrating. He listened as Dave cheered.

"*She's* the victim. *She's* lost her job. *She's* been innocently out looking for employment. *She's* been set up. Yada, yada, yada." Dave took a drink of hot coffee. "She's 'fessed up to the brush fire and to Brie's tires, even said she got in the garage through an unlocked door that she carefully locked before she left. It's only a matter of time before we get the rest out of her. We're taking it slow. Everything by the books. No mishaps. She'll go away for a very long time."

Nathan nodded. "Yeah, you're right."

"Then why don't you look as excited as I'm thinking you should be?"

"I am. Brie's so different. She seems...lighter somehow." He ran his fingers through his hair. "It just seems off."

"Oh, no, you don't. Where is this coming from, man?" Dave leaned forward and placed his elbows on his desk. "Nearly seven years of this shit. Be happy."

Nathan took a deep breath. "But how do you go from an evidence-clean arson to a shoddy brush fire set downwind of Brie's house? With a fingerprinted lighter left at the scene?" He shook his head side to side. "Shit. It's just me. That's not really why I'm here anyway."

"How so?"

"I want to know where you got Amanda's ring."

"No kidding? I'll be damned." Dave rubbed his plate-sized hands over yesterday's shave. "Congratulations, man. Mincemoyer's. I'll get the address."

"No, shit? I know where it is."

Nathan and Brie drove to Rochester for the afternoon. They ate salmon steaks with Chardonnay at a sidewalk café before stopping at the jewelers.

"You're quiet. Are you nervous?" He pulled up to the jeweler's to drop Brie off at the door.

"Just a little. I'm a pick-out-an-engagement-ring virgin. You don't need to drop me off. I'd rather walk."

He put the Saab back into gear and parked away from the door. "We could go into the city if this doesn't work out."

"All right." She pulled on her ear and smiled warmly.

"Mr. Reed, we've been expecting you." The man in black slacks and crisp, white shirt held the door for the two of them. "I'll take you to the back room. Mr. Mincemoyer would like to assist you himself." The man turned to Brie. "And this must be the lovely Brianna." He took her hand and kissed the back of it. "Such a pleasure to meet you. Please, follow me."

Now she was nervous. They sat in ridiculously ordained, velvet chairs at a table covered in glass. They didn't wait long for the owner.

"No, no. Please don't get up." Mr. Mincemoyer gestured to her. "How are you, Nathan, my boy?" She lifted her brows at their embrace. "When will we see that project of yours? You've gotten my furniture requests, have you? Are the offers up to your standards?"

"I'm not sure about a showing, George. And are you going to

charge me more if I tell you I'm still not in business?"

They laughed like old cigar-smoking friends before turning to her.

"So this is her. What price range are we talking, son?" he asked as he pulled out some boxes from under the table.

Brie looked over at Nathan with wide, puzzled eyes.

He took her hands and kissed her knuckles as he shrugged his shoulder at George. "Sky's the limit."

She leaned over to Nathan and whispered, "What if I don't really want the sky?"

"I figured," he said.

She turned to Mr. Mincemoyer, or George, not knowing how to address him. "Sir, I'd really like something I can wear. Actually, all the time."

Nathan saved her. "She works with her hands. I suppose a raised solitaire wouldn't work. Yes?" He looked over at her.

She nodded, relieved.

"She teaches first grade and owns her own landscaping business. What do you recommend?"

"An entrepreneur. A woman of my own heart."

George drew his hands dramatically to his heart before dipping back under the table. He pulled out an assortment of sparkling ring sets with imbedded diamonds. She sat patiently and listened as the jeweler explained golds and platinums, clarity and color. But, her eyes locked almost immediately on one toward the side.

Nathan followed her gaze and nodded his head to his friend.

She slipped on a slightly raised round diamond circled with smaller ones encased in a band of white gold. It fit. She couldn't remember the last time words had escaped her. She decided the jeweler must have thought she was a little slow.

"That's an exquisite choice. Nearly FI with a shallow cut that should meet your needs. What else can I get out for you today, Miss Brianna?"

She glanced over at Nathan once more.

He lifted one corner of his mouth. "George, I think we're done here."

"Well, my boy, you are an easy customer. Shall I wrap that up for you?"

She spoke up this time. "That won't be necessary. Thank you.

I'd like to wear it if that's okay with you. It doesn't seem to need to be sized."

"Of course, my dear. It looks beautiful on you." George turned to Nathan waving his hand at his wallet. "Just put this toward my sleigh bed."

"That's bartering, George." Nathan smiled.

"That's bartering plus bribery, boy. I'm in no hurry." George held out a hand. "You come back any time, and I expect an invitation to a showing soon." He winked at her and led them out.

They drove with the windows down. "Showing?" Brie asked.

"Ah." He took her hand and rubbed his thumb over her ring. "There is rumor of a showing of the house when it's finished. I didn't start it."

"Wow. Are you going to do it?"

He took a deep breath. "I left a lot of people hanging when I made the move to Northridge. People who got me where I am. I feel like I owe them, but I also want our house to be a home, not a museum."

Her heart sunk at the sound of *our* home. "I see." She looked down at their joined hands and the ring between them. "Have you thought about what we'll do with my house?"

"Sure. We could build a huge sky walk from one to the other." He lifted her hand and kissed her ring finger.

"I'm serious. I can't sell it. It's been in my family for three generations."

"I've thought about it, yes. It would make a perfect guesthouse. Your brothers would have a place to stay when they visit. We could even put in another bathroom...if you want."

"A guesthouse. Why didn't I think of that?" she responded sarcastically.

She watched his eyes humbly tilt with his head as he shrugged a shoulder.

"I'll never get used to having money." She smiled from ear to ear. "But I'll try."

"The kids fly in tomorrow." He moved his hand to underneath the wisps of hair flying in the wind.

She bit her bottom lip. "Last night alone?"

"Mmm."

"At least I won't be grounded to the guestroom anymore. I might even sleep on my couch. I've hardly even sat on it."

"We need to make a stop at Lucy's before we go home. She'll have my head if she hears about our news from someone else."

They pulled the car into Brie's drive and walked next door.

She found herself uncomfortable at the very platonic scene of Ethel leading them back to Clifford and Lucy. They were sitting in her four seasons room laughing like children.

"Brianna, dear. Come. And Nathan, what a lovely surprise."

Lucy stood with Clifford to greet them. Kisses were exchanged and small talk passed before Lucy asked what brought them to visit.

"Brianna, it's about time."

Brie was caught off guard with the first hug she could ever remember from Lucy. "I may get some grandchildren, yet. Nathan, your mother will share, won't she?"

Lucy led her to the kitchen to fill a plate with an assortment of congratulatory cookies and helped Ethel with the coffee as she addressed her. "Don't think I didn't see you running with those dogs the other morning, Miss Brianna."

She put her hands up in surrender and forced back a smile.

"We are two grown, single people and can live with whomever we please."

Oh jeez, they're living together. Brie stifled a choking fit. She wondered if Amanda knew. If Molly knew. If anyone knew. Oh, dear. "I...I... Yes. That *is* your business."

Ethel stood at the kitchen sink. "Are you kidding? Do you know how *old* they are? My mama, rest her soul, would roll over in her grave if she knew how these two are carrying on."

Brie sat with Nathan on the porch, waiting for his folks and the boys. Brie pulled on her ear and looked at her watch. He doodled a sketch of the beams and railings for the porch. The rocks from the creek would build up half-posts, and he planned to finish the tops with custom twelve-by beams. He didn't want anything too showy at the top, but big and bold enough to blend with the look of the house and Brie's work there.

When the Bonneville turned the corner, they walked down to meet them, the dogs at their heels.

Andy bounded out of the car first. "Hey, guys." He rubbed the dogs' heads. "Did you miss us? Huh?"

Nathan turned to his mother. "Why do the dogs always get first greetings?"

"Because they give the most dramatic welcome." She reached up on her toes and kissed him on both cheeks, then held his chin in her hand and looked at him.

Duncan stretched and meandered over.

"We climbed Pike's Peak. It's fourteen-thousand feet in the air." Andy spoke even faster than usual. "And we had on shorts but there was snow. And the plane was loud and made my tummy sink and do we still have to call you Miss Chapman, 'cause you're not my teacher anymore?" Andy stopped talking long enough to notice that everyone was quiet and looking at Brie's hand. "I know what that is. You got married while we were gone! We don't have to call you Miss Chapman anymore." He jumped up and down in circles. "We get to call you mom!"

Nathan put an arm around Brie and pulled her next to him. "I guess he approves."

Duncan knocked the side of his little brother's head with one hand while using his sleeve to wipe away a tear with the other. "They're not married, stupid. They're engaged. That means they're gonna *be* married."

"Don't mind me." His mother wiped away her own tears. "We're just so happy to have you in the family. This has been a big week for you."

The rains eventually came. The herons stood at the spillway and caught their fill as the fish washed over in the rush of the water into the creek. The floodplains came alive with the color of the mature wildflowers on one side of the creek and the tender greens on the side that had been burned.

Teenagers carried the pieces for croquet and badminton across the log over the rush of the water. Baked potatoes, burgers and brats cooked on the grill. The smell was mouthwatering and blew throughout the yard.

Brie and Liz wrestled with the badminton net while the rest of the ladies hammered the croquet wickets into the ground. Inadvertently, Liz held her hand beneath the lower part of her stomach while reaching up to untangle the net. This didn't go unnoticed.

The groups seemed to change places as most of the children went to the back to tie water balloons and fill squirt guns. Clifford and Sylvester stayed to man the grill. Adults went inside to start the massive hauling of food out to the tables on the deck and patio. Chairs were scattered around the yard and nets for the plates were set out, ready to place over the fruits and salads.

"The kitchen is amazing, Brianna dear." Lucy lined her basket for her homemade croissants with a red and white checkered towel.

"Thank you. I'm still finding all of the hidden drawers and compartments."

They piled their arms with chips and veggies for another trip out. Brie stepped in front of Liz before she got out the door, trapping the two of them and Amanda, who was stuck in the wrong place at the wrong time. "You're pregnant."

Liz folded her hands in front of her and tilted her head up at her.

"Whoa." Amanda's head bobbed between the two of them before she stopped at Liz. "She does that, Liz. It's creepy. So, are you really?"

"How can you tell? I've barely found out myself." Liz shrugged her shoulders. "Oops."

"Oh, wow. Does Tim know?"

Liz shook her head. "Wait 'til he finds out the little guy needs a sibling close to his age."

The three of them circled and hugged before regaining their composure and heading for the picnic. Food was eaten, games were played and s'mores cooked over the wrought iron and ceramic fire pit. Eventually, Andy and Rose crashed together in the hammock that lay under the deck.

CHAPTER 32

Molly was right, Lucy thought, she had been spending most of her time with Clifford and hadn't been out to see her condo in weeks. She relished the feeling of being in love again and could have argued that Molly was out of town most of the time, but didn't.

She felt like a teenager as she watched Clifford walk over to kiss her goodbye. "I won't be too long. I can't help but worry about her. She's still my daughter." She looked through her purse for her keys and felt that familiar chill when Clifford placed his hand on her arm.

"Take all the time you need. I'm going to beat Ethel in cards."

"She doesn't answer her phone, and I did tell her I would stop by." They walked together to the front door. "Let's have lunch in the four season's room when I get back. We'll invite Ethel." She smiled. "Unless she beats you in cards. Then, she'll be unbearable." Clifford kissed her gently, and they parted.

"Is Rose meeting us at the lake?" Duncan asked as Brie went over her mental list of supplies. He took the tub of earthworms from the fridge and set it in his tackle box.

"She's too young to walk there by herself. We'll walk over to get her before her mom leaves for work."

"Do you know how to put worms on a hook? I can show you

if you don't know how," Duncan offered.

"Anytime I can get out of stringing a worm on a hook, I'll take it."

Andy came in from the garage carrying an extra bucket. "This is for crawfish. You know Rose will want to catch crawfish."

"You know *you* want to catch crawfish," Duncan said under his breath.

The boys wore their swim trunks and worn-out sneakers. They smelled of sunblock and carried their chairs, buckets and tackle boxes over their shoulders. Brie carried a cooler with drinks and snacks. She couldn't figure how they packed so much stuff for an adventure that was just seventy-five yards from the house.

They walked down the shallow hill in back to the creek. The boys chattered while she analyzed the charred field on the other side. Indeed, nature survives. Lush, bright green plants sprouted from the fertile ash and soot. Rains washed away much of the black and refilled the lake and creek.

The day would have been perfect if it weren't the anniversary of the fire. She wondered if she should have told Nathan but convinced herself there was no need. She would spend a beautiful day outdoors with three of her favorite kids and her two favorite dogs. They ran without leashes and took it as a pass to run the fields and through the water.

Walking around the side of her house, she pulled her keys from her pocket with her only free hand. "The timer to the lights isn't working again."

"I know where it is." Duncan set his tackle box and chair down.

So mature, she thought.

Tossing the keys to him, she and Andy headed toward the Piper's house. Walking hand-in-hand she decided to prevent any bloody noses. "Now, listen. Don't tease Rose about her fair skin...or her freckles...or her red hair. You two could try—"

Brie's feet stopped before the rest of her. The smoke detector screamed. Her heart ripped into shreds. She whipped around and saw her blinds drawn. She never closed her blinds. Fear gripped her from the bottom of her feet to the top of her head.

She spun back to Andy. "Go, now. Tell Cliff—tell Mr. Piper to call for help. Go, Andy. Run."

He nodded quickly and took off down the street.

Fear gripped her lungs, her legs. She could hear the dogs splashing madly across the creek. Fighting the urge to drop to the ground and curl into a fetal position, Brie forced her legs to inch along the concrete and through the door.

"Stop," Molly yelled.

Under the piercing sound of the smoke detectors, all Brie could see was the gun digging into the temple of Duncan's trembling head.

As Lucy drove, she felt guilty that she hadn't visited more often. Molly really didn't live that far away. Just a short fifteen-minute drive through town. The drive was actually very pleasant. She made a silent vow to make this a habit. They wouldn't be able to set a day each week to chat, of course, with Molly's job taking her off who knew when.

She pulled in the drive of the tidy condo and locked her car doors. As she climbed the steps, she noticed the front door was cracked. Ah, she thought, she is home. "MollyAnne? It's me, dear." Lucy walked in and shut the door behind her. She made her way to the back thoroughly disgusted with the way her daughter kept house. The door was open to the basement and the light was on.

"MollyAnne, honey, it's your mother. Are you down here?" The silence created a mix of annoyance and worry.

Light came from a room she didn't remember. She pushed open the door to the tiny space and clutched her shirt in the middle of her chest. In it were dozens, no hundreds of pictures of Brianna. Years of pictures, some of them personal. She felt light-headed and set her hand on the short counter for balance. Her hand tapped a wooden bat, and it rolled. Lucy gasped at the sight of the blood splatter on one side.

Panicked, she slammed back against the wall and inadvertently turned out the light with her back. She screamed and cried and ran back up the stairs. Putting together the pieces of what she'd seen, she fumbled with her keys, dropping them on the ground by her car. "Why," she mumbled as she put the shaking key in the lock. "Why, why, why." She drove straight to the police station.

"Lock the door."

Brie couldn't move. Please. She pleaded with her body to move and help Duncan.

"Lock the door, or I swear I'll blow his fucking brains all over your precious house."

Brie obeyed, walking backward while focusing on the floor. She shut the door behind her and turned the lock. The dogs hit the door just as it clicked. They barked wildly, then ran at the windows.

Molly stood at the top of the stairs next to her old bedroom door. She sounded different, she thought. Crazed. Her hair was uncharacteristically tattered and her shirt untucked. Lines of black makeup smeared under her eyes.

"All these years." Molly's hand shook the gun against Duncan's face. "All these fucking long years and look at you, standing here in your perfect house with your perfect life. You think you can do whatever you want. Do whoever you want."

Brie inched closer to the stairs as she watched, terrified at the yellow smoke that blew under the door next to them. A nearly empty bottle of whiskey lay on its side on the floor. When she allowed her gaze to turn on Duncan, she blinked. His face was twisted in a petrified grimace, and he was shaking, sweat starting to bead along his brow.

The sight took her back to when she was the younger one scared stiff in this déjà vu. The memory gave her strength. Strength and clarity. This time, she would make it right.

"What do you want, Molly?"

"Hmm. What do I want? I want a life," she screamed. "One without you in it."

"What can I do for you *now*?" She held her arms out, palms down, creeping up the first stair.

"Don't take another step or I swear the next thing you'll see is the brat's head in pieces down your hall!" Her hand shuddered. Her eyes were red with rage. "I want you to listen to me. That's what I want."

"Okay. Okay, Molly. I can do that. See? I'm listening."

After his morning planning meeting with Detective Tanner, Dave organized his office. His intercom buzzed. It was the receptionist from downstairs.

"A Mr. Brian McKinney to see you, sir."

Great way to start the morning, Dave thought sarcastically. "Send him up."

Professionally, he met him at the top of the stairs. He noted that Brian still had on his work clothes and decided he must have gotten off his shift that morning. Holding a hand out, he nodded at Brian. "McKinney. What can I do for you?"

"I think I need to do one of those..." He looked around. "...missing persons reports or something."

"Why don't you come into my office and tell me who you think is missing." Dave turned and led the way. He shut the door behind the two of them and gestured for Brian to sit in one of the chairs opposite his desk.

"It's my friend, Rob. Robert Brusco," Brian said. "He didn't show up for work. He did this once before a couple years ago. I thought he was just sick, but I looked in his locker and it's empty. I talked to my boss and he never called. So, I went by his house and no one answered. I looked in the windows and, and it's empty. No furniture, no nothing."

"All right. Do you know if he has family in town? Anyone we could call to check up on him?"

"Not in town, no. I think one of the guys at the station might know his mom's name and where she lives, though."

"How about you get me what you have, and I'll do some digging. Sounds like he may have just moved on. There are some forms you can fill out, but we'll need to wait forty-eight hours to file since he's over the age of eighteen. I'll have the receptionist at the front desk get those ready for you."

Molly's face distorted. "Do you know how many years of my life I've had to listen to 'Brianna's so bright, Brianna's going to make something of herself. Brianna's got such a great eye for men.' You were like the daughter she never had." Molly spit at the floor.

Brie willed herself to stay calm. The smoke detectors pulsed their shrill scream. The dogs hit the windows with their heads. Duncan squeezed his eyes shut and shook violently from sobbing.

"Your mom wasn't fair, Molly. I see that now."

"Don't you talk about my mother! You think you're so smart. Always the one who gets the bright boys, the good guys. I get

243

the cheaters and your leftovers. Why can't they see you for the fat girl who fucking teaches two plus two and how to read *Dick and Jane*?"

Brie looked Molly straight in the eyes and smiled softly. "You're right. It doesn't take much." She tried to shake her head in shame as she placed her foot on the next step. "Tell me what I can do."

"You can go to hell, that's what you can do. That's what you're going to do. Do you know why my ex and I divorced?"

Brianna cringed at the sight of the barrel of the gun digging furiously into Duncan's temple. "I don't know, Molly. I want to know, but can you release Duncan first? Then, you'll have me all to yourself. Just you and me. You can tell me about it. Neither of us liked him."

Her eyes loosened and she slowly smiled. "You're wrong. I loved him. I got tired of hearing him call out your name when we were in bed. That's right. *I'm* the one he married. *I'm* the one fucking his brains out, and *you're* the name he calls out time after time after time after time."

Brie shook her head fast and pleading at Duncan. She could tell he was about to snap. The tears poured down his face and his gasps for air came in hitches.

"I worked on Brian for years. He finally gave up on you and once again, I got your leftovers. I'm sure you just happen to miss the fact that he and I had started seeing each other before you finally decided to accept his offer. He could hardly spare me two minutes to explain. He couldn't wait to get in your crotch.

"Now you have two choices. You can either get up here and open this frigging door..." She held Duncan by the hair, gesturing toward the smoldering bedroom door using his head with one hand and the gun to his skull with the other. "...or I can let you watch while I have the brat do it. Either way, today you burn."

"Noooo!" Duncan exploded and pushed backward against Molly, knocking her into the wall behind them. The gun fell down the hall, and they both dropped from the impact.

Brie flew up the stairs.

The gun. The gun, she feared. Duncan scrambled on his hands and knees toward it before claws clamped on his ankle and dragged him back. He kicked furiously as he slid. He used the heel from his free leg to dig into her fingers.

She wailed and let go only to grab hold with her other hand.

"I'll kill you, you little shit. I'll kill the both of you."

Brie landed on Molly's boney body, swinging madly. "Run, Duncan! Go," she screamed as she punched and kicked anything and everything.

He crawled to the gun first and then ran past the two of them. Fists wailed and legs kicked. At the bottom of the stairs, Nathan tore through the front door, tossing his keys aside. He looked to Brie, to Duncan, then yanked the gun and Duncan away to the front yard before plunging back through the open door.

"It's going to blow!" Brie warned as she and Molly tumbled down the long line of stairs.

Nathan caught her near the bottom, shielding her as he carried her outside.

Molly stood up and scrambled for the door, screaming, "No!" when the explosion hit.

They stood outside watching the firemen douse the flames. Nathan rested a hand on Brie's back as she felt a sense of closure she didn't know was missing. Her hand sat on the back of Duncan's head as he wrapped his arms and legs around her, clinging like a small child. He was silent as he fisted the back of her shirt with both of his hands and laid his head on her shoulder. She rocked and swayed with him and rubbed the back of his head, whispering reassurances in his ear.

"You saved us, honey. You saved our lives."

Andy wrapped an arm around Nathan's leg with Rose on the other side of him. She reached for him and they stood holding hands together, watching the fire with Amanda on the other side of them.

Memories flipped through Brie's mind. She never knew. Molly was right, she was dumb. They watched as the EMTs finished prepping the burn across the side of Molly's head and then wheeled her into the ambulance. It passed Dave's unmarked car on the way down the cul-de-sac.

Lucy was with Dave. She stepped out slowly as Dave hustled to Amanda and Rose. Duncan slipped from Brie's embrace and locked his arms around her waist. Lucy's eyes met Brie's as she walked toward her. She was overcome with emotion for her favorite lifelong neighbor and had no idea what her reaction to this could possibly be.

Lucy stood with her arms straight at her sides in front of her. "I'm so very sorry."

Brie felt her heart sink out of her chest. "Me, too." They hugged there on the sidewalk. "The ambulance just left. She's going to be all right, Lucy. You could catch up to her."

Clifford stepped next to Lucy.

"I will, honey. Thank you." And they walked numbly to Clifford's car.

Brie felt like a pro at the routine. She, Nathan and Duncan answered the same questions over and over again as they watched the flames burn out, then smolder. Next came the black shine from the moisture. Nathan convinced the authorities to let them have peace for the rest of the day and finish the paperwork the next afternoon. They walked to Nathan's house, to home and tucked in for the evening. As a family.

Andy slept in Duncan's bed for the first time in weeks. It was Duncan's idea. Nathan knew it would be a long time before Duncan could get past this and was already planning options in his head as how to help him through it.

"Are you seriously going to sleep in here?" Nathan stood in the doorway of the guestroom.

"I thought I was done in here, but tonight it's for a good reason."

"You seem okay with this. You've already rebuilt that house once."

"I'm actually more okay than I can ever remember. I have some ideas for the house, and I'm not sleeping with you in the same house as the boys until we're married."

He sat next to her and pulled her on his lap. "Married. I like the sound of that."

This time, she welcomed the dream. She crossed her legs up on the seat in the back of the yellow cab. When she passed Molly, the blonde had that same unhinged look she had at the top of her stairs. So sad, she remembered. She felt a pang that she couldn't see the man she was with, but turned her head quickly to her parents' home.

It was sunny and the dianthus were blooming. She ran in without paying the imaginary cab driver. As soon as she walked through the unlocked door, the sound of the smoke detectors stopped. The house looked the same, but different. She could see the back of her sage couch from this angle and the kitchen table where Liz and Nathan sat. Macey came from around the mudroom wagging her tail in her happy dance.

Her parents stood at the top of the stairs with their arms around each other. Tears of joy fell freely around Brie's cheeks as they nodded their heads warmly to her in silent understanding. She watched comfortably as they became translucent and then vanished altogether.

Brie woke in Nathan's guestroom. Their guestroom. She closed her eyes and smiled before whispering goodbye into her pillow.

EPILOGUE

The house was lit to match the thousands of tiny white lights that twined the trees along the freshly plowed asphalt drive. Each massive beam on the enormous wraparound porch was circled with dozens of lights. The low-lying junipers in front also were covered making them look like dazzling icebergs floating in a sea of freshly fallen white. Greenery tastefully wrapped around the horizontal rails with a spotlight on the eight-foot wreath adorning the angle of the roof over the garage.

Cars lined the drive and formed a makeshift parking lot along the west side of the Reed home. They'd hired a temporary valet service and limousines dropped off and parked down the street. The garage was closed off to the public, but heated for the evening's help and used as both a coat-check room and an area to prepare food and drink.

Brie had wanted to limit the holiday décor to the outside, leaving Nathan's work exposed for viewing. He talked her into a few tasteful arrangements and thin greenery wrapping the stairs. Red candles were scattered throughout, and she had a glimpse of what he meant when he said he wanted to avoid turning their house into a museum. Just for tonight, she thought, although she could still imagine the dogs tearing through the foyer with the boys on their heels by midmorning the next day.

They were across the creek for the night. Her older nieces and nephews had agreed to make the drive just to babysit, even though they would be back in a few weeks for the annual New Year's Eve gathering.

Her brothers were like kids in a candy store. They stood under the beamed, wooden arched entranceway to the dining room. The two of them walked through the house with their wives like they were walking through that museum.

To the other side of the foyer were spectacular wall-to-wall, built-in bookcases in what was finally a library off the bottom of the stairs. Visitors drank champagne from rented crystal flutes as they browsed that room, commenting on Nathan's mahogany desk and the copper sconces at the entrance.

Liz, Tim, Amanda and Dave stood at the landing up the stairs. Liz wore flats under her tea-length dress, which was smart since she looked like she was about to give birth at any moment. Brie watched her flirt with her husband as she inadvertently placed her hand under her enormous belly.

As aimlessly as she may have appeared to her guests, Brie was itching to find Nathan as she mingled her way to the back of the house. She wanted so badly for him to feel the evening was successful.

She glanced out the back kitchen window. The dogs were playing in Liz's backyard. Beside Liz's house. Brie warmed each time she thought of her sister as her new over-the-creek-neighbor. Her parents would be so proud they'd kept the house in the family. Liz would be the official hostess of the New Year's Eve gathering this year.

Nathan watched her through the crowd. Brie looked beautiful in her flowing silk ivory gown that reached to just above the heels she wasn't supposed to be wearing. He had reminded her not to wear them tonight. A corner of his mouth lifted as he decided it was likely the reason she did. Her hair was bundled in an intricately laced and braided mass with curled strands falling around her bare neck. The spaghetti straps lay flat against the delicate muscles in her shoulders.

On his way to her, he passed Lucy, Sylvester and Mackenzie as they sat chatting in the family room. Brie had been embarrassed that they used her sage couch and loveseat for that room thinking her furniture didn't quite fit with the evening. He was relieved that Lucy would have Clifford to help her get through

Molly's sentencing. She was looking at thirty to sixty years.

She had mingled with the crowd over the subtle sound of the quartet that played below the arch of the stairs. He wondered if anyone noticed the painting of Niagara Falls, courtesy of an eight-year-old boy, lit up behind the small orchestra. He was pleased with the floor-to-stairs wainscoting with burled walnut panels.

Walking up behind Brie, he kissed a bare spot just under her ear. "You look ravishing, Mrs. Reed." He traveled his arms around her protruding sides and rested them on the round tummy that carried their child.

Brie shivered as he raised her arm and moved his lips to her fingertips. He wondered if the thrill of the feel of her would ever ebb. She turned and adjusted the crooked tie that lay underneath his charcoal black tux.

"You look as comfortable and casual as you would in your faded jeans and work boots. You haven't sweat a drop all night," she said accusingly.

He shrugged a shoulder. "Come. I want you to meet the governor of South Carolina. He's a great guy, you'll like him. And, oh...he is a Panthers' fan."

She tucked an arm at his side as they headed toward the front. "Not something a girl hears every day."

Turn the page for an

excerpt from

FLYING IN
SHADOWS

The Black Creek Series
Book Two

R.T. Wolfe

Walking in the dark, Andy readjusted his tackle box. Moonlight shone on the dark ripples creeping down Black Creek. He spotted a raccoon as he crossed the bridge. Startled, the animal hissed at him. Andy stomped his foot and hissed back; he was in no mood for it.

In his peripheral vision, he saw movement. Larger movement. A man? The shape disappeared as quickly as Andy imagined it. When you let yourself get this worked up, you start seeing things, he chided himself.

He needed Rose.

She would calm him down and lighten his mood, help him feel normal again. He looked at his watch and winced. What were friends for if you couldn't count on them to be there? Even at this time of night. Or morning.

Rose slept soundly in her twin bed dreaming of her favorite spot at the zoo. In the small rain forest building, she allowed a newly emerged monarch butterfly to dry its wings on her apron while sharing facts about the insect to one of two visiting young boys. The other threw pebbles into the nearby wishing pond. The sound of the small rocks plunked as they hit the stone wall before dropping into the water.

Oh, crap. She woke and sat up straight. The plunking noise came from outside, not in her head.

Heart in her throat, she ripped off her blankets and hustled across the hard floor to the window. It was still pitch-black out.

Grabbing the flashlight she always kept on the windowsill, Rose paused for moment. It had to be Andy, but...

She found a familiar shadowed form with the beam, then hissed loudly. "Andy! I thought you didn't get home until tomorrow."

"It *is* tomorrow." He held up fishing poles and tackle box.

"It's not tomorrow until the sun comes up." Tugging on a pair of jeans, Rose smiled wildly to herself. This reaction she had to Andy Reed had to stop. It was *not* healthy.

"I've got the worms." he called. "Get down here."

FLYING IN SHADOWS
available in
print and ebook

MEET THE AUTHOR

Its not uncommon to find dark chocolate squares in R.T.'s candy dish, her Golden Retriever at her feet and a few caterpillars spinning their cocoons in the terrariums on her counters. When R.T. isn't writing, she loves spending time with her family, gardening, eagle-watching and can occasionally be found viewing a flyover of migrating whooping cranes.

R.T. enjoys hearing from readers. You can contact R.T. through her website: www.rtwolfe.com